The Portals of Tartae

THE LANGUAGE OF TREES

MARCIA SOLIGO

THE PORTALS OF TARTAE SERIES

In reading order:

The Portals of Tartae: The Land with the Two Moons
The Portals of Tartae: The Language of Trees

For my husband, Glaubert Queiroz, with whom I live a fairy tale every single day.
For Valente, the best friend and pup one could have. Love of our lives.
For my parents, who always believed in me and taught me that my dreams could come true.
For my sister and best friend, who helped so much in this journey.
For Thiago Gusmão, who first traveled to Tartae with me.

Cover illustrations by Marina Henry © 2021
Editor: Cecilia Lewis

ISBN: 978-1-7339607-4-8

The Portals of Tarthe

THE LANGUAGE OF TREES

PROLOGUE

A blazing light fell over the dark forest, enveloping and blinding everyone. It smelled as golden as it looked. Metallic and cold, and its touch paralyzed all living creatures in those hostile woods that night.

And after that, Lars fled.

Bran, Alegra, and Orion were again running between the trees, retracing Belenos' steps and heading to the circle where the final Portal would be opened. The night was cloaked in deep, dark hues and their footsteps echoed around them, the only sound they could hear. Orion's rhythmic gallop was the loudest it has ever been, sounding like thunder from a tormented sky.

"What happened?" asked Alegra as they arrived at the edge of the circle. Her eyes studied what she found there: Cordella, Alavro, and Belenos were still standing with indecipherable looks on their pale faces. Alavro held the Book of the Portals in his hands, and they seemed too still, as though they had been carved out of marble. The Portal Keys lay on the forest floor looking torched, all bent and worn.

"They're gone," answered Cordella. "The Portals … Olivia and Trevor." She looked into the eyes of everyone and appeared to be taking this notion in herself. The night around them was calm and silent; no crickets, no animals made any noise.

Mourning fell over them like heavy rain, damp, cold, constricting, weighing on their hearts.

"So it worked. There are no more Portals in Tartae," whispered Bran, and these words stabbed him deep in his soul.

"Yes. I believe so," answered Cordella. "And Lars?" She turned firmly to Orion.

"He ran away after the blazing light fell upon us. And so did all his companions," he answered.

The drawings on the forest floor were still there, but somehow, they seemed to have lost their lives. Right now, they were only meaningless symbols, as if they had been drawn by a child who played carelessly with a stick in the dirt.

Every single word they said came out with effort. They were all lost, unsure of what path to take now. This was a night of shift, and the rotten smell of that strange-looking forest reminded them how unwelcome they were in that place.

After a long silence, Belenos spoke.

"Everything is different now." His tone was low, but not a whisper. It was strong and deep, like a forgotten god of the seas, and they all shivered with the sound of his words.

There were no more questions after that. It was time to leave that foul place.

CHAPTER ONE

THE WAY BACK TO TARTAE

The water quickly spread through the white, cold floor of the movie theater's restroom until it touched Olivia's feet, making a chill climb up her body—this was real and happening fast. The smell of the phookas took over the place as they continuously jumped around like giant fleas, laughing in that irritating way of theirs. She missed a lot of things about Tartae—the phookas were not one of them.

"Why does Lars keep sending messengers? What does that guy do all day to prevent him from taking care of his business? Don't you all get tired of doing this for him?" challenged Olivia. In her mind, she tried to make sense of what was happening. Not only she had failed in her mission of destroying the Portals of Tartae, but they were now open, and there were phookas in Leve, ready to kill her and whoever entered that restroom. She needed to be careful and decide fast what her next steps should be to stay alive.

Neither the phookas nor the man said a thing. The phookas kept bouncing around, and this man—or man-like creature—looked fresh out of a grave, with deep dark circles under his eyes, as pale as death itself.

"Why are you here?" Olivia asked, now staring deeply into the man's black eyes. She was more serious now; the energy inside the restroom was palpably changing into something even worse. She needed to prepare herself.

He never answered. He took a moment, standing motionless, as though he were a painting or the photograph of a spirit snapped accidentally inside a haunted house, and then he attacked Olivia. The man moved his arms fast, making the white and blue tiles in the bathroom break free from the walls and fly in Olivia's direction. She threw herself onto the wet floor and crawled, taking cover under the white porcelain sinks. There was no time to ponder what she should do; the man was again raging in the middle of the restroom, yelling and destroying all that was there. Olivia's mind ran through her options while he marched in her direction. The phookas only watched and hysterically laughed, always annoying and loathsome, and obviously trying to distract her from her way out of it.

Olivia closed her eyes at once and silenced it all. Darkness filled her brain, and she got up with only one thought echoing inside her mind: She wanted to live. The water danced on the floor and stretched all around her until it became a thick, impenetrable wall, separating her from the rest of the room like a shield. She opened her eyes, and her heart ached in fear; she was protected now, but for how long?

The man stood in front of her defiantly and closed both of his fists, gathering strength, to the point that his veins seemed about to burst. He opened his hands in a purposeful movement and everything around them: The toilets, the wooden cabinets, the mirror, everything exploded in a rush of energy.

Olivia shut her eyes instinctively, covering her face with her arms and staying like this for what seemed an eternity. When she was finally able to open them, there was water splashing everywhere; the wall she had created was no more, the bathroom was empty, and she was quite hurt, having bruises and cuts all over her body.

She ran back to the movie theater, dripping water and blood all over the place, leaving a reddish trace all the way to her seat. The lights were out, and the movie was already on, painting the enormous room in its romantic yellowish colors.

"You sure took some time in there—Olie, what happened?" Lara asked, noticing Olivia's pitiful state. "You're all wet and … Is that blood? Are you hurt? What the hell happened in there?" Lara stood and couldn't hold her tone. Fear grew in her voice.

"We *gotta* go," said Olivia, her eyes as wide as they could be. "NOW! WE MUST GO NOW!" she yelled urgently, paying no mind of where they were.

People around them complained and shushed, but Olivia and Lara didn't even hear. Olivia's blood was running fast through her veins, and her mind was somewhere else already. Lara took her purse in a swift movement, and they both ran out of that place, stumbling onto people and yelling for them to clear the way.

Olivia led Lara outside, pulling her by the hand, and headed to the car. She looked around attentively at every second to make sure no one was after them; she looked with suspicion at every shadow, asserting that it wasn't a phooka or any other surprise sent from Lars.

There was an icy wind outside that froze Olivia's heart as soon as the mall's doors closed behind them, and the fact that she was completely wet didn't help with the cold at all.

"We must get Trevor. You need to drive us to the university, Lara," said Olivia as they approached Lara's gray car. A million thoughts danced inside her brain, and she had a hard time piecing them together. *What had just happened? Who was that man? Were the Portals really open?*

"WHAT? Trevor?" protested Lara. "What the heck is happening, and why are you hurt? We must call the police, not Trevor."

Olivia looked around once more, and that cold breeze she knew very well filled her lungs and awakened her skin, reminding her of everything she could never forget. She gazed deeply into Lara's eyes, and sadness filled her heart.

"Get in the car, Lara." She said it softly, a motherly tone in her voice. She was so serious and certain that Lara didn't question and just sat inside waiting. As soon as they were both in, Olivia looked around one more time and continued, "Lara, I don't have time to explain every little detail—and maybe it's not even possible—but yes, I was attacked in the restroom, but I'm fine now. The thing is … What attacked me in there was not from this world. And now I know for a fact that we are in danger, all of us. And Trevor is the help we need."

Lara stared back at Olivia with a puzzled look and seemed to be about to start laughing … or crying. Her expressions were all mixed, and she was clearly waiting for more information, something that could make sense and could make her decide what expression to choose. After a while in deep silence, Olivia spoke again.

"Trevor is who we need now. We've been through this before. Please, let's go, Lara."

Lara sighed and started driving. Olivia could tell that her friend was completely lost, in the same position she had been just over a year ago when she had arrived in Tartae unexpectedly, falling into a hole that had suddenly appeared on a calm street in Leve.

Lara didn't say much while driving to the University of Leve, but she kept shaking her head continuously, like a never-ending 'no'. Outside the car, everything seemed normal. The mid-afternoon traffic was light, and people were strolling up and down the quaint streets of Leve, unaware of anything out of the usual.

As for Olivia, she found a way to clear her mind, and the only thing in it now was to find Trevor. The rest was too much to handle. But every time she touched the tip of those thoughts, every time they unavoidably found a way into her head, she trembled and stopped breathing.

"We are here," said Lara, parking the car right outside the opulent building. The place was like a castle: big, gray, and old. A huge green field filled the front, and many students all around walking in groups and alone, carrying important looking books. Some laughing, others too serious, but none aware of anything strange that was happening in their own world.

"Let's go." Olivia sighed and stepped out of the car. She walked fast, willing her legs not to run. They were already getting too much attention as it was, since Olivia's clothes were still wet and stained with blood. Lara followed, and after going through several long and bright hallways, they arrived at the office where Trevor was working, digitalizing books from the university's library.

Trevor wore a white coat over his clothes and protective gloves to preserve the delicate books and documents he was handling. The whole assembly made him resemble a scientist, an impression even more accentuated by the concentrated expression on his face and the glasses he wore. He stood by a huge table with many books and loose pages laid out in front of him, and he was carefully analyzing every one of them. Olivia banged loudly on the large glass window, until Trevor was taken out of his absorption and looked at her. His eyes faded a bit when they met Olivia's. His face fell as he walked slowly to the office door, dreading his next moments.

"They're here," Olivia said, and her eyes watered. There was an enormous lump in her throat as she mouthed the exact words she knew Trevor was afraid to hear. They exchanged a look that only they could understand.

"What are you saying, Olie?" asked Trevor in a whisper, his voice now trembling too. For a moment that sense of urgency that was weighing the air around them dissipated, and there was slowness, as though everything had paused in order for them to choose their future.

Olivia took a deep breath.

"I was attacked by phookas and some other person, or creature—because he looked half dead—when I was at the movies with Lara. They used magic, and so did I," said Olivia.

Trevor pulled her close to him and hugged her tightly. Words were lost, and only an embrace seemed to speak what they both needed to hear.

"We must find a way to go back to Tartae," said Olivia as she let go of Trevor's arms.

"I know, but how? The Key we had disintegrated on our way back to Leve."

"If phookas can do it, so can we, Trev … We just have to find a way," concluded Olivia.

"What are phookas?" asked Lara, who Olivia had completely forgotten was there. Lara had kept quiet for a while, probably trying to understand and keep track of what Olivia and Trevor were discussing but seeing that she was nowhere near achieving that, she gave up. Her confused look would be comical, if it weren't so understandable.

"Oh, Lara … I'm so sorry," answered Olivia. "We can't explain it all to you, we don't have time. But I can say this: Last year we went to a place called Tartae. It's another world completely, where time runs differently, and they have two moons in their night sky. We ended up there accidentally when we fell into a Portal that opened right here in Leve. So there's also that … Portals between the worlds. We thought we had destroyed all of them and everyone was safe, but as you can see, we were wrong. I was wrong."

"Are you joking? You don't look like you are joking. Is this real? Why are you doing this?" Lara's eyes were now wide in despair and moving from Olivia to Trevor restlessly, searching for an answer much more ordinary than the one she had received.

"Yes, it's real," said Trevor, resting his hand on Lara's shoulder. "And I felt just like you once. I thought I was having a very bad dream, but at least you were not attacked and almost killed by the phookas. Who, by the way, are disgusting. They look like giant flies and they smell like garbage. You don't want to meet them."

"If the phookas were here, that means that the Portals were opened again. I know something has changed; my magic is different. I was able to connect with the elements in a way that I haven't since we were in Tartae," said Olivia.

"Were you able to do spells after we came back? Have you ever tried here in Leve?" asked Trevor.

"Yes and no. I don't quite know how to explain, but it wasn't magic … almost. I'd do something and then it would go away quickly, as if it had never existed. I don't know, Trevor … I just know that I wasn't feeling very magical, but now I am. Something has woken up all around and within me."

"Guys … This is too much … Magic? What are you doing?" scoffed Lara, her face twitching with the questions she wasn't asking.

"In Tartae, I was able to connect with nature and do some stuff … Magic, as you might call it." Olivia snapped her fingers, producing pink sparks that resembled little fairies. "See?"

Lara's mouth opened, letting out a squeak.

"Trev, I think it's better if we go and try to find a way back to Tartae, and Lara, you go home and just stay safe. Be careful, and don't go anywhere near our houses. I'd say that they are the worst place to be right now," continued Olivia.

"You cannot just dump me and go to Tartae. I *wanna* see this place too and help, if there's a way to help," protested Lara.

"I don't think that's possible, Lara. You should stay here and keep an eye out for things while we are there, and even maybe try to warn the authorities if something else happens," said Olivia.

"Yeah, believe me when I say this: You don't want to be in Tartae not knowing anything about how things work there. You'll be safer in Leve. And also, we don't even know how we are going to go there … So, definitely safer here," concluded Trevor.

"We have to move. I say we start in my house and try to find something there. If they are looking for me, that would be the place to go. Lara, could you give us a ride?"

"Well, yes …" answered Lara, seeming quite unsure of what to do, but then leading the way to the parking lot.

They drove through Leve's calm streets, full of trees and green lawns where evil seemed not to exist, and for some reason, all that peacefulness made Olivia even more worried, as if that false sense of safety would be the doom of the small, quaint city of Leve. She didn't dare to voice those thoughts, especially in front of Lara.

As they arrived at Olivia's house, she said goodbye to Lara and left the car with Trevor. She could tell Lara was uneasy and having a hard time following the orders to stay put, but deep down, she probably knew it was for the best and wanted to avoid an exceptionally weird experience. Lara took a moment, staring at the steering wheel, and then left without looking back.

"Do you have any idea where to start?" said Trevor as soon as they stepped inside Olivia's house. There was no one there. Her grandmother, Mrs. May Halin, was once again traveling around some pacific island and her things were just lying around. "Your grandma has a lot of stuff for someone who is never home …"

Olivia laughed and said, "Let's try to retrace our last hours in Tartae. There was that circle in the forest …"

"There were symbols there. Do you remember what they were? Maybe we can recreate them and open a connection," said Trevor.

"Not exactly. It was all so fast and dark. Alavro had the Book of The Portals, and we had one of the Keys in our hands," added Olivia.

"But it became dust when we got to Leve," said Trevor, sitting down on the couch and scratching his head in a pensive way.

"Yes. I think they all became dust when we *destroyed* the Portals, but even so, Lars managed to come here. I guess there's no need for Keys anymore," concluded Olivia. In her mind, the possibility of Lars traveling through the worlds freely arose for the first time. She wondered if it had become that easy.

"Do you think he can come and go now without a problem?" Trevor asked, as though reading her thoughts.

"I don't know, Trev. Maybe … But once again I think that he was still testing the Portal he managed to open, because he didn't come himself. He did the exact same thing with Baltazar last year, so I think it's a pattern. He's afraid of dying during the trip or maybe losing his powers. But we are still a menace to him; he's out for us once again," said Olivia.

"Why didn't he send Baltazar? He survived his first trip, and he knows us. He hates us. He would gladly try to kill us again."

A shiver ran through Olivia's back, and something fell inside her stomach like a heavy rock. The memory of her sword perforating Baltazar's flesh took over her, but she didn't have the courage to tell Trevor that she had possibly killed him in the room of mirrors on that dreadful, desperate night.

"Did you bring anything with you that day?" Olivia said, moving away from that subject quickly, trying to erase Trevor's question from her mind and maybe even from his.

"No, and I threw all of those clothes away because they were completely ruined. Oh, and I left my bow and arrows there at the circle; I didn't think I'd ever need them around here," said Trevor.

"I left my sword in Lars' mansion, but I still have the clothes I was wearing that day," said Olivia.

Trevor met her gaze and stared at her for a second, and Olivia knew he could read the emotion behind her actions. She had a harder time with the idea that she would never go back to Tartae, so she held on to the clothes, even though they couldn't possibly be worn again. She was clinging to a memory, maybe holding on to some kind of hope.

Trevor was graceful about it and didn't force a conversation on the subject.

"Speaking of clothes, you might need to change," he finally said, laughing.

Olivia had forgotten her clothes were damp and stained with blood. In the rush she was to find a way back to Tartae, everything else seemed unimportant. She decided to quickly change and wash her face, while Trevor continued the search around her house, trying to find something, anything that could give him a clue of how to open a Portal or spark some sort of idea.

Olivia got ready fast and resumed her side of the search in no time. She kept the clothes she was wearing during their last night in Tartae inside a fabric bag, hidden in her closet. She went through everything, looking inside all the pockets and even smelling the clothes, which now only had the scent of the lavender laundry detergent she used.

"Nothing," she said as she came downstairs and met Trevor's eyes. "There was nothing there. No clues whatsoever. I don't see how we can find anything here, Trev … What could we possibly find that would help us in my grandma's mess?"

Olivia sat down on a step, looking around, trying to remember everything she'd learned about the Portals and the way Cordella used to take them to Tartae: They went during the night; time passed differently; they didn't remember what had happened; the friends she made there … Bran, Belenos, Emma… *Emma*!

"Oh! The stone!" Olivia screamed. She stood and ran to her bedroom. Trevor followed her.

In there, resting over her nightstand, there was a small, beautiful wooden box engraved with a tree, which Olivia had carved herself. And inside was a stone that resembled a galaxy.

"Do you remember this? Emma gave it to me when we were leaving Belenos' house so I could remember her and Tartae," said Olivia excitedly.

Trevor studied the stone carefully, a gleaming, small beacon of hope. It sparked in silver and purple, and tiny rainbows formed on its surface when touched by light. Trevor smiled.

"This is it, Trev. This is our way back to Tartae!"

CHAPTER TWO

THE SATYR

They stared at the stone as if waiting for the object to do something. Seconds turned into minutes, and silence brought them no answer.

"What now, Olie?" asked Trevor. His eyes drowned in uncertainty.

"Well, now I have no idea," scoffed Olivia, twitching her lips.

"What if this is just a rock? If that's the case, we're only wasting our time," said Trevor. "Do you really think Lars knows where you live?" He peered out the bedroom window. The light was coming in gently, for the sun was weak and almost setting.

"He knew I was at the movies, and they even managed to portal there. Last time, they knew about Lucent Bookshop … That's where I saw Baltazar for the first time. So let's just assume that they know everything … It's safer for us if we are overly careful," stated Olivia.

Trevor closed the curtains and sighed, visibly worried. Olivia sat cross-legged on her bed, with the crystal in her right hand, shaking it, studying it carefully. The thing was cold and still beautiful, although lacking the appeal it once had. A warmth that was connected to Olivia's memories of Emma and Tartae and had nothing to do with magic or their way back to that place.

Trevor sat across from Olivia, and they both looked at the crystal. At the height of her despair, Olivia just talked to the thing:

"Please, show us the way to Tartae. We need to go back."

Trevor chuckled, but Olivia didn't look away from the stone. Maybe it was a silly thing to try, but she had hope. Her mind emptied, and something clicked inside her heart. All the smells that lingered around the room got stronger: the recently washed linens, the wood from the furniture, even the grass outside found a way through the walls and windows, as though everything had woken up.

The crystal vibrated subtly but visibly in Olivia's hand. The two friends looked at each other in expectation, barely breathing, and inside the rock, an image took form, but it went away quickly. For a moment, the thing went all dark blue, like a starless and cloudless sky, and then there was a metallic cluster of sparks in the middle that swirled until it burst all around the room.

Olivia and Trevor were petrified, mesmerized by what they were seeing. They were now inside this blue dome, full of stars moving slowly around them.

"This is not our sky, Olie. The constellations … They just don't make any sense," said Trevor, frowning and studying the dots that glimmered around them.

"That's because it's not the sky," said Olivia, her eyes shining with amazement. "This is a map. We must follow it!" Excitement grew inside her.

"But do you understand where it's going? This is not making any sense to me."

"I guess so," answered Olivia, smiling. "Come on!"

They both rushed outside, running down the stairs and through the living room. It was night already. The streetlights were on, and the houses were lit too. Crickets sang, and there was no one around, which was the usual way of things around this time of the day in Leve. Everybody was probably just having dinner and unaware of the peril they were in, of the uninvited guests in their calm land.

"Are we going to walk around in this? Not very discreet, I have to say," said Trevor. They were enveloped in a thin veil that allowed them to see through it, but was undeniably there.

"I don't think anybody can see this, Trev … just us. It's magic, remember?" said Olivia airily.

"If you say so …," said Trevor. He studied his surroundings so much that his actions were almost too slow; he seemed to be having a hard time accepting that this was happening there, in Leve, where virtually nothing ever happened.

"Trevor," said Olivia, gently grabbing both of his arms. "Look at me and breathe. We just have to follow the stars. See? They are shining for us, guiding our way. We just have to follow them. Emma knew what she was doing, and you know she'd never hurt us."

Trevor still hesitated. His face was heavy with worry and all wrinkled up, like a dried date. "Let's just hope so," he said, a little confidence growing in his eyes.

"Good. You'll have to drive," said Olivia.

Trevor nodded. They headed to his house, walking across the lawn that stretched over every house on that street; it was the quickest way to Trevor's, which was luckily very close to Olivia's. As they reached his place, it was like crossing city limits. The difference was palpable: It smelled like roses, love, and family. Something heavily missing from Olivia's place.

The house was painted light yellow, and its garden was lit by pale peach and white roses planted many springs ago by Trevor's mother. Mr. Meris took great care of them as if nurturing an undying love.

As they neared the garage, the sound of pots and pans got louder: Trevor's father was preparing dinner for him and his son while listening to some old jazz song. The smell of rosemary and sage found their noses outside, and worry grew all over Trevor's face again.

"Maybe it's better if you text him and say you're not coming, Trev. You can tell him that you're with me," said Olivia, trying to avoid a possible problem. Last time, it wasn't easy for Trevor to convince his dad that everything was okay and that he wasn't lying about the true reasons he was missing for a whole night.

"I hate lying to him …" said Trevor with a sigh.

"I know … But you *are* with me. That's not a complete lie …" observed Olivia.

Trevor stopped by his garage door to text his father: *"Something just came up with Olie. Can't make it to dinner… Sorry, Dad. Have to take the car!"*

He then opened the brown garage door and slid inside the car quickly, before his dad could show up to ask questions. They left in a hurry, and he just honked on his way out.

"I just hate that …" he said again, squeezing the steering wheel mindlessly.

Olivia guided, telling Trevor to go left, right, up that street, down the other. They drove around Leve for hours, getting far from where they lived and still having no idea where exactly they were going. The glistening dots coming from the crystal kept changing, pointing in different directions and reinforcing the hope they had that they were heading the right way.

"Trevor, I think we're here! The stone is glowing," said Olivia.

Trevor parked by the curbside and peered at the crystal that now flashed a bright white light, as though it had become a star itself. The dome around them disappeared and they were now at the struggling art district of Leve—a charming place idealized to resemble a Parisian street, with cozy cafes and beautiful lamplight. But people in Leve didn't really buy art, so it was quite sad, for virtually no one visited the galleries, and they were always going out of business after challenging months.

It was the end of the day, and people were leaving their offices, shutting and locking the doors behind them, and one of the galleries caught Olivia and Trevor's attention. While many of them had big glass windows that allowed customers to see what was inside in the hopes that something would spark their interest, this one had a small blue iron door that was wide open and no windows whatsoever, only two humongous paintings decorating its façade. Its walls were egg-yellow and old, beaten by the weather and the years. Unlike many other galleries on this struggling art street, this one seemed ancient.

Olivia and Trevor stepped inside, crossing the intimidating paintings hanging by the door as if they were guardians of the threshold: The one on the left was of a lady sitting on a chair; she carried a terracotta vase over her head and had a mouth for eyes—it was quite somber. The one on the right was colorful and geometrical, with many triangles filled with different bright colors, and inside the gallery, the walls were fully covered by art in every size, arranged in a Tetris-like concept. There was a style for every liking: still nature, modern, collage, weird ones, paintings too scary to describe, paintings too beautiful to describe. A single blue door was located at the end of the main room; wooden stairs led to the second floor, and an almost overpowering smell that seemed a mix of paint and hydromel lingered.

Olivia and Trevor studied the gallery openmouthed. They walked in slowly, amazed by what surrounded them. This room was alive with art, and it was contagious, like being dragged into a catchy song. Each painting showed them a path they could choose, a different door into the unknown. It was all strange and intriguing.

And then there it was: a tiny painting of two moons glistening in the sky, casting their light upon a deep valley.

"Trevor, it's Tartae!" said Olivia, pointing to the small painting, which was almost hidden at the top of the back wall.

"Oh, Olie … It could be a coincidence," said Trevor, studying it from where he stood.

"There's no such thing." Olivia shook her head and stared deep into Trevor's eyes. Excitement and fear grew inside her.

"Looking for anything in particular? We have more paintings upstairs if you'd like. A present for Mom and Dad, I'd say, huh?" said the man walking out of the office in the back. As he got closer, the smell of hydromel got stronger, and every single wrinkle on his face became so clear to Olivia that it was like reading a book that told all sorts of stories. His kind black eyes were framed by his round glasses, which rested on top of his large nose. His chin-strap beard was full and all white. He shot Olivia and Trevor a big smile, showing them his crooked teeth.

"Oh, thank you, sir. Can you tell us more about this painting?" asked Trevor, pointing to the one with the two moons.

"I guess you can find something better for your parents, young man. Maybe a bigger one, or more colorful. What do you think about flowers?" the man said, already walking away from where Olivia and Trevor stood and heading closer to a painting of many red roses.

"We need to go to Tartae." Olivia said, resolutely. Her voice broke the energy in the room, as it put all of their intentions and secrets out, open for whatever destiny had in store for them.

Trevor and the man looked at her.

"Olie …" warned Trevor, trying to be discreet.

"No, Trev. We have no time to lose!" she said, urgently. "We know that it's Tartae in that picture, sir. And this stone brought us here, so I guess you know something about it. Will you help us?" Olivia asked while she stretched her arm and showed him the glowing crystal.

The man smiled and, in complete silence, walked to the front door to close it, which made Olivia and Trevor more scared and uncertain.

"First of all, my name is Aeron Dunes. And you are?" he finally said. His eyes gleamed.

"I'm Olivia Halin, and he's Trevor Meris. We need to go back to Tartae, Mr. Dunes. Is there anything you can do for us?" insisted Olivia in a business-like tone.

"Call me Aeron, please," said Aeron, airily, as he observed Olivia and Trevor.

"We thought that the Portals of Tartae were destroyed. But we were wrong," said Trevor.

"And why did you think that?" inquired Aeron, frowning.

"I'm afraid I won't tell you that part," said Olivia. "Can you help us? Please, just say if you're able to, because if you're not, we need to keep trying to find a way back."

"You don't trust me, but you want my help?" Aeron continued, a mischievous look in his eyes.

"We don't have a lot of options," answered Olivia.

"Do you have any clue what we are talking about, Mr. Dunes?" asked Trevor.

Mr. Dunes' lips arched a little, a draft of a smile. "Yes, I know about Tartae. Did someone from the Svender family give you this?" he asked, his eyes fixated on the stone.

"Yes, Emma Svender did. So you know her?" asked Olivia eagerly.

"I knew her family very well; I used to live in Lirianthis too. I moved here a long, long time ago … Things were very different then. May I ask why you need to go back?" asked Aeron.

"The Portals of Tartae are open again, and people are using them who shouldn't be. We must warn the Clan," said Olivia.

Mr. Dunes looked at Olivia while pondering.

"Oh well, I guess it's time to help." He headed to his office, and Olivia and Trevor followed, stopping by the door while the man looked through some old papers. Hanging on the wall was a painting of him as a satyr. "Oh yes, my dear. That's me in my most unearthly way," he said dismissively. "Now, let's go."

Aeron led Olivia and Trevor upstairs; the steps creaked loudly under the weight of their bodies. The second floor was even more flooded with paintings, and a big window let the breeze dance inside, touching all of them gently and reminding them that the night was getting old.

"A long time ago, I was also protecting Tartae, but I fell madly in love and came here. I like this place, even though some things here seem forgotten. Here, this is your way back." Aeron removed some gigantic paintings that were leaning over one wall, leaving just one of a beautiful, enormous tree. "If the Portals are in fact open, you will be able to go back to Tartae; if not, I'm afraid you'll be stuck in the painting forever, and there's nothing I can do about it. Are you certain?"

"Yes, I am," said Olivia.

"Are we?" asked Trevor with uncertainty, and Olivia just looked in his eyes, twitching her lips and shrugging. What else they could do?

"So may it be. You can step inside the painting whenever you're ready," said Aeron.

Olivia and Trevor looked at the painting awkwardly; the thing appeared too normal to be a Portal, and Trevor reached to touch it.

"No. It doesn't work that way," warned Mr. Dunes, shaking his head. "It will only be a Portal when you step inside with all of all."

Olivia looked at the man and took a deep breath. "It was nice to meet you, Aeron. Thank you."

"Thank you," followed Trevor. "Here goes nothing."

And they stepped inside.

CHAPTER THREE

THE HAWTHORN TREES

Olivia and Trevor were now covered in paint: Yellow, green, blue, red, and black thick brushstrokes everywhere; it touched their skin and enveloped them like colorful dresses, ever-changing, fresh. It pulled them deeper into the white canvas, spreading and dancing in front of them, but never forming a clear image, never painting a picture that they could make any sense of.

The two friends floated like leaves falling from a tall tree with no control of their direction, only sinking deeper into the white void. The smell of paint was so strong that Olivia could taste it in her mouth, and it made her sick. This Portal wasn't like the other ones they had known; it wasn't fast like the last time, and they weren't pushed and pulled around. They were not falling into a dark hole either. This was slow and seemed somehow hopeless; they danced inside the paint to no sound, moving slightly to one side and the other, rocking their way down. But eventually, it ended, and they arrived.

A forest materialized in front of them, at first blurred, and then its image became sharp and real; it revealed itself like when one wakes up and opens their eyes in the harsh light. Olivia's feet met the mossy ground, and she drew a deep breath, taking in the night around her. There was no vestige of paint in their bodies anymore, although Olivia's stomach still turned, and the scent of it lingered for a moment.

"Where are we?" Trevor broke the silence, speaking softly as if trying not to break a delicate spell. "Is this Tartae?" he said, looking at the sky and seeing no sign of the two moons.

"Yes," answered Olivia.

"But do you know where we are?" Trevor asked.

Olivia only shook her head. They had landed in a dense forest, where the trees were wild and emanated ancient energy, revealing that they must have arrived inside an untouched woodland. Here, the scent of nature caressed their noses, sweet and flowery. The night sky was covered by thick clouds, those that hold buckets of rain. And the forest was unusually silent.

Olivia and Trevor chose a direction and walked carefully, afraid of their next steps. The forest floor was dry and cracked as they followed a path chosen by chance, and the night got darker as they went deeper into the woods.

"Olie, I'm not sure if we should be here. These woods are getting denser, and those bushes seem so thick that I don't think we'll be able to cross them. We should turn back," said Trevor.

"I know where we are, Trev," said Olivia. A wall of hawthorn trees stretched in front of them. Their branches were covered in white flowers and formed something of a wild white fence, much different than what one would find in Leve. "We are at the edge of Lirianthis. Hawthorn trees protect the village, look! Even in our world, they're known for their protective powers, some people even call them 'The Fairy Trees' because they believe guardian fairies live under them and can take you to another world. Come, we must find a way in."

It was as though something had lifted from Olivia's shoulders. She now carried a smile on her face and guided their way into the cluster of hawthorn trees—and there were many of them, all very close together, making it impossible to see what was guarded beyond their trunks and leaves. Olivia opened the way for Trevor, pushing the branches carefully away and venturing between the protective plants. As they passed through, the trees seemed to close the path behind them: Olivia and Trevor were being led into Lirianthis.

"I guess that after all this time, you'll finally see Lirianthis, Trev. The forest is inviting you inside, can you see it?" said Olivia, searching for Trevor's eyes and finding two sparkly big brown acorns, gleaming with amazement. "And here we are …"

The trees became sparse. There were still many hawthorns and other trees all around, but they were now scattered throughout the landscape. That beautiful mossy landscape that Olivia would recognize anywhere. Lirianthis was still pretty much the same. A secluded haven well-guarded by the forest itself, with stairs climbing up the tree trunks, green and blue houses on top of rocks, and the veil of magic blessing everything.

"So this is Lirianthis ..." said Trevor. His expression was almost hidden under the shadows of the night, but Olivia could read his voice very well: The wonderment was undeniably there.

"I wish you could see it in other circumstances ... But I don't think you'd come here happily or willingly. So this is as good as it gets, I guess," joked Olivia.

Trevor chuckled. "Oh, well. I can barely see it anyways. It's so dark without the moons, and no one seems to be up. There's no light. And this silence ... It's giving me the creeps," said Trevor, looking around.

"It wasn't like this last time ... It felt secluded, but it was alive and bursting with good energy, people walking around and enjoying themselves. But we don't even know what time it is. Maybe it's late at night and everyone has already gone to bed. Come, let's try to find Emma. If I remember it well—" started Olivia, but Trevor interrupted her.

"Olie ... We have no idea how much time has passed or what happened in Tartae while we weren't here. Who knows what could have changed? Do you think ... that ... they ..." Trevor didn't find the courage to finish, and his voice fell to a low whisper. He found Olivia's gaze, somber and afraid.

"Let's not even go there, Trev ... Let's just try to find her," said Olivia, being assertive and deviating her thoughts from a possibility she didn't even want to consider. "If I remember it correctly, Emma used some flowers to make her house easier to find, and it should be in this direction. Come."

Trevor followed her, they went on and on through Lirianthis pathways for about ten minutes, passing the giant birch trees with multiple houses attached to their trunks, and then by the clearing where Olivia had attended to the summer festivities what seemed like many lives before. It was still a splendid forest, but it had no sound, and under the heavily clouded sky, they could barely see what was in front of them. Everything around seemed to be asleep: the forest, the animals, Lirianthis as a whole. Plants didn't move at their own will anymore, not like they did the first time they'd arrived in Tartae. Olivia tried to pay no mind to it, doing her best to ignore what could easily be the truth. Time ran differently in Tartae, and too much of it could have passed. Lirianthis could be full of other souls. She had no idea. Closing the Portals could have destroyed more than what the Clan hoped for. But then again, Lars seemed to be alive. Those thoughts were quickly pushed away from Olivia's mind using the best of her ability; she kept focusing on the moment, on walking the next step, finding the next sign that they were on the right path to Emma's house. They took a right by a fragrant hawthorn tree—the only thing that appeared to be alive in that place, for its smell was potent and followed them around—and there it was, red flowers coloring a window.

"That's a good sign," said Trevor between breaths, trying to appear hopeful and upbeat, almost to the point of sounding fake.

They climbed the spiral stairs that led to Emma's house as fast as they could, hurrying up the narrow steps. But it was hard; not only with as steep and tiresome as it was, but Olivia and Trevor were now half-breathing, as though fear had its menacing hands on their throats. Olivia didn't remember how high Emma's house was. On their way to it, they were met by low clouds that wrapped them in a cold, wet blanket. The wooden steps cracked under their shoes, and the night became heavier as they reached the door.

After knocking three times, Olivia's heart pounded in her chest, finding its way to her throat. Beating like a drum.

"Olie, Trev! You're here!" Emma's hoarse voice greeted them, smooth and warm like a lullaby. "Come inside. Please! Come!"

They walked in between hugs, laughs, and one or two discreet tears. Olivia's heart was like a flower once frozen and now blooming again under the warm sun. For a heartbeat, she wondered if everything she loved wasn't there anymore, if she were about to encounter an unfamiliar Tartae, if the people she loved were long gone and only stories remained. If even that. "Oh, Emma … We're so happy you're here," she finally said, breathing out.

Inside Emma's house, little had changed, which was somehow a comfort to Olivia. There was still a lot of papers spread out, open books and notes about flowers and incantations. Emma looked the same, as though no time had passed since they last saw each other, but she seemed tired and less energetic than Olivia remembered, with deep circles under her eyes, and there was something in them that Olivia had never seen before.

"How long has it been?" Olivia asked as she sat on a wooden chair, removing a pile of papers and books and putting them on the floor.

"Too long, but not long at all," Emma answered. "And I'm not being poetic or anything, I actually don't quite know. Things have been strange and slow, almost paused for a while. You'll see it for yourselves."

"What do you mean?" said Trevor, his eyes studying Emma carefully.

"I mean exactly what I just said, Trev … You left and things went on pretty well for a while. After, I don't know, a couple of months, time slowed down, and we all lost count of it. Sometimes, days seem to last seasons, nights are too dark to count. I don't know if you noticed, but it's all drying up. There has been no rain since you and Olivia left and—apparently—didn't destroy the Portals … On that note, how did you get here?"

"Using this." Olivia showed Emma the crystal. Its little dots now glimmered like stars in the sky. A calming and assuring sight. "How did you know we might need it?"

"I didn't, but I had a tad bit of hope. Sometimes you just have to cling on to that … I'm glad it worked and that you figured it out!" Emma's face brightened as she smiled. "I couldn't let you leave Tartae without a way to get back … If there were still a way. The stone was supposed to show you a Portal, in case they still existed. I suppose you met Aeron, then?"

"Yes. Interesting guy, he is …," said Trevor.

"Interesting satyr, you mean!" said Emma with a laugh.

"How were you able to open a Portal?" asked Olivia, piecing together the information she had.

"I wasn't …," said Emma. "Aeron was. You are here because of his talents and my guessing. Aeron went to your world a long time ago; he was a friend of my grandparents and they talked about him constantly, for he was extremely talented in healing and loved to experiment with Portals. He went to your world to help cure some disease, in one of the travels organized by the Clan, and fell in love with a woman there, which led to his decision to stay. He came here once more to say farewell and gifted my grandparents this crystal, assuring them that, if one day the Portals were unblocked and there was no more need for Portal Keys, they would be able to find a good Portal and visit. My grandparents passed away, but satyrs live extremely long lives. I figured if something went sideways and you needed a way back to Tartae, this was it."

"So, you weren't even sure if there was going to be a Portal?" asked Trevor.

"Oh, I was sure … Aeron wouldn't disappoint the Portals. And satyrs were known for having a special way with Portals before Ourivio Brut closed them; it's said that they still carry on those abilities. So, I just put two and two together and hoped for the best." Emma seemed proud of herself; her smile was honest, and she sounded lighter somehow.

"Do other magical creatures live in our world?" Trevor inquired.

"Of course! But not many forest beings find it appealing, at least not after people in your world started to forget the Old Ways. They think it's quite boring and soul-crushing most of the time," Emma explained.

"And how come I've never seen a satyr anywhere? Neither here nor there?" Trevor continued.

"Because they wear pants!" Emma laughed.

"I don't know if this is interesting or scary … or both," Trevor said.

They laughed, which seemed to bring Emma fully back to her old self, bubbly and warm, and that made Olivia's soul at ease.

"But I'm sure you're not here for satyr stories … What happened?" asked Emma, her tone suddenly grave, and a gray cloud back to her face.

"Someone attacked me in Leve. Lars sent them, I'm sure. There were phookas and sorcery, and it was a complete mess. The Portals didn't open only for Trevor and me; Lars is at it again. The Portals are unprotected, and we needed to warn the Clan," said Olivia, her voice firm and contained.

Emma took a moment and looked into Olivia's eyes as if collecting clues of what she needed to do next, or the words she needed to say. "I'm going to let Cordella know of your arrival; you need her. As for right now, let's go to Diana." She sighed, saying nothing else. She got up at once and walked to a room deep in her home, coming back with a leather pouch that she was now closing carefully. "There, Cordella is aware of everything."

"Medallion messengers, I suppose …" recognized Olivia.

"Yes. And I sent word for Orion too. We'll need the centaurs' fast pace to move quickly," said Emma as she got ready to leave. She belted her pouch around her waist and grabbed a long sword that rested next to the door, and with her sage green pants and dark brown boots, she resembled a warrior elf.

Emma led the way to Diana's house, stepping into the night that was smooth and cold, like velvet. There was no one around; Lirianthis still seemed too quiet, almost abandoned, and everything in Tartae was strange. The place appeared to stand still in time. The trees didn't move even an inch, for there was no wind, and their leaves were in the air as if they had forgotten how to fall. It was all frozen in some moment.

"It's sad. I haven't seen the two moons yet. I miss them," said Olivia, shaking away the thoughts creeping into her mind and peering at the sky, searching for the two pearls that used to show them the way during every journey in Tartae.

"You better get used to it." Emma sighed. "We can barely see them these days."

And for some reason, neither Olivia nor Trevor had the nerve to ask her why. They only exchanged a look that meant a thousand words, all of fear and complicity. The sky was still covered by heavy clouds, dark gray and thick, never moving, never changing.

"Emma, what about the others?" Olivia asked, as she could wait no longer. This pressing question had repeated itself constantly in her mind for the past year or so.

"You can ask me what you *really* want," Emma said with a half-smile.

"I guess Cordella is well—we're going to her and she seems to still be fighting for the Portals. But what about the others?" Olivia repeated.

"They are fine, Olivia. *Bran* is fine," she answered. Her eyes rested on Olivia for a moment. "You must prepare, for things are different here. And I feel that they're about to change even more," Emma said, her face stern, and something in her voice made Olivia think that she had lost some hope, some innocence. "Come, on. We can't waste any time."

Relief eased Olivia's heart, and her mind cleared a bit after receiving the news that all her friends were well. Bran was well. Knowing this sparked a light inside her, something that made her stronger. The fight with Lars and his lackeys wasn't as fatal as she'd feared, a certainty she'd desired for such a long time, but this warm feeling of relief didn't last long; it was drained away quickly as she remembered the urgency in Emma's voice.

They passed by Lirianthis' trees, through the pathways drawn by stone and dirt, and finally arrived at Diana's house. The charming cabin at the edge of the Lirianthis forest was surrounded by ferns, heathers, and bluebells.

"Look what the Portal brought!" said Emma with an exaggerated tone as soon as the tall, white-haired woman opened the door. The woman's hair was like snow, and her small black eyes studied Olivia and Trevor for a second.

"Come on in," she said, her expression empty. "You can sit down. I'll call Diana." She left, walking swiftly through the hallway door, her slender body moved like a ghost through the ill-lighted room.

Olivia and Trevor stood there, quiet like two standing stones. The energy around the place was unsettling, quite different than the first time Olivia was here. There was a lack of warmth, and of words. She could almost hear Trevor complaining about this trip to Lirianthis being quite disappointing. Not at all what he had dreamed about. The question was: *why*?

After they waited a while in the dark living room, Diana appeared, dressed all in blue, and broke the cold silence with her deep voice.

"So, you returned. Welcome back." Diana smiled politely, no warmth there either. "It's wonderful to finally meet you, Trevor. I'm Diana and this is my wife, Drusilla. Cordella is aware that you are back in Tartae, and I'm afraid I can't do much for you at this time. You must go to her now."

"Isn't it best to wait for the sun?" asked Emma. "I've called the centaurs already, but I'm unsure."

"No. Now is the time," Diana answered softly.

"What's going on here? Is there something pressing Olivia and I should know before going?" Trevor's tone was louder than anyone else's; his voice broke the reverence hovering over the group as though waking them from a dream. "You're all acting weird, and I have to say that I'm afraid. What is happening here?"

Olivia chuckled. It wasn't actually funny, but it was like old times in Tartae, and she knew that only Trevor would be able to bring that exact sensation back.

"I think Cordella should tell you all there is to tell; it's not my place. She was the mind behind it. But not everything had gone according to plan, or to what she had planned." There was bitterness in Diana's tone, especially when she said Cordella's name. She took a while in each letter, as though every part of it made her think of something else, something that was painful or wrong.

"I don't think it's fair to put it like this, Diana," Olivia said, something squeezed her insides with anger and fear. She was unable to hold her tongue, out of admiration and friendship, and like nothing in any world could have stopped her. "Cordella wasn't the only mind behind the plans to destroy the Portals. We were all behind it, if I remember it well, and this time I didn't forget anything … We all agreed that closing the Portals was the best solution. That fighting Lars was what we should do." Olivia's tone was calm and restrained; she didn't want to seem disrespectful to Diana in her own house, but when the woman talked about Cordella with that tone, it hit a nerve.

Diana only smiled in response, barely showing her teeth. A very fake, complacent smile that didn't seem to belong to her face. Silence fell over the room again until Emma broke it.

"Can you hear it?" she said and walked to one of the windows. "The wind is blowing."

Diana and Drusilla walked to the window and stood next to Emma openmouthed. The sound of the wind rushing through the leaves was nothing out of the ordinary, but that didn't seem like the reality for the three women amazed by the sight and sound of the breeze.

"The Portals … isn't it?" said Drusilla with surprise in her voice.

"I guess," said Diana. She stared at the night outside, and then at Olivia and Trevor. "It's time. The centaurs are here; you must leave now. You know what to do, Emma. Follow the shadows and stop for nothing. With the help of the centaurs, you'll be fast as light."

Outside, Orion, the tall and majestic centaur, waited for them, and with him were Firlo and Arden, a young red-haired centaur who didn't talk much.

Olivia and Trevor ran to Orion as fast as rockets. They held the centaur in a warm embrace, and Olivia's heart slowed down for a bit. Seeing Orion was so calming, and his smile was so honest that everything got a bit more colorful. As if the forest had just received a fresh coat of paint.

"Please, my friend. Just get us out of here! This place is weird …" murmured Trevor as he got closer to Orion, who just laughed and patted Trevor's back.

"Not so fast, Trev," said Emma.

"What now? Can't we just leave?" protested Trevor. "I don't think she likes me very much." He glanced at Diana, who was standing on her porch still as a statue.

"It's better that I do a glamour on both of you."

"A what?" asked Trevor.

"A glamour. A disguise … a concealment spell. You must not be seen—as I said before, things have changed a lot around here. Let's keep your arrival between us, at least for now," Emma answered. She moved her hands in circles, one over the other until a pink sphere materialized between her palms; it became translucent, and white clouds appeared inside, moving like a living rose quartz. She then blew the sphere in Trevor's direction, transforming him in a blond man with long braided hair. Trevor was still the same, but somehow, delicately, his features had changed enough for him not to be recognized easily, especially covered by the blanket of night.

And then Emma did the same to Olivia, who became paler, her hair now short, as white as the moon.

"There you go, now we're ready," said Emma, proud of herself.

As the group galloped fast through the woods of Lirianthis, agony filled Olivia's heart and stole her breath at once. She strengthened her hold on Orion's waist; his body was warm and muscular, and he didn't seem bothered by her. She found Emma's eyes gazing at her and encountered in them the confirmation for her suspicions: The forest was suffering. Something had hurt Tartae deeply.

The centaurs were as majestic as ever, galloping into the night. They seemed to glow a bit, making the group's way brighter than it would have been otherwise. Their braided hair moved to the wind created by their own swift pace, spreading the scent of wildflowers and earth that brought magic to the air around them.

Their way to meet Cordella was through dark paths in the forest where light, if there was any, didn't find a way between the branches and leaves. The road was so unkept that was probably only used by the forest beings, and the centaurs—of course—knew that place well. Olivia had yet to discover what time it was and there was no sun or moon to give her a clue. Her first hours in Tartae went by much differently than what she had imagined.

The air was cold around them; the mist rose, and they were now passing by enormous trees, all a blur of green and brown as the group rushed through them. Orion led, so Olivia couldn't see Trevor or Emma most of the time during the journey. After a while, the road became larger and the plants scarce. The sky was still dark when they took a left turn into a paved way, reaching the edge of a city. They kept the same hurried pace as they passed through houses and shops until they finally found a street of paving stone, with austere-looking townhouses and commercial buildings on each side. After going up a slight hill, they arrived at a Greystone building that bore that aura official buildings usually do. In the front, it read in big black letters: Official Council of Tartae.

"Do you think we were followed?" said Emma. Her eyes studied everything around the group. She dismounted Firlo and thanked him. Olivia and Trevor followed suit.

"No. I didn't see or feel a living soul crossing our path or lurking. Animal or otherwise," said Arden. His voice was soft and calm, much like the sun and the moon, which seemed to have forgotten how to fully rise.

Emma nodded. "Did you smell it?"

"Rain? Yes. It's filling my nose," answered Orion. They exchanged a look, only clear to them. "Come, let's go inside."

Olivia and Trevor followed them up the large stone stairs and inside the building. As soon as they stepped in, the glamour spell Emma had cast over them went away, and they were back to their usual appearance. It happened fast, as though it had been washed over as they crossed the Council's huge iron doors. And when it did, there was a shiver all over Olivia's body, running from her neck to her feet, lasting mere seconds. She looked for an answer in Emma's eyes.

"Not a lot of enchantments allowed inside," Emma said, shrugging as if saying there was nothing she could do about it. "Especially ones for disguise …"

The place seemed to subjugate Olivia with its high ceilings and gray stone walls. It was uninviting and made Olivia question if this was where she should be. Until now, Tartae was giving them such a different experience that Olivia wondered if all the magic she remembered had really existed, or if she had just romanticized an awful experience due to her eagerness to flee the boring life she knew in Leve.

The lobby had big glass windows on every wall and a number of paintings on each side, displayed maybe to make the room warmer. They portrayed places in Tartae and also some important people in its history. Olivia was able to recognize Cordella, who looked younger and held a black aquilegia in her right hand. The flower was between her long fingers, and her hand rested over her chest languidly. There was also a painting of Belenos, who didn't seem to have changed at all, always glowing and young as a mythical god.

"By Ourivio's socks!" Cordella entered the room through a broad hallway to the left. She walked fast, her usual pace when times were alarming like this, and Atlas flew just above her, making the lady also resemble a goddess of some kind. "What are you doing here? How did you—?"

"Cordella!" Olivia and Trevor said in unison. A happy call followed by an even happier embrace that broke Cordella's train of thought.

"Oh, I'm glad to see you too. To see you all." Cordella looked at all of them over her thin nose. "So, I can see the Portals are open again …"

Olivia and Trevor nodded.

"It changes it all …" said Cordella airily, more to herself than to the others around her.

"How are things, Cordella?" asked Orion, his voice low.

"Not very good, I must say. The Council is in session right now, and I don't think you should come in," said Cordella.

"Why?" asked Trevor, his eyes looking for Olivia's.

"We failed, my dear. If I had a problem before they knew the Portals were open, now … I can only imagine what they are going to say. Our plan failed, and the Council can barely stand the sound of my voice—not that I care—but I hardly think you all should endure the same absurdity I'm having to endure now," said Cordella. "Lars is still at large, a danger to all … and Tartae is hurt."

"So we must do something! We must—" said Trevor loudly.

"Shush. Be quiet!" Cordella interrupted him kindly, but with urgency, turning back.

Freya appeared in the hallway, coming from the same direction Cordella had come from minutes before. Her hazel eyes gleamed like big stars under her thick eyebrows, her aqua dress flowing gently to the movement of her legs, almost dancing down the hallway. She smiled, looking deeply into Olivia's eyes.

"The president wishes to see you all. Cordella, you know you shouldn't do this," said Freya, her tone as empty and aethereal as always. Her words were like an ancient song echoing around the room.

The way Freya spoke fell like a spell over Olivia; everything went numb, and she was hypnotized, diving deep into the sound of Freya's voice as though it were the ocean, as though she were being carried by its waves, slowly, rhythmically, out of control. Freya's voice vibrated inside her. Olivia was only awoken by Trevor's touch on her arm, guiding her down the hallway to the room where the Council was meeting. She then noticed that Freya knew very well what she was doing, for she had a half-smile after Olivia was back to her senses. Freya walked away and quickly disappeared inside the meeting room. Once more, Freya's intentions were a mystery to Olivia, and she knew as well as ever before that she had to learn how to shield herself from Freya's influence.

"Be prepared for what you're going to find inside that room," said Cordella, her eyes serious.

"Aren't they members of the Clan?" asked Olivia.

"Members of the Clan, our president, and some other elders. Not many, you'll see. But you must keep in mind that people don't usually remember when they agree with failed missions. They tend to rebel and forget their place in all of it, and the power of the decisions they made. They are eager to find someone else to blame," said Cordella.

"But we tried our best, and we were the ones out there, doing something. They must know that we couldn't foresee that we wouldn't be successful," said Olivia.

"I know, Olivia. But you're speaking with reason, and here there are a lot of emotions involved … The most composed person can feel lost right now."

"Are all other members of the Clan like Freya?" asked Trevor. "Because then I could understand the amount of trouble we are in."

"Oh, well … There are Guardians and there's Freya. She's … well, something else," replied Cordella, rolling her eyes.

Cordella led the whole group inside the room where the Council was holding a session. The place was lightly decorated, with iron chairs everywhere and some open space in the front, like a stage of some sort. There, chairs were organized side by side, but they were more sumptuous than the rest, made from wood with black upholstery. There were only two small windows, very high on two opposing walls, making the air inside the place stiff, especially since everybody inside the room was so deep in heated discussion.

As they stepped in, everyone went silent and turned their eyes to them. Freya stood next to some empty chairs located deep in the room, her fingers intertwined. A few chairs down, there was a short, bald man, with the biggest and most impressive mustache Olivia had ever seen: it was white, imperial, and maybe an effort to compensate for the lack of hair on his huge head. He waved his hand, ordering silence and calling for attention, and without further ado, he said, looking at Cordella, "How did you dare to bring them here, when you were under strict orders not to do so?" the man asked. His words were full of anger, his lips trembling with hate.

"She didn't," said Olivia, and every pair of eyes in the room turned to her. She had a sudden realization that maybe she wasn't allowed to talk.

"Did you fall again?" asked Freya bluntly.

"Not this time," answered Olivia, and Cordella waved discreetly at her; she should stop talking.

"The Portals are open … Oh, that much is clear!" said the president with disgust. Outrage broke inside the room; elders, Guardians, everyone was yelling and pointing, and some of them stood in protest.

"Even after we prohibited you from opening the Portals again, you just went there and did it anyway! Against all better judgment!" said a tall man, his hair as yellow as the sun and his formal dress very purple, making him look like a mean clown. "As if we didn't have enough trouble around here! We haven't had any rain in ages because of your doing, Cordella. Most of our elders are under a weird spell, completely disconnected from what is happening. You must be stopped!"

"Mr. Evon, please sit down," said the president. He took a deep breath, waited a moment, and continued in a calmer tone. "Cordella, you know very well that your plan didn't work and now we are living in this … in this *state* of things. Your plan was to destroy the Portals and put an end to Lars; however, you failed at both. You're all forbidden to keep chasing the Portals, to keep studying them, to keep doing anything connected to them," he said, waving his hand dismissively.

Again, there was a murmur in the room, and some people revolted. They all spoke so loudly that Olivia couldn't tell who was with them and who was against them. In their anger, they seemed all the same; it didn't matter where they stood. Cordella stood in front of the mustache man, looking somewhat impatient. After a while in that mess, he continued.

"I'll designate other members of the Council to take care of this matter from now on, and I hope that we can bring Tartae back to its glory. I believe that it's time to redirect the Clan's attention to some kind of celebration, which you seemed to do fine. There's no harm in that. And now, Ms. Halin and Mr. Meris, please leave the room. You're excused, and you will be out of trouble if you just leave this matter to us. You have no business meddling with *our business*, and you'll be notified as soon as possible of your way back to your home. Until then, behave and just wait for our message."

Noise exploded in the room again, and Olivia and Trevor left, walking quickly out of that place and not looking back. Soon after,

Cordella and Atlas appeared, followed by Orion, Firlo, Arden, and Emma.

"Did they say something else, Cordella? Who is going to take care of the Portals now?" asked Olivia.

"It doesn't matter what they said; they couldn't tell the difference between a Portal and a boot, if they had to. This is the Clan's job, it always was," said Cordella. "But then again, Olivia, would it really make a difference?"

Olivia stared back at Cordella, reading between her words. "No, it wouldn't."

"I figured." Cordella smiled.

"What was that about elders being under a spell?" asked Trevor, stretching his neck a little, trying to see inside the meeting room from where he stood in the large hallway.

"Not every elder understands what's happening. Something strange fell over Tartae and its inhabitants when the Portals were destroyed, and not everyone is awake," answered Cordella slowly.

Olivia and Trevor looked at her fearfully.

"Oh, if it isn't the troublemakers!" a familiar voice broke the conversation. Alavro walked to them with his arms open and hugged them, like too much time had passed. He wore a black suit and seemed thinner, but his face was happy as always and his smile very inviting.

"We missed you, Alavro!" said Trevor happily.

"We missed you too, my boy! And you, Olivia. Later today, you must tell me how you ended up here again. I bet you never thought you'd be back, and I bet you never could have imagined such an unhinged reception, and I'm the sorriest for that," Alavro continued, shaking his head in disapproval.

"I don't think you need to apologize, Alavro," said a short woman, dressed in a deep red gown. The hair on her head so white that it could easily be made of clouds. "It's not you who went bananas!" She laughed.

"Olivia, Trevor, this is Adaelta Maelura, one of the Guardians," said Alavro, wrapping his arm around her weak shoulders in a friendly gesture.

"It's a pleasure to finally meet you two. I only wish this had happened under better circumstances," said Adaelta. Her voice sounded ancient, and the wrinkles in her face resembled a tree that had seen a thousand winters.

Olivia and Trevor shook her hand and smiled in relief. At least they still had others who believed in them.

"I guess there will be no better time for you to meet all the Guardians, at least the ones that are still around," said Cordella, walking up to other elders and bringing them to Olivia and Trevor. "Trevor, Olivia, meet Genevieve Brandin, Mocer Alba, Fara Slasor, and Cerceluna Kassis."

"Oh, at least something good came out of today. We've been in that room for more hours than I can count, and it was only sadness and stupidity, I might say," said Mocer Alba, a tall, interesting man, with small black eyes so profound that they seemed to have seen too many ages. "It's a pleasure to meet you."

"Yes, it is," added Genevieve Brandin, with what seemed like a fake smile jumping out of her thin lips. "But I'm afraid there's not much for you to do around here. I hope we can trust in you, Cordella, and Alavro, to keep things under control. We don't want more problems," She shot a judgmental look at Olivia and Trevor, and quickly, Olivia knew where the woman stood.

Mocer seemed displeased with her addition and excused himself quickly, as to avoid any trouble or hearing anything else he wouldn't like. He pretended some other elder had called him and left the group as quickly as a sneeze. Genevieve followed his lead, excusing herself and finding solace with a group of elders that seemed to agree with her position, since they kept looking askance at Olivia and Trevor.

"Oh, my dears … Most unfortunate time to meet, I'm afraid. But I'm pleased anyway. I've heard of your accomplishments and I admire them, but we all must recognize when it's time to retire … Yes, we must," said Fara Slasor, a short woman who seemed quite tired of it all. She grabbed Olivia's hand with her tiny and fragile one and tapped gently before leaving the group to their thoughts. The other Guardian, Cerceluna Kassis, didn't say anything, only smiled and followed Fara, moving away from the "troublemakers."

Quickly, they all mingled and mixed. To Olivia, they seemed the same at a distance: all confused and blinded by fear of the unknown. There was no difference, from what she could tell, between elders and

Guardians, friends and foes. There was this sea of characters, their group of troublemakers, and Freya, who always stood out somehow.

"I told you they were old ..." mocked Alavro, waking Olivia from her wonderings.

"I understand now why you didn't call them for the fights," added Trevor, still studying the other members of the Clan while they spread out through the hallway, joining different groups.

"So, the Clan is broken," acknowledged Olivia. Sadness sank her heart and made her limbs weak, almost numb.

Everyone in their group looked back at her, agreeing in silence. After a moment, Cordella led them to the main room of the building, and when they were in the center of all the paintings, she said calmly, "Atlas, please."

The eagle, who was perched on Orion's shoulder, flew high, almost touching the ceiling, and as she opened her colossal wings, a protection rose, and a dark blue circle enveloped them. Olivia and Trevor looked at it, intrigued. All the noise around them, all the voices inside the room and coming from the hallway were canceled, and Olivia figured no one could hear them either.

"What should we do now?" asked Olivia.

"Now we go after Lars," said Cordella. Her direct tone made Olivia and Trevor widen their eyes and skip their breath a beat.

CHAPTER FOUR

WHAT HIDES IN THE SHADOWS

The world around them stopped, and for a moment, Olivia thought that it was still a result of Atlas' spell until she noticed they weren't inside the magical dome anymore. Everyone remained silent, but in their eyes, there was the confirmation that they were all on the same page.

"You don't think I didn't see that, Cordella," challenged the president of the Council, approaching the group fast. His eyes were on fire, and all the ruffles in his black clothes made a funny sound as he marched quickly in their direction.

"I haven't done nothing forbidden, Thoman," said Cordella calmly. "If you excuse us …" She made a motion to leave, but he went on, stopping her.

"Remember what I said: You are forbidden to chase the Portals, destroy them, or whatever is your idea right now. Forbidden!" he barked, his index finger pointing madly at them, waving uncontrollably in the air.

"I see, Thoman … But, for all that I know, you don't have such authority. Controlling the Portals was never part of the President of the Council of Tartae's responsibilities," declared Cordella, and before the man exploded into a lecture, she continued, "However, you don't need to mind us. We will leave quietly and be out of your sight before you can say Portal Keys. Good day."

The man seemed eager for a fight, and his face fell when he noticed that Cordella's desire wasn't the same. He stood there shakily, mumbling words that no one could hear.

"Thoman Maugre, everyone … Not our best president, I must say," said Alavro with a sigh as they left the building.

Outside, there was no sun, or moon, or stars, even though hours had passed, but the fresh air brought some solace to Olivia. Leaving the Council made things look instantly better, like a rush of positive energy, a waterfall of cold water that had the power to awaken one's body.

They left quickly; Cordella didn't want anyone else to reach her or give them any more time to say their minds. She found her horse and led the group to her house, where they were to discuss the current situation and decide on a plan. The centaurs kept a slower pace, following Cordella and Alavro through the path of stones and charming houses of Victro, and Atlas hovered over them the whole time, sometimes flying a bit higher, probably to scout the place for danger.

Wind gusts made the trees nearby dance from side to side, some of them almost breaking with the violent motion. When they arrived at Cordella's cozy terracotta home, the sky was filled with lightning, and all they could hear was thunder. Everybody stopped to contemplate it, as the lights webbed throughout the whole grayish sky, which was still covered by heavy clouds.

"What's happening?" asked Trevor, his eyes widening, studying the menacing vision.

"Honestly, Trevor, I don't know," answered Cordella. "Come on, let's go inside."

They walked into Cordella's house slowly, still peering at the spectacle happening above them as they entered the small porch. The garden looked wilder than last time, its plants spreading throughout the whole area, but there were no flowers anywhere. Somehow it looked sad.

As soon as Olivia stepped into the living room, it was as though she had crossed another portal: Comfort filled her heart, and the smell of allandrio reminded her of everything good about the last time she was there. It reminded her of Tartae. For some reason, she was sure that this was something that she had to hold on to no matter what; she could never forget this feeling, her friends, the forests.

Cordella went about lighting the place, then the fire, and finally closed the front window curtains. Her house was the same: warm, full of mementos of her life, but now with piles of books resting over every table. Emma quickly sat down by the fireplace and was followed by Atlas, who rested over the top of the couch's back. Trevor stayed close to the window, peering outside from time to time. The centaurs stood by the stairwell, and Alavro sat down on the big yellow armchair. Olivia stood like a statue for a while, rooted to the floor and just taking everything in until thunder exploded outside so loud and strong that it made the house tremble.

"Is this normal, Cordella? I've never seen anything like it," said Trevor, his eyes fixed on the piece of sky he was able to see through the curtain crack.

"Neither did I, Trevor," she answered, walking in his direction and curving her eyebrows. "I believe this is happening because of you."

Trevor's eyes widened. "What?"

"Because of your use of the Portals, I mean. The weather had been strange since a short while after our failed attempt to destroy the Portals, but it was still, like it had forgotten how to pass. Now, what we are seeing is movement. Thunder, lightning, wind, rain … all in motion. Tartae needs the Portals," said Cordella. "But yes, I also think that you and Olivia have something to do with it."

"Cordella …" said Alavro, exchanging a meaningful look with her. He leaned forward, resting his elbows over his knees and rubbing one hand against the other, and then as though he had to explain himself, he continued. "Since the changes in Tartae started to be impossible to ignore, Cordella has been saying to me that we should bring you back to Tartae. But I didn't agree … I thought that you two were safe in your world. It wasn't our place to bring you to this mess again, especially considering that we failed last time."

"We were not safe … Olivia was attacked at the movie theater. There were phookas all around, and who knows what they could have done to others if there was anyone else close by?" protested Trevor.

"That's how you came here?" asked Orion.

"That's *why* we came," answered Olivia. "I didn't see how the phookas and that man got there, they just appeared, and we fought.

After that, we managed to find another Portal, one inside an art gallery in Leve, thanks to Emma and her intuition."

"Aeron ..." murmured Cordella, and Olivia nodded.

"We knew we had to come back and help, or at least let you know that the Portals still existed and were opened again ... Probably by Lars," added Olivia. "What happened here after we left?" she inquired, finding a place on the couch next to Emma and gazing at everyone in the room.

Alavro took a deep breath and, staring into the fire, he broke into it: "At first, everything seemed better. Victro was full of life again, people were not afraid anymore, and some were even commemorating our accomplishments. There was no fear. The Clan took some time to organize itself again, but there were no more Keys or Portals to protect ... We couldn't go on just protecting what didn't exist. Some Guardians wanted to end it all; they were tired, and they felt that there was no point. Cordella didn't feel the same way, and neither did I. In this we agreed. We knew in our hearts that Tartae still needed protection. Lars was still at large and a real danger to all. Who knew what he would do next? How long it would take for him to find a new plan? Cordella could barely sleep. I was very stressed myself."

"What about Freya?" asked Olivia.

"She didn't believe it was the end, and neither did Belenos. They were waiting for something to come, but they mostly kept to themselves during this time. I am pretty sure that they knew that most of the people weren't ready to hear what they felt in their hearts," added Cordella, a hint of worry in her expression. "Things were changing ... Freya was aware of that, but right now, even though we believe in much the same things, I don't think she's willing to fight with us anymore."

"We noticed the shift first in the forests," said Orion. His low voice echoed in Olivia's heart. "Tartae fell asleep so slowly that most of the common people didn't even notice it when it started. The birds stopped singing, and later disappeared completely. Then, there was no more rain. And so it began."

Olivia shivered at the ominous sound of Orion's last words, as though he were narrating the end of times. Her heart fell; once more she was broken by the realization that she had abandoned someone of her own kin.

"In Lirianthis, the scenario is somewhat better than in Victro and other cities," said Emma. "Some people actually felt the complaints of the forests and other things changing. They are awake and aware. But even some of those believe that you're to blame. In Lirianthis you'll still find allies, but outside, the scenery is bad ... That's why I've cast a glamour over you."

"None of the Guardians and forest beings caught this slowness," said Cordella. "We believe that those who are more connected to Tartae were unscathed, but you heard what Evon said about the elders who are half-asleep ... This is happening everywhere."

"They keep on living life but are now much like the time that has forgotten how to pass. They don't see what's happening around them, they don't see danger, they don't protect themselves," continued Alavro.

"And all of this is happening because we failed. The Portals still exist, and Lars is still a threat. All that effort was for nothing," said Trevor, his eyes lost.

"Yes, we failed. We must admit that," said Cordella with a sigh. "This is the first we've heard about Portals, we thought we had succeeded with that at least for a while. But at some point, Belenos, Freya, and I were all awakened by this tremor, and the sudden realization that Lars had started again. He wasn't opening Portals yet, but he was definitely trying. I tried to warn the Council, but they didn't want to hear and—of course—they didn't want to pursue Lars."

"They keep doing meeting after meeting about the state of things but never how to correct it," added Alavro. "That's what we were doing in our last session ..."

"I wonder if it's possible to destroy the Portals ... Ourivio tried, we tried ... Has anyone talked to Belenos?" asked Olivia. "Belenos was never convinced that destroying the Portals once for all was the best solution, and maybe he was right."

"I don't know what to believe myself, Olivia," said Cordella. "All I know is that when we tried to destroy the Portals, we broke something important. We had good intentions in our hearts, but that's what we did. So, in some ways, I can understand people's frustration."

"There's frustration among the centaurs too. And having seen what I saw in the forests and felt in the air, I get Cordella's point," said Firlo, speaking for the first time. His voice grave as Orion's, but younger. "Some of the centaurs believed that what the Guardians did wasn't right, and they rebelled, disappearing into the woods."

Cordella looked beaten. She kept pressing her lips together, pondering what everyone was saying. Olivia didn't know what to think. The air inside Cordella's living room was heavy, and the rain started to fall outside.

"Rain!" exclaimed Orion, walking to the window and forgetting any precautions. He opened the curtains and stared outside like some happy kid.

Everyone looked out through the window, observing the small drops falling from the sky. The rain seemed still shy, afraid of coming down with the strength it really had.

"What should we do now?" asked Trevor.

"I advise that we go after Lars," answered Cordella resolutely. "I acted with caution every other time and it didn't work. We have too much to discover about the Portals; we have too much to study. We cannot delay dealing with Lars and his lackeys for that long, hoping that we will find an answer fast enough."

"But what about the Portals? There are no Keys ... There's no control. Aren't you worried that they might open at will? Or worse?" inquired Emma, anxiety wrinkling her forehead.

"Of course, I'm worried, but one thing at a time. And right now, I believe it's best to go after Lars. Can I count on you?" said Cordella.

Silence filled the room for a while, and only the fire sang its crackling song while the wind still roared outside. A million thoughts traveled through Olivia's mind: every Portal she had seen and remembered to or out of Tartae, the one in the forest, that whole night of fighting there, the fight with Baltazar, the incredible strength of Lars.

After what seemed too long, Atlas flew around the room and landed in front of Cordella, who bowed her head in agreement. Everyone else followed her lead.

Too many hours seemed to have passed while they were in Cordella's living room. Olivia could now understand what Emma had meant when she said they had no idea how much time had passed since she and Trevor had left. It was hard to explain or make sense of it; it was just this sensation of ages dripping through her fingers. But then again, she wondered if time was always something relative, or if it didn't exist at all. It was a concept created by someone to help society, and maybe there wasn't a point in finding much sense in it.

Later, Orion announced that they had to leave. They would discuss the matter with other allies and meet Cordella and the group at the Forest of Lis using medallion messengers, to keep track of the time.

The group was also to meet Belenos, Alegra, Bran, and Kirk at their hiding spot, which they called Treestone. It seemed to be a place hidden in the Forest of Lis, a shack made out of trees and stones, extensively protected by a number of spells that made the place almost a fortress.

Now, only Olivia, Trevor, Atlas, Alavro, Emma, and Cordella remained, all looking very tired—even the eagle. Alavro and Cordella went to the kitchen for about half an hour and came back with some sandwiches for everybody (a special one made with fish for Atlas); it was only then that Olivia realized how hungry she was and how loudly her stomach was growling.

As always, the food was amazing: homemade sourdough bread filled with herbs and something that tasted like cheese but was lighter and fresher.

They ate while the thunderstorm raged outside. Olivia had no will to talk or ask anything, and she wasn't sure if it were because she was starving or if there was just too much information inside her head already. But after a couple of bites, Emma spoke with a serious tone.

"What's a movie theater?" she asked, frowning.

And Olivia and Trevor broke into laughter. After all they had heard today—a council that was out for them, phookas, traveling through an improvised Portal—this seemed an easy enough question to answer. Emma kept waiting, not quite understanding why this was so funny.

"It's a place you go to watch movies … Uh, movies are stories that you can see on a very big screen. People act the story and you go watch," Trevor explained, almost talking with his hands, trying to draw the image. Everyone else in the room seemed confused, and Olivia almost choked on her sandwich.

"I thought it was something dangerous … Olivia was attacked there, I mean," added Emma, shrugging.

"I'm just glad to see that you were not looking for trouble in Leve," said Cordella, resting her back on her couch.

"I'd like to see a movie theater …" Emma added.

"Maybe one day you will," said Olivia. "It's fun, you'd like it."

Emma had a dreamy expression now, probably trying to visualize how a movie or a movie theater should be. They were all sitting around the coffee table in Cordella's living room: Cordella and Emma on the couch, Alavro on the yellow armchair that he seemed very fond of, Atlas perched over a creepy statue of a faun holding a leaf, and Olivia and Trevor sitting on the floor. For the moment, all seemed normal enough, and Olivia almost forgot to worry. She and Trevor went on and on about their favorite movies, the ones with powerful heroes who saved the world and still had time for romance. The classics, the scary ones. But this didn't last. As soon as they were all finished eating, Cordella got up and announced where everyone would be sleeping, that they would have to be up soon, and that they couldn't be late. And time now was unpredictable, and it was very possible to get lost in it.

To Olivia and Trevor's surprise, their bedroom was still exactly how they left. The navy quilt full of stars, the chests, the books were even tidier.

"She was waiting for us," whispered Olivia, meeting Trevor's eyes.

They walked inside slowly, recognizing the smells and revisiting the first steps of their last—failed—mission. The fear they had of seeing traces of themselves in a place they didn't remember, the constant dance with the unknown, the many discoveries and the strength they never knew they had.

"Aren't you exhausted?" asked Emma, entering the room at once. She'd be sharing it with Olivia and Trevor and was already ready to sleep, wearing one of Cordella's white gowns. "I'm so tired, I think I'm going to faint …" She threw herself on one of the beds, quickly passing out.

"That was fast," said Trevor. "We should just let her sleep here. We can rock paper scissors to see who can get the bed."

"Fair enough," agreed Olivia, already stretching her hand. She won.

Trevor fixed himself an improvised bed on the floor, and Olivia helped with some magic, making the once thin sheet become a very comfortable mattress. She was proud of herself. Magic came easier this time since she hadn't forgotten anything. That spark was inside her, and just needed a little encouragement.

Cordella's home went silent. Nearby, there was only the soothing sound of Emma and Trevor's breaths, in and out slowly, deep into sleep. Outside, the rain still kissed the windows and the earth slowly, and the thunder rumbled far away. This lullaby put Olivia to sleep without much thought. She rested quickly, just a little bit afraid of waking up in her other home, even farther away than the thunder.

Cordella woke them by opening the door, and the floor cracked enough to bother their sleep, making her job a little easier.

"But it's still dark outside," Trevor complained.

"Yes, it's going to be one of those days," said Cordella, leaving the room.

"What does she mean?" asked Trevor.

"Sometimes the sun takes a while to wake now. Sometimes he doesn't come out at all ..." completed Emma; she looked sad as she opened the window and peered outside. The rain was still at it, and the weather overall seemed to be pleading for them to stay in bed.

Trevor didn't argue or ask any more questions; mornings were not his time of day, even if they were disguised as night. They all got ready without making too much sound and went downstairs for breakfast.

Just as last time, they found a bountiful meal waiting for them: apple juice, elderberry muffins, strawberry jam, and many other delicious treats. They all ate, talking lightly about how it had rained all night long, and how rare this had become, but always trying to avoid the most important subjects: the Portals, the dangers, the allies they needed. Atlas ate and quickly became restless, showing them that it was time to go. They all helped cleaning the kitchen and preparing the food they didn't eat for the travel, and as they stepped into the living room, Cordella touched Olivia's shoulder and said, "You need to get your weapons."

"Were you able to ..." Olivia started.

Cordella nodded. "They are in the same place as last time."

Olivia and Trevor ran upstairs, and there they were, lying beautifully inside the wooden chests: Olivia's sword and Trevor's bow and arrows.

"Now I'm prepared!" chuckled Trevor, running his hands over the bow.

"I wonder how they found my sword …" Olivia said, guilt turning her stomach as she remembered how she had lost it.

"I don't think it matters now, Olie. Let's go, they are calling us."

They left Cordella's home quickly, looking like seasoned warriors bearing their weapons confidently and out for a mission. To Olivia, it sounded, sometimes, like she was reading a story about herself, this warrior lost in a forbidden land. And it was scary and exciting at the same time.

Cordella and Alavro guided them to some horses just outside her house. Sadly, there was no sign of Myrrh or Lito, but according to Cordella, they would be seeing them soon enough. They mounted their horses and rode into the dark and mysterious morning. The sky was still full of clouds, with no sign of the two moons Olivia missed so dearly and no sign of the sun either.

As usual, the company found a comfortable pace for every member and a formation, which they followed most of the time. Since now Olivia and Trevor remembered everything, it was easier to ride and feel at home, or something close to that. Cordella rode in the front, guiding the way for the rest, with Atlas flying right above her head. Olivia and Trevor were in the middle and Emma and Alavro in the back.

They rode into the Forest of Victro, which began as soon as the houses stopped, where they would gallop to the clear creek in the Forest of Lis. There, they would find Treestone, the meeting point. Something insisted on jumping inside Olivia's stomach every time she thought about meeting the others. Bran's face would pop into her mind, and she was suddenly very unsure of what to expect. So many things happening, and this simple one disturbed her mind …

The rain was still the same, falling faintly. From time to time, Cordella would turn her face to it, to feel the drops on her skin, breathing in deeply the smell of rain and damp earth. That simple sight made Olivia think about things people took for granted. And that resounded in her head for a while.

Their pace was fast, but nothing that Olivia and Trevor couldn't follow. They went through the trails until some pink clouds appeared in the sky, announcing the sun, and then the wind howled again, blowing strongly as it did after they had arrived. It seemed to follow them, swirling only where they were. Cordella slowed her pace, and Atlas flew very low now.

"Beware!" Cordella whispered. She galloped so slowly that she almost stopped.

"What is it, Cordella?" Alavro asked, getting closer to her.

"Something in the woods," she answered.

And slowly, coming out of the places hidden by the shadows of the forest, shapes formed between trees, revealing a number of centaurs, ogres, men, women, and phookas bearing huge grins. They were surrounded.

CHAPTER FIVE

THE FOREST BATTLE

Cordella looked from side to side, studying the situation. Her expression remained unchanged, although Olivia caught the despair in her eyes, the many calculations of the different outcomes the situation could have. Every time Olivia looked around, she counted one more person or creature staring at them, drooling for a fight. They all bore weapons of different kinds and sizes: axes, swords, all already in their hands, almost alive with will and purpose. She brought her hand to her scabbard, and Trevor and Emma also reached for their weapons, but Cordella signaled for them to stop. Her right hand paused in the air ceremoniously, intentionally visible to the attackers; she hoped to come out of this without a fight.

Olivia's heart beat scandalously inside her chest, traveling up and down her throat. There were too many of them, and those were only the ones she could count. On a day like this, with a weak sun shining over them, there could be hundreds hiding deep inside the forest, and this would be a massacre. Olivia's heart was emancipating from her, almost creating a life of its own and jumping out of her chest, but her hands were still, and her thoughts gave way to patience.

Minutes stretched even more than what was now normal in Tartae; uncertainty and fear hovered over them, and soon, Cordella's hope crumbled down: coming out of the shadows, on a beautiful white horse, Edmund Lars appeared.

He came out of the woods smiling, his red hair longer than the last time Olivia and Trevor had fought him; it fell down in waves, heavy over his skinny shoulders, and it was darker too, maybe for the lack of light to reflect on it. He showed all his teeth when smiling, proud of himself and confident of the outcome of this encounter. He was dressed in fancy clothes but prepared for a battle, for he wore a very tight dark purple shirt and pants that matched. His posture, his figure, his confidence, everything about him made him look regal, not so ordinary as the last time Olivia had laid eyes on him.

As he got closer to Cordella and the group, Trevor's horse trotted a little, and the sound broke the reverent atmosphere. Olivia's heart skipped a beat, and Emma looked at Trevor with concern, but Cordella, Alavro, and Atlas didn't look away from Lars.

"You were not being very discreet," he said with a mocking tone, almost singing and pointing to the sky with a dramatic movement. His voice resounded in Olivia's ears, and anger grew inside her. "There's no element of surprise when wind, thunder, and rain follow you around."

No one responded. Olivia was under the impression that his troop was already moving, closing in on them, hardly waiting for Lars' signal.

"Cordella, Alavro, hear the voice of reason. You have no way out and no way to win; surrender and give me what I want. We'll leave without spilling a single drop of blood." He said these last words slowly, a *single drop of blood.* Making it so visual that it hurt.

Cordella's face trembled with anger, and she spoke. "*You* should hear reason, Edmund, and you should remember fairness. I suggest we do this the right way." Cordella's voice was calmer than she herself appeared; it was firm and intense.

"Fairness?" mocked Lars. "The Clan can never preach about fairness. What is fair about stealing the right to power from people?"

His troops cheered in agreement.

"Where is fairness when the strongest and brightest have to subdue to the old and weak?"

Weapons banged on each other—it was clear that they were many.

"You see?" Lars pointed to his troops. "Your time has come to an end. They want change, and the change is *me.*"

The crowd now clanged their weapons even louder, and Lars grinned with satisfaction. His power had grown; he took advantage of the confusion that was instilled in the Clan and the Council of Tartae.

He gave voice and hope to those who felt unheard or unworthy, and this had become his greatest strength.

Cordella and Alavro were dismayed. Their faces, for the first time, seemed weak and even far away from that imminent fight. Cordella took a deep breath, put her hand on her sword, and turned from Lars' followers to him.

"And so it is," said Lars. "You choose blood." He gave a derisive smile and reached for his staff, raising it high over his head.

Cordella drew her black sword and looked back at the rest of the group. "Fight for your lives!" she yelled, her brown eyes as wide as they could be, gleaming with focus and courage.

Olivia wielded her sword and looked for Trevor, finding in his eyes almost a goodbye. Olivia shook her head, silently saying that he shouldn't give up; he had to believe even if it looked like they were walking into a lost battle. And, imbued with that notion, she dove into battle.

Phookas came from every side and, by now, Olivia knew better how to deal with them. Those creatures were disturbing but not that smart, and their main goal was always to puzzle their victims enough to make them easier prey to something else.

"Don't be distracted by the phookas!" she yelled, not sure if anyone could hear her.

The phookas resembled shadows dancing around like in a ghost movie of some sort; they jumped on her horse and grabbed her legs, trying to pull her down, and it took Olivia a while to remember how afraid they were of fire and that she didn't have to trust only in her sword—she had another weapon. She closed her eyes to center herself, and something stirred inside her, something luminous and clear, so real that she could taste it in her mouth … magic.

Olivia opened her eyes and grasped the grip of her sword with both hands, setting it completely on fire. She then touched the ground with the tip and made the flames stretch and run through the forest floor like snakes, chasing away the phookas, which ran and climbed the trees. But it wasn't enough; the rest of Lars' troops kept coming, and they were many, and they came from everywhere. This simple sight was enough to make everything much harder. Olivia kept doing what she knew with the best of her abilities. She attacked trolls with her sword, green blood oozing everywhere; she dismounted her horse and stepped heavily on the ground, making it shake where Lars' lackeys stood so they would lose balance and fall. But all around her was a complete mess. The five of them fought fiercely but were still drowning in a sea of enemies, and everywhere she looked, she was met by a fearful sight.

Cordella fought like she had been blessed by the goddess of war. She used both her black iron sword, which was long and majestic, and her powers as a witch, which were even more interesting to watch. She fought human warriors, trolls, and centaurs, but they kept coming at her like violent waves, barely giving her time to breathe.

Alavro was also deep into the fight, using his silver sword and showing a talent for war that Olivia had no idea he had, but nothing appeared to be enough, and in Alavro's eyes, Olivia saw their last moments approaching. Trevor and Emma fought next to each other, and Trevor's arrows flew all around but were not as precise as they used to be. Emma kept the enemies at a distance, using a lot of magic and her sword to fight, and above them, Atlas, the eagle Guardian, attacked with spells while flying over the others, but even she seemed tired.

That was merely a glimpse of what surrounded Olivia, and the moments kept happening, one strike after the other until the unavoidable would finally meet them. Her friends were all still alive, but the end of that battle was settled if it kept going this way; she herself was already hurt in the arm after a centaur attacked her from the side, and there was blood all over her friends' bodies.

Olivia ran to Cordella, opening her way through other warriors with fireballs and her sword.

"Cordella, where is Lars? We need to take him! It's our only hope!" she said, out of breath. Cordella looked twice at Olivia as if to make sure she was not hallucinating.

"Come with me," answered Cordella, and, turning to Emma, she yelled, "Emma, you know what to do!"

Emma fought so swiftly and was surrounded by so many figures that she had become just a blur to Olivia. Cordella pulled Olivia by the arm, leading her out of the path where the battle was happening, and everything went silent. Olivia looked back, and there was a big cloud of dirt covering it all. People and creatures coughing nonstop.

"A good ol' distraction," Cordella said, running with Olivia into the woods and reaching the trees.

The area, where some of Lars' troops had hidden before, was now empty, but there was still a heavy energy lingering. The forest floor was muddy, marked by footprints of many different species. Inside the woods, the sounds of the battle were lower, giving the false impression of safety.

Cordella walked slowly. After all, who knew who would be in there, behind or up in a tree, waiting for them? But the only one they found was Lars, still on his horse and looking at the direction of the battle, as if he could see it clearly from here, even on this somber gray morning, or was it afternoon already?

He seemed surprised when he finally noticed Olivia and Cordella, although he tried to mask it with a grin. Olivia's stomach turned, not because of fear or anger, but out of disgust. Lars made her sick. So many things were wrong, and he was preaching them all around Tartae, preying on others.

"You sicken me." The words jumped out of her mouth. Lars looked at her with the same disgust she was showing, as if she were a rat invading his party.

"Oh, come on! I have no patience for this. Just get out of my sight!" said Lars, contorting his mouth while he waved his hand, and with a blast of wind, he threw Olivia far away.

Olivia fell on her back in the mud, splashing dirt everywhere. Her stomach hurt as though she had been punched right in the middle of it, and her head was dizzy from the fall. She was now a few feet away from Lars and Cordella, who were now fighting barbarously; he was still on his horse, and Cordella stood on the forest floor but seemed taller than ever before. They both used magic, and being both so talented, their spells always met in the middle. Cordella was able to protect herself every time, creating shields or ricocheting Lars' attempts to hurt her, and he did the same.

Olivia ran to them, already preparing a fireball to throw at him. She figured he would be distracted by Cordella's efforts, and it would be easy, but she wasn't as good or fast as Cordella. He not only protected himself, but he was also able to make Olivia get stuck to the ground, mud covering her feet and pulling her down like quicksand. Tentacles made of mud embraced her feet and restrained her.

"OLIVIA! DO SOMETHING!" yelled Cordella, looking at Olivia with a desperate expression. Her arms were raised high, and blue light ran through her fingers, creating an ethereal chain that fell all over Lars. He struggled with it for a while, but before Cordella was able to cast another—more dangerous—spell, he freed himself and attacked her again.

Olivia opened her mouth and screamed at the tentacles, annoyed, trapped, desperate. The slimy things stretched themselves and succumbed to little pieces, and then it dawned on her: emotion! She walked out of the mud and in Lars' direction, waving her arms like a maestro, making the tall branches from the trees move and reach for Lars. He tried to avoid them and threw her another blast of wind, which Olivia was able to dissipate only by closing her eyes.

Swiftly, the branches wrapped themselves around Lars' arms and pulled him out of his horse. He landed awkwardly on the ground, fighting the trees. Olivia and Cordella were ready to strike him again when he turned the trees into ashes. He stood up quickly, and in his face, anger took over, making his gray eyes red. He removed a whole tree from the ground with his powers; red and green tentacles of light came out of his hands, and he threw it in Cordella's direction. The motion made her slide backward. Olivia threw a fireball at him. It was robust, the size of a watermelon, but Lars stopped it in the air, halfway to him. He then made it bigger and threw it in Cordella's direction, grinning.

Cordella, who was walking back to the fight, was caught off guard and hit in the chest, flying backward and falling on the ground unconscious. Olivia quickly manipulated the mud, making it cover Cordella to avoid the fire taking over her body. When she turned to Lars again, he was one step away from her, his hand reaching for her neck.

Lars was extremely strong. Maybe it was his magic or just his anger, but he was able to bring Olivia over the ground with just one hand on her neck. She struggled, shaking her body and trying to free herself, but on his face, she found such a strong will and hatred that she knew it would be hard to find a way out of this.

Olivia brought her hands to his face and calmed her mind; a gush of metallic light came out of her hands, like a lightning strike, and Lars lost his grip of her. His face, at first, seemed burned, but quickly it disappeared, and fear took over Olivia once again. He was so powerful, what else could she do?

He sent another blast of wind at her, and this time, he kept pushing her back and advancing with it, until they landed on the path where the battle began. Olivia flew back without control, and when she was finally in the middle of the battleground, she fell on the floor, her stomach hurting as it never had before. All her muscles were sore, and she had a growing urge to puke.

She stood, staggering, with one hand on her stomach and the other one on her mouth; there was blood all over her chin, dripping from her lips. She took a deep breath and prepared to fight again. Everyone else stopped. There was no sound of swords banging against each other; they all paused to witness their fight. Olivia didn't look at them; there wasn't much that could help her now, and no one else should get involved. She got ready to attack again, arms prepared for casting a spell. Lars smiled mockingly, and then it started once more. Olivia fired at Lars the same electric light she had manipulated before, while he gathered all his troop's weapons in the air, to then throw at her all at once. Her lightning-like spell created a sort of web in front of her, similar to what the sky was like the day before. It connected all the weapons like a magnet, and they fell at once on the ground. But before she could take a breath and think about her next move, Lars' face filled with horror, and she had no time. He kneeled on the ground and punched the surface, a punch so strong that the whole forest floor shook, and the trees too; it was as though the strength in his arm had left his body in the form of air and mud, and it traveled underneath the earth through a tunnel until it reached Olivia. The world stopped while she waited, but it was also too fast, and there was nothing she could do. The power of his spell came from under her feet, strong and inescapable, and in a matter of seconds, she was flying in the sky to then free-fall into the earth, diving deep into it until it all became nothing.

CHAPTER SIX

A DIFFICULT CHOICE

Trevor couldn't process what had just happened. He didn't have time, for it was all so fast while unfolding right in front of his eyes. The whole situation was much like a figure that passed by in the shadows so furtively that one was never sure if it was really there. *Did this just happen?*

"OLIVIA!" He broke into a scream so strong that his body bent. *What happened?* he kept thinking.

"We are done here," said Lars, his voice bursting with satisfaction, and his troops cheered.

Lars' voice shook Trevor out of his trance. He looked around, and Lars' troops were leaving loudly, stepping heavily into the mud and dragging their axes and swords. They left a foul scent behind and a dreadful scenery, for many trees had fallen during the fight, fire had burned others, and mud had been splashed everywhere. Trevor caught a glimpse of Alavro, who ran into the woods where Olivia had appeared minutes before, flying backward due to one of Lars' spells; Atlas followed him.

"Where's Olivia?" Trevor asked. Emma shook her head, a dreadful look on her face, and she reached for his hand. The idea that Emma was trying to comfort him was revolting; he hated her at that moment, and then he ran into the forest to where Olivia had fallen.

Trevor had never run so fast in his life; it was as though the speed of his arrival would make things turn out differently. *From that height? It's impossible …* These words popped into his head, and he hated himself for it. Emma followed him, running between the pine trees that smelled so festive, and—of course—so wrong, but instead of finding a place wrecked by a heavy impact and an evil spell, all around them seemed normal. The trees stood tall and danced to a delicate breeze; the rain had stopped but left its soothing smell behind, and the earth seemed untouched, except for a huge hole a few feet in front of them.

Trevor halted at first, and then walked slowly to it, his steps making light noises on the muddy forest ground. Fear rose in his throat; he strengthened his grasp of his bow, and Emma called, "Trev, maybe it's better …"

He didn't let her finish, waving his hand at her but not looking back. As he got on the edge of the hole, there she was: Olivia was deep inside the earth but not covered by it. She was lying on her side, hands crunched underneath her head, twigs intertwined in her chestnut hair, and flowers and leaves surrounding her, growing out of her hair and contouring her neck, arms, fists.

Trevor and Emma stood there for a minute or two; the image was unforeseen, and neither one of them knew what to do with it.

"I'll go check," whispered Emma. She manipulated the roots entrenched in the walls of the hole to create some steps and walked down carefully. After a while, she returned. "She's alive," she said, hardly believing it herself.

At this moment, Alavro appeared with Atlas and Cordella, helping the elder witch walk, which she seemed to find excruciating. Alavro had covered Cordella with a plaid throw, but she still shivered. Atlas flew high when she saw Olivia and then dove down at once, staying in there for a while.

"She's not dead," said Emma, as Alavro and Cordella got closer. "She's not waking up either, I tried." Her face was blank.

Tears ran down Trevor's long, young face. He bit his lips and couldn't find words for what was happening; he tried hard to organize his thoughts, but he couldn't. It was as though he were frozen, unable to move, to say just a few words. *Maybe this is what shock feels like …*

Atlas arose and chirped, looking deep into Cordella's eyes, apparently exchanging information in a language only the two of them could understand. Cordella sighed and looked down, scratching her forehead and then passing her hand through her hair, which was down and free for the first time since Trevor had known her.

"We cannot stay here …" she said with an effort, her wounds paining her almost to the last of her strength.

"We can't leave her alone," Trevor said weakly.

"Trevor," said Cordella. "I know your pain, but she must stay in there. I believe that's the only way she has to recover."

Trevor was rooted to the ground, his head down and tears dripping all over the edge of the hole, drained by the rich earth under his feet. Atlas came near him, flew right above his face, and met his eyes as Trevor lifted his head.

"I don't believe you," said Trevor, looking at the eagle. "I'm not leaving her here."

Atlas flew around, and Trevor followed her with his gaze. She gave a loud cry that brought some peace to Trevor's heart and echoed in the forest. Then, she swirled over the hole where Olivia lay deep in sleep, and from her wide wings, a yellow light illuminated that gloomy day; deep orange flashes were born from Atlas' long talons; they hugged many trees and then found Olivia, falling all over the hole and sealing it in a protection made out of twigs and leaves, like a cocoon for Olivia to rest inside while she needed to. Trevor only hoped that it wasn't long.

Atlas gave another cry and flew away, disappearing into the dark gray sky.

Trevor got closer to the cocoon; it had enough space for the sun to come between the thin branches. He figured that it was for the best, for it wouldn't be the first time Olivia had become a plant. Last time they were in Tartae, she'd turned green and had flowers in her hair … Maybe this was the same. But even so, Trevor had a hard time walking away. The forest was big, with many creatures walking around, and many of them hated Olivia, hunted her. Would they be able to find her in there? Would Lars?

"Come on, Trevor. We *gotta* go," said Emma, touching his hand and pulling him gently. Her eyes were red, and there were tracks on her cheeks left by the tears that ran down her dirty face.

"Let's go, my boy. It's going to be alright, I tell ya …" said Alavro, a stern expression on his round face.

Trevor walked away reluctantly. His body was heavy, and his heart still too unsure of what to do. He kept reminding himself that he had to trust, especially because when he thought rationally, nothing made any sense. Not even being there. His only option was to believe in those who understood what was happening better than him.

This time around, Tartae wasn't so strange or new. He was lucky enough to remember everything and everyone, to see reason in some of it. But remembering it all was also traumatic. Months after the experience, already in Leve and living safely with his father, phookas still haunted him; fear was still there, crawling to him every time there was a noise he didn't recognize … and at first, even with the ones he did recognize. The memories of when he, Olivia, and Bran got lost in the forest kept coming to his mind. At that time, Olivia had created such a strong connection with what was around her that she had blended with it, becoming almost green and flowers bloomed from her hair. Was this the same thing at some level? If it was, why? Trevor needed answers, but right now there weren't many.

Trevor, Emma, Cordella, and Alavro spotted their horses eating grass under some trees. They were now back to the path where it had all started. It was quite dark now, and Trevor had no idea of the time; it could be night, afternoon … But an eternity seemed to have passed. Seeing the state of things refreshed the memory of the latest happenings, and everything was even more disturbing now.

Trevor, Emma, and Alavro helped Cordella mount one of the horses. Emma was now going to ride with her—even though Emma didn't have the power to perform any kind of healing spells, she could make Cordella more comfortable with some enchantments she knew. Cordella was too hurt to do any magic; she tried to hide her pain and concern, but it was very clear across her face and body.

"We must go back to Cordella's house fast …" said Alavro, preparing to mount his horse and taking a look around. He was pale and tired, and clearly very apprehensive about Cordella's health.

"Who is going to take care of Cordella?" asked Trevor. "Isn't it better to take her to a hospital?"

"We can't go to a public healing place, Trevor. It's too dangerous for us now … I'm going to ask Olea, she's the best we've got around here. It's going to be alright … It's going to be alright." Alavro repeated those last words more to himself than to Trevor, as if trying to convince his soul that this would all be under control soon. He analyzed the scenery one more time, sighed, and mounted his horse. Trevor followed him.

They left for Cordella's burdened by defeat. Trevor couldn't hear everybody's thoughts, but he was sure they were all much like his: full of guilt and loss. The silent group galloped into the dark, retracing the steps that had led them to their doom. It was almost like rewinding a movie and feeling that you could change what was to come somehow. Take a turn, go back, try this another day …

They arrived at Cordella's house quite fast, considering their pace and conditions. Emma and Trevor took Cordella inside, and Alavro quickly contacted everyone who could help. Soon enough, Cordella's house was full, which Trevor didn't believe was going to be very good for her health, and Olea believed the same: "Please, would you keep it down! Cordella needs her rest!" she said repeatedly, every time the conversations fevered.

Olea, a gifted healer who was good friends with Belenos and had lived her whole life in Lirianthis, had arrived soon after themselves. She got to work quickly, and everybody helped. Trevor sanitized Cordella's bedroom to avoid any infections or dark energy during recovery; Emma helped Olea with healing potions and foraging for curing plants, and Alavro cooked meals that were specifically created to aid the recovery, all under the strict supervision of Olea.

Cordella's wounds were deep. Her whole chest and some of her arms and legs were burned, some of her bones smashed, and she had a bad concussion. But Olea was adamant that she would be fine. They should expect a slow recovery, especially if they didn't have sun for many days.

Belenos arrived in the house a while after, maybe a day or two; it was still dark outside and very hard to keep track of the passing days and nights. Just after him came Bran, Kirk, and Alegra. Seeing her made Trevor's heart stop for a second; her eyes were even fiercer and her hair as dark and magical as a crow. Trevor couldn't hold his impulses. Seeing her was such a balm that he jumped into her arms as soon as she came through the door, making it very clear to everybody in the room the place she held in his heart. But he didn't care. A lot of things didn't matter much now, and seeing her and hugging her was much more important than hiding his feelings from everyone else. "You're all welcome for the distraction," he said as he let her go, noticing every eye in the room was on them. They both laughed.

The conversations would boil every time someone brought up the Council, the lengthy night outside, their next steps, Olivia. No one knew clearly what to do now, and Trevor noticed how important Cordella's part was in orchestrating and organizing it all. She was the compass that kept everyone on the right track.

And as for Olivia, Trevor wasn't allowed to go to the forest and check on her. There could be another unwanted surprise behind the trees, and they couldn't fathom losing someone else. They had to trust that she would be out of the woods (figuratively and literally speaking) soon. Atlas was the only one who visited her spot frequently, and she would then give updates and mostly just say that nothing had changed.

When they discussed what had happened to Olivia, Belenos had the most indecipherable look on his face. He kept staring through the window, deep in thought, and he didn't say a word. Bran didn't receive the news very well; he fell into the same questions Trevor had: *Why did you leave her there? We must go to her.*

"You weren't there, Bran, you don't know how it was or what it meant," protested Emma, her eyes watering.

"I wish I were," he answered.

"It wouldn't make that much of a difference," Emma replied. "We would still be outnumbered and unprepared. Your presence wouldn't mean a different outcome."

Bran ran his hands over his face. "She shouldn't be alone there," he whispered.

"She's not. Let's give it some time," said Belenos softly.

All that happened in those days felt urgent and slow at the same time, as in a dream where one is supposed to be running but when they look down, they realize that they had never left their spot. They were always moving in the same place, for nothing.

Some days, the sun would cast a faint light in the sky, trying to rise but having no strength, and when that happened, it also cast some kind of hope. Cordella's house became the headquarters for lost Guardians, where everybody stayed most of the time discussing their next steps, wishing well for Cordella, waiting for Olivia.

CHAPTER SEVEN

THE SEED

Olivia walked inside a thick forest. Her bare feet touched the humid grass and refreshed her whole body. The night was dark, deep, dreamy. Bathed in dew. Millions of stars decorated the pieces of sky visible between the leaves of the tall trees that surrounded her, and there was an ancient quality about it all, but it was also fresh, and as new as the first hours of the darkest night. There was something to discover in there; she had to keep looking.

There was nothing unusual about this place. It was only a forest during the night, like many others Olivia had seen, especially in Tartae. The song of the nightingales, the water dancing in some creek not too far away, the perfect balance of the stones, all so common and homey that she couldn't quite understand this agitation inside her. It was like hearing a melody but having a hard time placing the song, being bothered by it all day. This weird simple comparison made her remember something her mother used to say: "Sleep, let your dreams run wild, and what you need to know will come to you in the morning … as simple as that."

A noise came from deeper in the woods, and Olivia followed it; maybe it was the clue she was looking for, or what she needed to find in there. She didn't give it much thought and just ran until she came face to face with a deer. They both halted and locked eyes for a while.

"Did I give you a scare?" Olivia asked, smiling. Her voice was hoarse, unused, and sounded like something she had never heard before. She reached for the deer's head and petted it; its long antlers were like branches, twisting, brown and perfect, full of flowers. "You are different, aren't you?" she said kindly, noticing that she was in front of something even more otherworldly than what she was used to seeing in Tartae.

The creature stood there for a while, calm, eating the grass under them slowly, doing it more like a habit than out of hunger; its antlers were massive, and from them, a number of pink flowers bloomed big and impressive, and ivies climbed up, decorating it like a crown. On its fur, there were patches of moss, so green and alive, so part of the whole, and a thought crossed Olivia's mind: This creature was much like her; it blended with nature and had become one with it.

And like that deer, many other animals passed by Olivia: other deer, bunnies, foxes, and bats, all connected to the earth. It was as though she were walking on a different level of nature where all was one so deeply and blissfully. And all was right.

Olivia took a deep breath and, as if she were being called, looked up, bathed in the light of the two moons of Tartae that floated rightly in the beautiful dark sky.

"It's time to wake up," a voice whispered.

And Olivia opened her eyes.

At first, she was quite confused. The sudden change of scenery hurt her eyes and was a shock to her senses, but quickly the images of her recent experience fell away into an unclear memory, much like when one is out of a dream, and what seemed like reality quickly stops making sense or occupying an important space in the mind. Little by little, everything else was pieced together in her brain: Lars, the fight, why she had ended up there.

Some things she knew, even though she wasn't sure how. It was just this certainty in her gut that made her not even question what came to her memory. After Lars' cruel and successful attack, she had ended up dormant in the earth—for how long, she had no idea. Right now, she was alone in the forest and it was a bright day. The place didn't seem to have seen any recent battles, and around her were many twigs and dry leaves scattered on the forest floor. She looked down at her hands and legs, and she was, once again, a greenish color; her jeans and white t-shirt were full of tears, but there were no wounds in her skin.

"The earth healed me …" she whispered to herself, still studying her body and standing slowly since her legs were weak. "This is just--"

Strong gallops took her out of her realizations; a group of small deer passed a few feet away from her, running down the forest happily, jumping high while the sun touched their fur. Olivia remembered her dream more vividly.

Everything was at a different pace. Olivia's mind was slow, but she realized that ought to make sense for her condition—after all, she had just woken up from a deep, strange, never-had-anything-like-it-before sleep. She was still unsure of what to do next but was appeased by the fact that there was no fear. She knew what the earth in that forest knew, who was around, what creatures, and how many.

Olivia wandered in the woods. She recognized the Forest of Victro and knew that she was still quite close to Cordella's house, but she wasn't certain of how long it would take to get there on foot with her shaky legs. The sun was low in the sky, announcing the first hours of the morning, and she was happy to see that the sun was in Tartae again … She only hoped for the moons.

Some branches cracked at a distance, and there was a presence coming near, someone familiar. Olivia stopped and waited; it could be her way out of there and to Cordella's house.

"Oh, you woke up!" said a tall woman, her shoulder-length gray hair in a low ponytail and a straw hat crowning the top of her head. She carried a romantic straw basket on her right forearm, full of mushrooms and herbs, and wore a rosy brown linen jumpsuit with rustic knots holding the shoulder straps in place. "Good morning. You brought the sunshine with you! For days, the sun rehearsed shining strongly but always gave up halfway through the dawn. Today he felt encouraged."

"Good morning," said Olivia, a frown building on her forehead. On some level, it was as though she had to get used to language again. "I'm Olivia—"

"I know who you are, Olivia Halin. I'm glad that you're well and know that there's no reason to fear me," said the woman ominously, cutting Olivia off in a kind way.

"And what's your name?" asked Olivia.

"I'm Malva Oakwood, and it's a pleasure to meet you," she answered, coming closer to Olivia.

"Could you help me getting to Victro? I need directions … maybe a horse," asked Olivia.

"Of course, I can, but I don't think you'll need any help; someone is coming for you. Now come, my dear. You need a shower and some fresh clothes …" said Malva.

Olivia followed her trustingly, and they walked together side by side for a while.

"You know, I have been visiting you. Every day I'd come and shower you with water from the creek. I thought it would help you bloom," said Malva calmly.

"Thank you, it helped, I'm sure. I'm here now," said Olivia.

Malva smiled. "As soon as it happened, you were protected by a beautiful spell. Your friends didn't leave you at chance. When I found your pod, you were planted deep down, but every day you came up a bit until you flourished in the soil, like a flower. Cordella wanted me to look after you, since she couldn't."

"Is she okay?" asked Olivia, concern filling her eyes.

"Yes, she is. I hear she has recuperated very well. You will see her in a minute; just give it some time. You need to rest a little more, I'd say. In this world. I'm sure you'll find my home very pleasing. I know I do!" exclaimed Malva.

"Thanks," Olivia said, not giving it too much thought. "How long was I in there?"

"We don't quite know, Olivia. Time is still resting around here … At least we seem to have the sun back. That's a good sign. Soon we'll have days, hours, ages," added Malva, looking up to the sky dreamily.

They were in front of Malva's house when she stopped talking. It was as though the cottage had sprouted out of the earth, out of nowhere. The place was small, made of wood and stones, with a lake a few yards away and misty mountains at a distance. A huge garden stretched in front of it, filled with purple flowers and vegetables. A little to the left, there was a greenhouse.

"See, things are blooming again," Malva said, pointing to the flowers and holding one gently between her fingers. "I'm just happy we never ran out of food." She sighed.

Olivia had never thought of that … Tartae was in danger, and she had yet to discover how to help. If plants ceased growing for good, there would be no more food, no more breathable air, and probably, life in that beautiful world would become extinct quickly.

Inside, Malva's cottage was simple. The living room was dark and cozy, and a big stone fireplace burned across a brown armchair, with a rustic wooden side table on its left. The armchair had several colorful throws on it, the only hint of color around the room.

"I've prepared this for you," Malva said, grabbing some clothes from a chest placed under the living room window. "I knew you were coming … Figured it would be better to be ready. In the bathroom you'll find clean towels, and I'll get you some shoes."

Olivia thanked her and headed to the bathroom, which she could spot from the living room, tiny as it was, the door ajar. She walked inside, closed the door behind her, and there was a little window to the forest outside, so green and quiet, so inviting. The bathroom was really compact, and its small shower had the coldest water that had ever touched Olivia's skin. She got ready, putting on the large gray linen pants and the white shirt Malva had given her and found Malva in the kitchen, where she had spread the herbs and flowers she'd foraged in the woods all over the big wooden kitchen island. She divided them according to magical properties, Olivia could tell.

"Olivia, please grab that jar for me, will you?" Malva said, pointing to an empty glass jar under the clean sink. She took it from Olivia's hand and placed pieces of plants she had cut in there, mixing them and pouring in some water.

There was a big clear window behind the sink with a view to the lake and mountains, framing the scenery much like a painting. The small wood stove had no pots on it and multiple shelves covered the walls, most of them filled with jars of spices and liquids Olivia didn't recognize.

"You're still not quite yourself, aren't you?" asked Malva, looking at Olivia kindly, showing that any sort of answer would be fine.

"I don't know …" Olivia whispered.

"Don't put pressure on yourself. It's the last thing you need," added Malva.

"But Lars … I need to do somethi—" started Olivia.

"Yes, you definitely need. And I must say that you have to. But time is running slow—here it always did. Tartae is allowing us to look at things and find out what they really are, especially things that are inside ourselves."

"Our truth." Olivia said it out loud, to her surprise, and blinked many times after as an automatic response to erase or understand it. Malva only smiled.

"Did the cold water help you find your truth?" she said, facing Olivia and holding some dark brown and juicy albeoit leaves in her long hands.

"Wow … Is there a way to make it warmer? I tried to find one but couldn't, not even with my magic," said Olivia.

"I know, I figured the cold shower would help you, and also figured you might try to fight it! I hope you forgive me, but in my home, I like the showers cold. It's the best for one's soul and health, you'll see … I'm one hundred and fifty years old, can you tell?" she laughed. "Now, would you like to help me prepare these potions?"

"Yes, I'd like that," said Olivia; the simple sight of so many plants made her happier, and the possibility to learn about them was also a way to learn more about life, for plants were powerful energy.

Olivia removed the albeoit leaves from the stalks carefully, always preserving the juices the leaves held inside. While she did it, Malva told her about the applications of that herb, how potions made from it helped people with afflictions like constant nightmares and sleepwalking; it also helped the ones who couldn't dream up to their actual potential, and got stuck on a life path far away from their purpose, which crushed their souls. Malva explained that for some cases, potions needed to be very strong, using the juice of as many as fifty albeoit leaves, and even a bit of the leaf itself. "Powerful little plants," she concluded.

Malva was a witch trained in Lirianthis at the same time Cordella was trained. That was where they met and became friends. She had lived in the woods for decades, always respecting the cycles of nature and asking for permission before removing anything from the forest.

"That's mandatory! Never forget that!" she said and then explained that if you weren't allowed to do it, you'd have a hard time cutting the plant out, for they would resist, and their effects would be deeply compromised. One should never go against nature's will.

Malva's main job was selling potions and other kinds of balms. She lived alone quietly in the woods and didn't seem very worried about Lars. Every time Olivia brought that up, she would say that many things might not be just, but nature always was.

That day, the sun set almost normally. It started to lower in the sky, but then it moved up again, staying there a while more, and before it decided to finally rest through the night, Malva called bedtime. She handed Olivia three warm blankets, a long blue nightgown with embroidery of darker blue flowers around the neck, and a nice fluffy pillow.

Olivia arranged her improvised bed in the living room, close to the fire that now burned in the fireplace. She used the same spell she did for Trevor's bed on the floor, making it all very comfortable. Being in that isolated cabin, curled up under many blankets, made her feel safe and experience a glimpse of how ordinary life in Tartae could be. She observed the fire crackling, and its sparks that reminded her of fairies, dancing up and down and then disappearing into thin air. She wondered how her life would be if Tartae was her home, how she could have a place in the forest to rest after adventures around wild mountains and rivers.

"Olivia, come here," Malva called from her bedroom, shaking Olivia's thoughts away from her.

Olivia went and received two more blankets, "just in case." According to Malva, nights in the Victro woods could be as cold as the snow. When Olivia was leaving the room, she passed a small round mirror hanged next to the portal of the bedroom door. Her face was viridescent, her eyes bigger than normal, and with a green hue so electric that it looked fake. From her hair, many flowers and twigs popped out; she had touched some of them during the day but hadn't realized how many they were or how her face actually looked.

She headed straight to the living room, and neither she nor Malva said a word. Olivia's heart raced. This idea of becoming part tree was never unwelcome to her, until now, until it seemed so real. Last time this happened, she had deepened her connection to the earth in order to move around quickly through the forest. It was intentional, and even though she had never seen anything like it, it was easy to trace where it was coming from. On that same occasion, she was hurt badly when there was a threat, once phookas stepped in the forest and it was so painful that she couldn't stand it. Now, after being in the soil like a seed, the connection was greater than ever, and she wondered what would happen if another threat came by.

Olivia crawled into her improvised bed and tried to come up with an answer, but before she could think of a good one, she fell asleep. It was fast, and to the sound of the lullaby sung by the burning fire in the room.

The next day came without any fuss. Olivia woke up with the fire dying and the sky still dark outside. Malva was in the garden already, and Olivia found bread, blueberry jam, and fresh water on the kitchen island, waiting for her. She ate while admiring the calm, pristine lake through the window until orange lights started to brighten the sky. When she was finished, she went to the garden to help Malva. The weather was frosty, and some plants in her garden were having a hard time staying alive.

"Sometimes these changes make it all very hard," Malva said sadly.

According to her, it had been hard to predict how the plants would react. Some of them kept flourishing even when the weather was against them, as if they had been programmed to thrive at that time of the year. Malva then said that she believed it was sometime around fall—or something that looked like it—for the pumpkins were strong and beautiful, filling the garden with orange hues and flowers.

Olivia ran her fingers through the rich soil; the plants' struggle was clear as crystal to her, and the solution unfolded before her eyes naturally.

"I can help," she said, sinking her hands into the ground.

Malva looked at her, but Olivia didn't look away from the plants. Something came through her fingers, ascending to her arms, freezing inside her body. She stopped it, making the ice-cold sensation warm like it was emanating from her heart. She felt it pump, beating back to the earth, and the plants thawed, green and healed.

Malva didn't say a thing. She smiled and rested her hand over Olivia's shoulder, squeezing it a little in a sign of affection. After that, they went deep into the woods, where they foraged mushrooms, herbs, and a number of weird little stone-like plants, which Malva said she would make into a powder to strengthen potions for trembling hands, very good for healers and nervous people. She taught Olivia everything she knew about what surrounded them in the forest: the magical uses for rosemary, cloves, moss, belion, bugswort, pine needles, oak's bark, love in the mist—which covered the forest floor at some point in the woods. As Malva had said before, time there ran slowly, and Olivia's mind did the same.

Every time something reminded her of all she had to worry about—Lars, the unhinged Portals, the attack—or even of what she loved—Trevor, Cordella, Bran, and the others—it was as though a cloud filled her mind, and she quickly redirected her thoughts back to plants. She didn't even have time to consider that she might as well be under some kind of spell.

Olivia waited in that cottage in the woods patiently, with no clear notion of the time, until the day someone would come for her. She could have left by herself now that her legs remembered how to walk properly, and her muscles were again strong and ready for a journey, but she had no horse, and quite frankly, no will to leave. Her time in the wooden cottage was packed with lessons about the art of brewing potions and helping others, and also with Malva's many great stories about the forest and her teaching days back in Lirianthis.

With time, Olivia's connection to that garden strengthened, and she helped make plants grow and bounce back from pitiful states using her magic. The sun seemed to be now more and more back to its schedule, and sometimes, Olivia walked alone to the lake in the last hours of the afternoon. She would then play with the elements for hours and hours, performing magic in a way she had never done before: natural, free, connected to the soul of everything around her. The water danced to her flowing hands, the clouds moved in the sky, the grass raised her high in the air. But when the night came—which was sooner or later—there were still no moons in the sky. And those heavy clouds—Olivia couldn't move.

During those days, Olivia knew her appearance was still different and quite otherworldly, but she never again looked in the small mirror or paid too much attention to the reflection in the still lake. Malva never said anything either. They both knew it didn't matter, and whatever was to happen was going to; it didn't depend on what they thought.

And in a day as any other, Cordella and Belenos arrived. They came galloping on tall and strong horses out of the Forest of Victro to Olivia and Malva, who stood in the garden. The sun was in the sky, and Olivia ran to them, hugging Cordella tightly when she dismounted her horse.

"Welcome!" bid Malva, cleaning her hands on her red apron. "It was about time. Come on in, I'll make a fresh pot of tea."

She headed inside, and the others followed her. Cordella was completely well again, and Belenos' gaze fell heavily on Olivia, studying her every move.

"I heard Olea took care of you," said Olivia when they reached the living room. They all stood awkwardly since the place didn't have much sitting space. Malva was already in the kitchen, brewing some fragrant tea.

"Yes. I most definitely wouldn't be here if it wasn't for her and for you. You put out the fire, I remember," said Cordella.

The memory flashed back inside Olivia's head, paining her heart.

"How are you feeling, Olivia?" asked Belenos, a caring smile on his face. He was still the same, as handsome and cavalier as ever.

"I'm feeling very well. Awake … But at the same time, half-sleep. It's all quite slow around me." Her own words were a shock. She had never stopped to really think about that, but that was it: a half-awake life.

"Do you remember what happened while you were sleeping?" Belenos continued, his clear eyes curious like a child's.

"Faintly …" answered Olivia, sitting over the chest, her back to the window. "It was calm. But it feels like a dream I should remember. You know the feeling? I remember waking up and having a hard time understanding what was real and what was not. I remember seeing two moons in there, animals I had never seen before … Much like mythical creatures of a forest," she said, unsure, squinting as she tried to recollect the images.

Belenos' eyes gleamed.

"Trevor and Bran told us what happened last time you were here in Tartae. How you started to present something much like what you're presenting now. We believe the two episodes are connected, of course," said Cordella.

"How are they doing?" asked Olivia eagerly. She had had no news about her friends and just now realized how this would have been a mess to Trevor. She needed to see him as fast as possible.

"They're very well, Olivia. All sleeping when we left. Actually, we caught them and Alegra trying to escape our curfew and visit you on more than one occasion. Good thing there are spells to contain the eagerness of youth!" said Cordella, smiling.

Malva entered the room with a tray and the tea, resting it over the table next to the armchair. Belenos stood with his back against the wall, very close to Olivia. Cordella sat down on the armchair after Malva insisted many times.

"There aren't records in Tartae of anything like what has happened to you, Olivia. We can only guess. It seems that your connection to the earth is much stronger than the rest of us when you open yourself to it—consciously or not. You blend with it, which I don't think is bad at all," said Cordella.

"When you fell into the earth, it healed you deeply. It saved your life," Belenos proclaimed, locking eyes with Olivia.

"How has it been around here?" asked Cordella.

"Olivia learned much and well. She rested and is ready for what's waiting for her, if you ask me." Malva smiled at Olivia, bringing her teacup to her mouth and drinking loudly from it.

"I like it here, and I even grew to enjoy the overly cold showers," joked Olivia.

"Oh, Malva liked that since we were young in Lirianthis!" Cordella stated, laughing lightly. "You needed time to heal, Olivia. And apparently Tartae too. I let you stay here for this long so you could do it fully, for from now on we have a long and tortuous way ahead of us. It has been a long while, and now even the days are getting back to normal again. It is time."

Olivia didn't question. Her days at the cottage were fulfilling, but at the very moment Cordella and Belenos entered the reality she was living in, it was as though she had stepped out of some kind of enchantment and things became clearer, which she later realized was probably exactly what had happened. In order for her to relax and have time to heal completely, some worries needed to leave her mind, at least for a little while.

They talked more in the living room, and the fire crackled slowly, sometimes reminding Olivia of a ticking clock. She got ready to leave quickly, for she didn't have much to carry with her, only some gifts Malva had given: a linen pouch to gather herbs, some potions she had made, and the clothes on her body.

She walked outside alone while Cordella and Malva said goodbye to one another, and headed to the lake. Saying farewell to that place was only right, and she did it after playing a bit more with the elements, making the water dance in tiny waves.

Belenos arrived from behind her, smiling under the aging sun. He waved his big hand, and one of the clouds that hovered over them swirled, spiraling down and passing through Olivia to then return to the sky.

"I'm a little scared," whispered Olivia. "I'm not sure why this is happening to me, and at the same time … I'm afraid it'll stop."

"I don't think you'll lose what you have now. You didn't forget anything from Tartae before coming back here, and this alone already made you stronger," said Belenos.

"Every time I left, I lost a little magic …" realized Olivia.

Belenos nodded.

"I feel like I don't manipulate the elements anymore, I weave them," she stated, looking deeply into his eyes.

"There's nothing wrong with you, Olivia. I've never seen anything like this before, but you just became the earth in a way the rest of us could only dream of, and I don't think there could be anything bad coming out of an experience like that," said Belenos, reaching for Olivia's hand. As they touched, there was a rush of energy around them, and everything trembled.

Olivia widened her eyes, and Belenos gave a side smile.

"Have patience with the ones who worry about you and let them know you're well. They are overly protective because they care," Belenos said.

"Yeah, I know," Olivia answered happily. She worried about them too.

"And enjoy it while it lasts, my sister," he said with a fraternal smile.

Olivia said her goodbyes to Malva in a slow and silent embrace. They needed no words. After that, she, Cordella, and Belenos left swiftly into the night being drawn in the sky. They galloped through the dense woods, avoiding known paths and, as silently as they could, heading to Cordella's house.

CHAPTER EIGHT

THE LANGUAGE OF TREES

"Olie!" Trevor ran to her as soon as Olivia walked through the door.

Olivia didn't even have time to see what or who was around her; she was quickly lost in Trevor's embrace, and warmth filled her heart completely. She closed her eyes and smiled, happy to be back.

"We've been waiting for you," said Bran softly. He stood right next to her, ready to envelop her in his arms as well.

"Bran ..." she said weakly, turning to him. His eyes shone with kindness, and little by little she was reminded of how it was to be less tree and more human. How it was to be filled by a different kind of emotion, anointed in a different kind of love. "It's so good to see you all!" she exclaimed, gazing at everyone who stood around the room.

"It was about time," complained Trevor, making a face to Cordella and Belenos, who came into the room right behind Olivia.

"He's right, it was too long of a wait," said Alegra. "We tried to visit you, but we were always busted ... Those old spells Cordella cast are unbreakable." She laughed and hugged Olivia too.

"I can imagine ... But you didn't need to worry. I was well taken care of," said Olivia.

"Are you sure? You're aware that you're green, right? I just hope it isn't of hunger," said Trevor, uncertain.

"I guess I'm just becoming a tree again." Olivia shrugged. "I don't know how it looks right now. It's been a while since the last time I saw my reflection. I wonder if anything has changed," she pondered, studying her arms and hands, which were still as a green as a young leaf.

"What happened to you? I mean, they told us some of it, but—" asked Alegra.

"I don't remember everything, but I was healed while I was in the earth. Kind of like a plant waiting for its time to surface … When I did, I had no more cuts. I was fine, only my legs seemed a bit stiff," answered Olivia, heading to Cordella's couch and sitting down.

She told her friends all that she remembered about the earth, and then about the time she spent with Malva. They told her about what had happened in her absence, how it was hard to deal with the fact that there wasn't much they could do, how they were hurt in the battle, and how scary it was to see Cordella in that state. She was now well, but she took a long while to recuperate and, for some time, all their efforts were pointed at her. In the end, it was a good way to distract from Olivia's situation and how doomed it sometimes felt.

Emma left for Lirianthis as soon as Cordella was strong enough to cast spells again, but she promised to come back and begged for updates about Olivia.

"I miss her," said Olivia.

"Me too," added Trevor.

"What about you, Alegra, are you staying here?" asked Olivia.

"Yes. Kirk is also here … somewhere. I think he's outside training or something," said Alegra, looking toward the backyard.

Olivia mostly listened to her friends' stories. They had planned many escapes to see her—and failed every single time—and had also spent hours plotting their next steps to save Tartae. Plans that were new even to Belenos, who listened attentively to them. Cordella and Alavro came from the kitchen carrying a honey cake and apple juice, resting the trays over the coffee table.

"Oh, Olivia! So glad you are back!" said Alavro, pressing her cheeks. "How are you feeling, huh?"

"I'm well, thanks!" she laughed.

Cordella's home was now tidier than ever; apparently, Trevor liked to channel his anxiety and frustrations to cleaning, something Olivia hadn't known about him and that Alegra thought was very funny.

Olivia wondered if the two of them were dating yet; if not, that would probably be happening soon … Unless Tartae's crazy misfortunes got in their way. A thought that made her stomach fall.

Olivia knew that her days living calmly and foraging herbs for potions were over. Everything they had to face was just outside that beautiful house, and it was now a matter of waiting. None of them had touched on the matter of Lars yet and what he had been doing for all this time. She knew it was coming and wondered who would bring it up.

"We need to talk about Lars," said Belenos.

"Do we?" asked Trevor. "I don't think we do …"

"I know last time was hard on you, but we need to decide our next step," continued Belenos.

"Does he know Olivia is alive?" asked Bran, his eyes locking with hers across the room.

"We can't be sure. But this time, I think it's best to believe so. I will never make the mistake of underestimating him again!" said Cordella firmly.

"After the last fight, he left victoriously, but he was hurt as well. I saw it," added Alavro. "He needed time to heal."

"Yes, and time to gather more followers, I suppose. I'd say he's stronger than ever, and I don't think he sees us as that much of a threat … We've lost so many times. And with the Clan broken, a Council that doesn't support our quest … He feels he has won already," said Alegra.

"Cordella and I have reason to believe that he has been opening Portals at will," said Belenos.

Everybody went silent at once.

"What else happened?" asked Olivia.

"There was a shift in the energy," answered Cordella.

"And is that enough to conclude that Portals are being opened?" inquired Trevor, frowning.

"Yes," said Cordella. She was so adamant that no one dared to question her.

"What should we do now?" whispered Trevor. His voice was much more serious.

"We must decide. Should we go after Lars and his followers or mend the Portals?" stated Belenos.

"You already know what I think," said Cordella, her eyebrows raised high and a stern look upon her face.

"Can't we do both?" asked Alegra.

"Not with the knowledge we have of the Portals at this moment. We have no idea what is happening … How to better this situation," said Alavro. "And we don't have enough people to confront Lars. We didn't think he had that great of an army. After the last battle, it became clear that our strategy against him needs refinement."

"Ourivio forged Portal Keys to close the Portals," said Trevor. "Can't we do the same?"

"We don't know how," added Cordella, shaking her head.

"Generations and generations protecting and celebrating the Portals, and you never learned that piece of information?" asked Trevor sarcastically.

"That information isn't anywhere to be found, Trevor," said Cordella. "Many tried … Ourivio didn't register that anywhere."

Trevor looked bothered, and Olivia could almost read his thoughts through his arched eyebrows.

"Cordella," said Olivia. "Where's the Book of the Portals?"

"It's here," answered Cordella.

"Can I take a look?" asked Olivia. A spark of hope glimmered inside her.

"Yes, I'll fetch it for you as soon as we are done here," said Cordella.

"I agree with Cordella. I say we leave the Portals alone for now," concluded Belenos. He looked at Cordella and nodded, his face still stern. "But we must gather more knowledge about Lars and his plans, and act with certainty this time."

"I agree. And we should assemble a group of allies to fight with us," added Bran.

"I say we do this," said Olivia.

Cordella and Alavro exchanged a meaningful look but didn't say a word.

"What?" asked Trevor as he noticed that strange, ominous exchange hovering over them.

"When we saw in the stars that Olivia should come to Tartae, there was also the omen of a war. We hoped to avoid that. We tried at all costs," said Alavro.

"How come I've never heard of this, Dad?" questioned Bran. His cheeks blushed, his eyes eager.

"Not that many people know. Not even Belenos. We figured that there wasn't a need for it," said Cordella. "That's the reason we've never called a great battle. That's why we've always tried to get Lars alone before it was too late. But it never worked … Not even his attempt of attacking us brutally when we were at such a disadvantage worked."

"I guess there's no way to hide," said Olivia.

The energy of the room turned into something heavy, and quickly after, Belenos left. They decided to gather allies and prepare for a fight, now using all they had: magic, strength, strategies. Bran, Alegra, and Kirk—who entered the house much later, exhausted from training—would leave in two days (or something close to it, since time was still quite tricky around Tartae). Olivia was asked to stay. According to Cordella, she was under strict orders from Olea to let Olivia rest until she got tired of it. And realistically, there was no way that Olivia could walk discreetly around Tartae considering her current plant-like appearance.

After dinner, Cordella handed Olivia the Book of the Portals, which was still big, heavy with knowledge and the intentions of those who came before her. Cordella was now responsible for keeping the artifact safe under her care, but since their last ritual to destroy the Portals, most of the Guardians believed the Book served no purpose other than being a piece of Tartae's history.

She sat in the living room to read it, crouching on the yellow armchair while everyone else in the house was taking care of their own business. There was no sign of Cordella and Alavro, and she figured that they were probably somewhere discussing more secrets; Alegra, Trevor, Bran, and Kirk were outside. The latter two training, and Alegra and Trevor giggling. Olivia laughed too. It was clear that they all had gotten a little used to her absence.

She read and read the thick pages of the book, and it was as though she was reliving moments in her history: spells for opening Portals, for destroying them, details about the blood of the other world, in other words, about her. She ran her hands through the old parchment; the scent of the pages screamed magic, and eventually, she found in there something she wasn't hoping to. Could others see this?

Olivia took her time studying what lay in front of her before announcing it, trying to understand it better so she could at least explain it in words. It was some sort of a language of trees written inside the pages, between the intricacies of the parchment, and telling every single detail of many of Ourivio's discoveries. It was as though Ourivio was talking to her.

She ran to the kitchen table and rested the book open over it, passing her hands through other pages, and finding many more of Ourivio's notes. Her legs went numb, and excitement rushed in her body, exploding out of her mouth.

"Guys, come here! You need to see something," Olivia called Trevor, Alegra, Bran, and Kirk from the kitchen door. They all came without question. "What can you see here?" she asked, pointing at the ancient Book's page.

"Ourivio's enchantment to open a Portal," said Trevor, reading it.

"Nothing else?" asked Olivia.

They all shook their heads.

"Cordella, Alavro!" Olivia called loudly with an urgent tone, and they came out from the library.

"Is something wrong?" asked Cordella, a pen in her right hand and a grave look about her face.

"Do you see something in here other than the instructions to open Portals?" asked Olivia again.

"No, I don't," answered Cordella, looking closely, her face almost touching the Book.

Olivia pointed to the top right of the page.

"Here Ourivio explains how he thought about using keys to harden the access to Portals, and how they would work well for their simplicity and their symbolism." She turned the page and pointed to the bottom right corner. "Here he explains how to forge Keys and why it is important to use the right kind of metal."

Everyone looked at her incredulously.

"Where are you reading this?" asked Cordella, analyzing the pages.

"He scribbled secrets in the parchment, using the language of trees. Yes, I guess I speak tree now …" Olivia said. "It's all spread throughout the book. I can write them down if you want. But some things I won't."

"Why?" asked Trevor.

"Because they are too horrible …" answered Olivia, her eyes wide and her face serious.

"Horrible how?" Trevor insisted.

"I guess Ourivio was not that good of a guy … or he really liked to experiment and made some mistakes in the name of his discoveries. He used the Portals to defy the natural order of things … That wasn't right." Olivia shook her head.

"Like what?" asked Kirk.

"Like to open Portals for the dead," Olivia answered.

"Alas …" said Cordella with a sigh, sitting down on one of the chairs.

"These spells are all hidden here, but I don't think he meant for people to find it," said Olivia.

"I've heard old tales about the language of trees, but we didn't even know if it was a real thing … No one has spoken that for a long time, of that I'm sure," added Alavro.

"I guess our people are not the only ones who forget about old customs …" said Trevor, irony in his voice.

"This must be kept between us," stated Cordella with a serious stare. "Olivia, don't translate any part of it yet. Let's think about this some more and then we see what we can do … We don't need Lars discovering that this Book is still relevant for him. We must keep this *weapon* out of his hands."

"Yes, I agree … I'll do that," said Olivia, closing the Book of the Portals slowly and ceremoniously as though the thing could break under her touch.

"If it comes down to it, would you know how to forge another Key?" asked Alavro, under Cordella's vigilant gaze.

"I know all the instructions," replied Olivia, something turning inside her stomach.

"Good, good. That we might need in the future," completed Alavro.

One by one, they left the kitchen. Cordella and Alavro left first, returning to the library in silence and slowly, as if something heavy hardened their movements. Then, Trevor, Alegra, and Kirk went back to their training, but Bran stayed behind with Olivia. She had been staring at the Book of the Portals for a while, and she wished for it to remain closed for as long as possible. In her head, the dangerous things she had read in there kept repeating themselves, menacing, unavoidable, and she tried to recreate Ourivio's train of thought. The reasons for him to write that down.

"Hey, come outside with us," said Bran. He stretched his hand in an invitation, asking for Olivia's. She took it and smiled, following his steps outside.

In the yard, the air was much lighter. Alegra, Trevor, and Kirk stood in a circle talking, weapons resting in their hands.

"Do you want to go for a walk? It will take your mind out of the Book and Ourivio," said Bran, looking at Olivia.

She agreed with a nod, and they crossed the yard together. The grass under their feet made a faint noise with every step they took as they headed to the rustic fence in the back. Night had been falling for a long while now, and the sky was painted orange, pink, and dark blue. Bran opened the small gate and took the trail behind it. A very thin path of dirt was surrounded by huge trees.

"I have never been here," Olivia said, studying the place, and Bran shot her a smile. "Have I? I guess I don't remember that …"

"It's not a dense forest; people mostly use it to take a stroll or even forage for herbs," Bran said, walking next to her.

"You know, my parents were adventurers. We were always off to some place, real or in our imagination. I guess that's why I'm so fond of venturing into new forests. Once, we visited one just to find some mushrooms and eat them. It was like a treasure hunt …" Olivia said, looking ahead at the trees and smiling. It was dark inside the woods, but Olivia was now very used to forests in the night. She could see everything in front of them, every stone on the ground and every bunny hiding away in the bushes. "Everything changed so much when they died … It sounds obvious that it would, I know. It's silly to wish otherwise."

"It isn't silly ...," Bran said kindly, his voice as soft as the ocean's breeze.

"I didn't have much to look for when I was in Leve. People had big plans, and I just felt kind of lost, different than what I had pictured for my life when I was little. But then, Tartae happened and I wished I had never forgotten anything about it. When I'm here I have a purpose, something bigger to look for," she finished, stopping and resting her back against a thin tree.

"You still don't remember anything before last time?" Bran asked, stopping too and facing her, his face almost completely shadowed by the falling night.

"No, but now it doesn't seem as important ... I remember last time, so I feel more prepared and even more connected," Olivia said.

Bran smiled.

"What about you? Was it always just you and your dad?" Olivia asked while they resumed their walk. The sun had set completely, and the sky was filled by those heavy gray clouds at once, leaving no place for the two moons.

"Pretty much. My mother died when I was ten, and I miss her every day," lamented Bran.

"I know how it feels," Olivia said, shooting him a kind smile.

"My dad never had another relationship. At least not that I know of ... I don't think he completely healed from some things that happened in his youth. I know that he loved someone very much before my mother, but his family never approved. They had many rules and were quite strict, not at all my father's style," he continued.

"I see," said Olivia, not sure of what she should say. It hurt her to think that someone as giving and sweet as Alavro was afraid to be happy.

They walked in silence for a while, ignoring that it was time to head back to Cordella's house. The night around them got darker and deeper.

"My family isn't very cool either," Olivia said, breaking the silence. "It's only me and my grandma now, and she doesn't seem that fond of me. She never liked my mother, so she never liked me as a result, and now she's stuck with me."

"I know ..." said Bran with a smile.

"You do?"

"Sorry … I mean, I understand." He chuckled.

"Have I told you this before?" asked Olivia.

"Yes, but I like to hear you talking," said Bran, smiling.

Olivia chuckled in return, and without giving it too much thought, she whispered, "I missed you. I didn't know what had happened to you during the battle in the ruins. It was hard to move on without knowing," she said, and Bran's gaze turned to her.

"I missed you too," he said, stopping on his feet. "We should come back; it's getting late."

Olivia nodded.

They walked slowly on their way back to Cordella's house, trying to make those last moments of the night last. Soon enough, it would be all of the same troubles again, all that rush they were by now so used to.

When Olivia and Bran entered Cordella's house, everyone had passed out all over the living room, from tiredness most likely, for they were all still sweaty from the training. Kirk was twisted on the yellow armchair, Alegra on the floor, with a throw pillow under her head, and Trevor on the couch. Olivia and Bran tried to wake them, but had no success and ended up just covering them with some throws Cordella had in her living room.

"I guess they are too tired," whispered Alavro, coming out of the bathroom with his funny nightgown on. The thing was sky blue and down to his feet, with golden dandelion embroidery all over the hem. "Where were you at?" he asked, squinting.

"We went out for a walk. Olivia didn't remember the trail outside, and she needed some air … You know, after the Book and all," answered Bran lightly, not at all bothered by Alavro's question.

"I see, but don't go back there … not with all of what is happening. Do you think anybody saw you? Was anyone else out there?" Alavro inquired, worried.

"There was no one else," answered Olivia. "Good night," she said, smiling for the both of them, and climbed upstairs to her bedroom.

***

Sooner than Olivia expected, the next day came into her bedroom window and woke her from her dreams. She'd had a silent dream about trees and drops of rain, and had the hardest time putting it together once she was up. All of her dreams had been like that as of late. It started with the one she had when still sleeping in the forest while physically connected to the earth. Even though she couldn't remember the whole thing clearly, the pieces she did never faded away. The vision of the two moons and her encounter with those animals were engraved in her mind, and she wondered if it all meant something more.

Olivia checked her hands and her hair as she did every morning, and that greenish tone remained on her skin. From her hair, white and pink flowers bloomed.

The door cracked open, and Trevor entered the room, still wearing the same clothes as the day before, deep circles under his eyes.

"I need a shower …" he said, looking for his clothes in the drawers.

"Did you sleep well on the couch? We tried to wake you all, but no one even moved …" said Olivia, her voice hoarse, still waking up.

"Didn't sleep very well … Nope … I was just so tired, I didn't even notice I was falling asleep," Trevor said, yawning and then passing his hands over his face and hair, trying to wake up. "What were you up to?"

"We talked," said Olivia.

"About?" asked Trevor.

"Life and its misfortunes …" Olivia answered with an exaggerated tone.

"Heavy."

Olivia laughed. "Yes, it was. But it was kind of nice too; it took my mind away from all the rest."

Trevor looked at her and sighed.

"Olie, are you really okay? You can tell me anything, you know." Worry clouded his eyes.

"Yes, I am. I'm not *gonna* lie to you, I'm a little confused and all, but I feel this sense of calm. I guess the urgency of things didn't catch me yet …" She sighed.

"I guess it's because of what happened to you in the forest," Trevor said bluntly.

"Yes … That too. When I woke up there, everything was slower, kind of like I was … I don't know … Half-asleep still. Or sleepwalking. But I feel much better now, and things are almost back to their normal pace in my head," she said, and Trevor only studied her with his attentive eyes.

"I've read a lot while you weren't here, and there's nothing quite like what happened with you anywhere, as they keep telling us. But, from what I know, I think it's going to start to fade away soon. This time it's lasting longer because you were connected for longer … It's pretty obvious," he concluded.

"Pretty obvious!" scoffed Olivia. There was nothing obvious about her situation, as it was unparalleled, but she believed the same as Trevor: soon, things would go back to normal. She just wondered if she would become part plant every time she connected with the earth. "Anyway, I think there are many upsides in this, Trev. One of them is that magic comes easily to me now. I barely have to think about it."

"Okay … That's good, I guess." Trevor shrugged. "But I don't think we should just ignore what happened to you and the way you're looking now. We should understand it and learn why this happens. Cordella, Belenos, and Emma also manipulate the elements and they don't become part plant. We have to understand if this is dangerous to you," said Trevor.

"I don't think it's dangerous. I feel fine—"

"But you're not sure. No one is. Last time this happened it was also very hurtful to you; the mere sight of phookas made you black out, don't you remember?" said Trevor gravely.

Olivia just looked at him, out of words. She thought of what would happen to her if she was to face all of Lars' lackeys at the same place, at the same time, and fear rose in her spine. This was just one more reason to avoid any thought about the oncoming war, and the prophecy no one had mentioned before but that seemed to have them doomed.

Trevor left for his shower minutes after that, still bearing a grave expression on his face. Olivia was left alone to think about what she could do to control her connection. After all, it wasn't only her appearance that had changed, but also her way of processing things.

She was slower and sometimes too dreamy, and there was no way of facing anything in that state. She needed to find a balance.

Over breakfast, Cordella said that the days appeared to be almost what they used to be. It was now manageable to count time with the sun rising and setting every day. But by her tone and the lack of enthusiasm in everyone else's response, Olivia knew that there was still fear of it all going off track again.

They didn't discuss anything profound during their meal. It was only the weather, the sun, and Cordella's neighbor who kept complaining about how wild her garden had become.

"The world falling into pieces and this sad man complaining about my lack of gardening skills …" she mumbled, annoyed.

After they left the table, they all went to the library and discussed finding more allies and who could they be. They would try the centaurs first; they would meet Orion and travel to the Mountains of Lotre to talk with the ones who lived there. After learning in their last battle with Lars that some of the centaurs had moved completely to his side, they had to act quickly. Olivia was sad that such powerful and intelligent creatures now believed in Lars' claims, but she guessed they felt hopeless and betrayed by everyone else and found in Lars their only solace.

Next, would be the Willow Warriors, a tribe of sorcerers who lived in the depths of the Eagle Forest. They had almost no contact with the outside and were skillful warriors, using mainly their magical powers that were so developed due to their deep and always uninterrupted connection to nature.

The group went on and on about who their allies could be and who they had known in their travels around Tartae who could help. Olivia and Trevor just listened, not having much to contribute, for they didn't know many except those in that very room. When it was almost time for lunch—mostly because of the sound of their growling bellies—there was a heavy knock on Cordella's door.

Three women dressed much like each other, with brown pants and white shirts, many weapons hanging on their backs and their waists, were standing on Cordella's porch.

"We have news about Lars," the tallest of them said. Her thick hair was long and dark, like her eyes.

Cordella let them in, and before she invited them to sit, the tall woman continued:

"His whispers are not mere whispers anymore. He now has magic folk on his side."

"Who?" asked Cordella nervously.

"Diana," she said, and her eyes filled with tears.

CHAPTER NINE

THE LOST ONES

"That can't be!" argued Cordella, bringing her thin hand to her mouth in disbelief.

"We had a hard time believing it ourselves," the woman said firmly, trying to stay composed but clearly as hurt by this news as Cordella was.

"How did Lars infiltrate Lirianthis?" asked Alavro.

"Only his words did. Diana wasn't the only one; others from Lirianthis joined him and left the place. Those who remain there are protecting it to the best of their magical abilities."

"What about Drusilla?" Alavro continued, frowning.

"She didn't join them."

"And Emma?" Olivia asked, addressing the woman for the first time. She glanced back at Olivia and frowned, and Olivia witnessed how every inch of her curiosity sparked; looking like a tree wasn't that common, after all, not even in Tartae.

"She is in Lirianthis, protecting it. We are doing all we can," she said. "Lars is coming out of the shadows, Cordella. Soon enough, he'll be at the council. He'll be everywhere, spreading his lies and gathering more believers. Listen to me."

Cordella sighed, and everyone fell deep into thought. She invited the group to sit and offered some water or tea while they found places on her couch.

The women were from Lirianthis; Cordella had known them since they were little, and she told this to Olivia and Trevor as they went to help her with the tea. They were now warriors who fought in different lando, traveling and helping people all around Tartae. The tallest one, who did most of the talking, was called Driona Mallet. The other two were sisters, Bea and Whilla Wood.

Driona explained that they had been in the Ancient Forest when her mother sent word for them. She told between sips of her mint tea that she had seen Tartae folk talk more about Lars lately, but she hadn't seen many signs of his influence: no burned grounds, no drying trees, nothing like the last time. So she hadn't quite believed in those whispers or in his strength until she had arrived in Lirianthis. She never thought that those witches and wizards would change sides like that.

"It was a mess when we got there, our folk running up and down, homes abandoned by those who chose to follow Lars. But strangely enough, it wasn't like the other times people with greedy intentions played with the Portals; there was not even one tree dying. Even so, those who could were protecting Lirianthis with their magic, trying to strengthen the elements and give those who were trembling in fear a bit of hope," Driona said slowly, holding her cup with both hands, covering the whole thing.

"Things are upside down …" sighed Alavro ominously.

"What should we do?" asked Trevor, searching for Cordella and Alavro's faces.

"If Lars lured some of the most powerful witches and wizards of Tartae to his side, his speech has become something else," said Alegra. "So much so that he's not afraid of being caught anymore. I think it'll be no time before he addresses people openly, and we must prepare for that."

"Calling our allies cannot wait, Dad," said Bran, looking at a very worried Alavro.

"Let's start now! I say we get ready and leave today!" said Kirk, his face serious with purpose and his voice already inflamed by the excitement he felt for war.

"Wait," said Cordella, waving her hand slightly. "Is there anything else we need to know, Driona?"

"People are scared, Cordella. All around. The ones who didn't fall under the Slowness Spell fear for Tartae. Our world changed too much. We had no rain and sometimes no sun. We hadn't seen the moons in what feels like ages. Now people know that the Portals reopened, the

Council had spread word about it, and everyone is seeing things falling into place again. We have days and nights, and there's no drought, so they think your attempt to destroy the Portals was a mistake and they still fear the repercussions," said Driona.

Cordella looked back at her, pondering her words. She stood by the fireplace with a cup in her hand, more like an accessory than anything since she hadn't take a single sip of the mint tea yet. The room was filled with a heavy energy made out of uncertainty, fear, and anxiety, all hanging over them now.

"We must get people's trust back," said Bran, his voice echoing in the room and turning everybody's head to him. "We need to be clear as water now. Tartae folk need to know about what we're facing, all there is to know about the Portals, Olivia, and Trevor. That's what's going to make them our allies: the truth." His words were deep and sounded too wise for his age.

"I agree," said Olivia, Trevor, and Alegra in unison.

"I as well," said Alavro.

"Very well, then," smiled Cordella. "There's no simpler answer than the truth."

"Cordella," Driona called, putting down her empty cup. "We also believe that there should be a new Key."

As Driona voiced these words, something inside Olivia turned so strongly that her chest constricted, and she coughed, almost choking. She tried to mask it, giving a faint smile and excusing herself, but deep down, she was annoyed and angry. The idea of controlling the Portals again with Keys was unacceptable, and she had a physical reaction against it that took her on a trip through her reasons and why she felt that way. Every sound in the room became indecipherable mumbles, and she was shaken out of this trance by the sound of her name faintly in the back of her mind. "Can you, *Olivia*?"

"I'm sorry, could you repeat the question?" she asked, taking a sip of the tea that was already cold and trying to make sense of what was happening to her; she wasn't even sure who had asked the question.

"Can you help us forge a new Key?" asked Alavro.

"Lars stole them before. He killed people for them," she said, twitching her face. "I don't know if that's the best way."

Driona looked offended and scared. "Who did Lars kill?" she asked, her expression now even more worried.

"I guess you really need to start telling the truth …" stated Trevor, widening his eyes.

Cordella told Driona, Bea and Whilla all about Lars' doings and the death of the Arbres and Grondes, as well as the reasons behind the Clan's choices. They seemed disgusted. By what exactly, Olivia didn't know. It wasn't clear if it was the Clan's behavior or the cruel ways Lars used. But even after that, none of them seemed very bothered by the idea of forging a new Key.

"We can forge a new Key and protect it again. I don't see why we shouldn't follow this path. The Portals cannot stay as they are now; things might happen," said Cordella. "But we can't wait for it and then go after Lars, we must do it all at once."

"Olivia, what kind of metal do we need?" asked Alavro.

"Lontyr," she answered reluctantly, her tongue trying to hold the words inside.

"Can you help us?" Cordella asked Driona, Bea, and Whilla. They nodded in agreement. "You three go get it; we'll organize for war."

The women left to accomplish their share of the plan. They still looked sad and worried but were now filled with purpose and didn't have a lot of space for all the other emotions that could easily mount. Olivia was deep in thought; a terrible sensation shrunk her heart, but she had no idea how to voice it.

"We need to find out exactly what Lars is telling people. Have any of you had any contact with Greedy Factions?" Cordella asked, finally sitting down on the armchair.

"I have," said Kirk. "I know where to find some of them, or at least some who will know about them, if they moved."

"Good," said Cordella.

"Tomorrow we leave," continued Kirk, looking for Bran and Alegra's eyes. They all agreed.

"Be even more careful now; hide under the cloak of shadows and trust only the ones who can hear the truth. But tell it to all," Cordella said, and Alavro cringed.

"What about those under the Slowness Spell?" inquired Alegra. "Should we approach them?"

"Yes, it's better that they hear from us than from Lars. Even under this slowness, they might have to decide," said Cordella.

"Aren't they waking up, like the rain and the days?" asked Trevor.

"The moons remain unseen," said Kirk, finding Trevor's gaze.

"I wish I had all the answers," said Cordella, sighing.

"What we know now is that Tartae was a mess without the Portals," pondered Alavro.

"I'm not so sure—I'm not so sure this was the only reason," said Cordella, and everyone looked at her, shocked. "Don't be so surprised, Alavro, you know this. I believe that things are also falling into place because Olivia and Trevor are back."

"But things were fine before we ever came here," protested Trevor. "I don't think we have anything to do with the chaos or the recovery."

"Perhaps, Trevor. But maybe there's something more now. Something we need to discover." Cordella looked deeply into Olivia and Trevor's eyes. "After all, this is how fate works: A piece of history clinging to another, calling the next chapter, making it impossible to remove one."

Cordella's words brought to Olivia and Trevor a sense of responsibility that they hadn't had since last time they were in Tartae, when they learned about their past trips there and how crucial their position was, and how little they remembered.

Memories from before their last mission seemed to be long gone now; they barely talked about getting them back and even the thought of it seemed pointless. This time, they remembered enough for them to be more helpful: their training, details about that world, and Olivia recollected all about her magic, which seemed to make all the difference, since every time she traveled back to her world and was taken over by Cordella's spell to forget everything, she also lost her connection to nature, weakening her powers.

The mood among them was weird; they all left the living room slowly and barely said a word after all that conversation and the first sketch of their new plan. Olivia and Trevor exchanged a complicit look before going to the yard. They both knew they were back again at the middle of something, but they didn't know what. At least this time, Cordella was the only one thinking so. It wasn't so hard as being under everyone's expectations.

Olivia crossed to the kitchen door and removed her shoes, stepping barefooted over the earth outside; the feeling grounded her instantly, and calmness filled her heart at once. Trevor observed her from the kitchen.

"We need to talk to Cordella about this, Olie," he said, a very serious look in his face.

"I told you, Trev. This isn't all bad," she protested.

"I know, but we can't go to war with you that way. You won't survive. There must be a way for you to do what you have to do with nature, but without actually becoming a plant. Have you tried to disconnect from it like you did last time?" Trevor asked, getting closer to her.

Olivia took a moment. "I didn't have the strength," she finally said, unsure.

"You didn't try." Trevor shook his head. "This can be dangerous, Olie. Not because of becoming a tree or whatever, but if we were attacked again … I don't even know what would …"

Olivia looked back at him and took a deep breath. He was right, but this was so hard that it didn't feel that way. She was afraid and shivered.

"Try now," he said firmly.

Olivia closed her eyes, and quickly her mind went blank. She was suddenly lost in a void of slowness and depth, as though she had dived into the forgotten parts of the ocean—dark, lonely, whole. There was no other thought in her mind or sensation in her body, only the ancient song of the elements.

"OLIVIA! OLIVIA!"

Olivia opened her eyes with Trevor yelling and shaking her. She took a step back and looked around, confused.

"What happened?" Trevor had worry all over his face. "What happened?" he repeated, urgently.

"I—I tried to disconnect, but then … I don't know," Olivia mumbled.

"This is serious, Olie …" Trevor said.

Olivia agreed. Her connection to nature now was so strong that she couldn't even begin to detach; calling for it only made her sink in deeper, until she was left with no trace of anything else. After that, she was back to that half-awake sensation. It wasn't so strong now, but it made all of her reactions and thoughts slower, as though she were still under the water.

Trevor was restless, and he kept listing all the many reasons they had to worry: she could lose her human senses, she could be hurt when phookas appeared, she could lose her mind, she could die. Olivia tried to appease him, even though she knew he was right and fear was now making her insides tremble. She was already convinced that it didn't matter how good it was for her magic, or how wonderful it made her feel, this was something that had to stop.

They sat together under a tree, breathing deeply and striving to calm themselves, and then discussed telling Cordella all of it, which they did later that day. The elder witch seemed equally worried and inquired about every single thing that had happened. "We'll do something about it tomorrow; it's late now and you need your rest," she finally said, and it was only then that Olivia noticed how the night had taken over the sky.

CHAPTER TEN

BETWEEN REALMS

Bran, Alegra, and Kirk left the next day to find allies. They were up and out so early that Olivia and Trevor didn't even see them leave. Alavro was quite disturbed by his son's quest; he had not spoken a single word about it, but he kept mumbling incomprehensible things around the house, barely paying attention to anything else.

It was a dangerous mission. No one knew who would be against them and already siding with Lars. They could step into an ambush, and Alavro was well aware of it. Their main goal was to reach enough people to build a strong offense and, hopefully, with word spreading about Lars' deeds and the danger upon Tartae, they would have a lot of volunteers.

Olivia and Trevor spent their morning outside in the yard training for fighting and spells. Trevor had been practicing since he returned to Cordella's house and recovered from his wounds. It was nice to train just the two of them; they could plan attacks together and combine their strengths, ways to add magic to bow strikes, and use the elements to give Trevor high ground. In some ways, it also seemed that they were two kids playing, pretending they were in a war—a much nicer thought than the reality.

When Alavro called them inside for lunch, Cordella wasn't around. "She's out for something," Alavro mumbled dismissively, not paying too much attention and leaving the kitchen without eating. The two friends only looked at each other and shrugged, not sure of what to do with that information or even about Alavro. They ate and were back to their training in no time.

The day went by slowly. The hours seemed to stretch and stretch until Olivia and Trevor had no more energy for training. At night, after showering and preparing dinner, Olivia sat in Cordella's living room to study the Book of The Portals while Trevor read a book Alegra had given him: *The Sounds Of The Breeze*, by Kirst Kings. Alavro had been locked inside his bedroom since midday and didn't even come out to turn on the lights when night came or to have dinner.

After what seemed like a day with a thousand hours, Cordella walked through the front door, followed by Belenos, who wore a peacock blue cape that made him look even more dashing.

"Some light reading, huh?" joked Belenos, approaching Olivia and removing his not-very-subtle cape. He sat on the couch next to her.

"Did Cordella tell you about what I found?" Olivia asked.

"Yes," Belenos answered, studying the Book's pages carefully. "I'm afraid I can't see any of it either."

Olivia looked discouraged and sighed.

"But that doesn't mean anything, Olivia. We're similar, but not the same," Belenos said, putting his hand over her shoulder.

"Where is Alavro?" Cordella asked, looking around while she hung her purple cape, much more discreet than Belenos'. She seemed worried, and so did Belenos, but they didn't say much about it.

"He's been in his bedroom almost all day," answered Trevor. "Is everything alright?" he asked, catching the same uneasiness in the air as Olivia.

"Oh well, I'll deal with that later." Cordella sighed and ignored Trevor's question. "I brought Belenos here to help, Olivia. We can use his talents to understand what's happening with you."

"You think you can help?" asked Trevor, his eyes full of hope.

Belenos looked into Olivia's eyes as if trying to see what her thoughts about all of this were, and then he finally said, "if she wants to."

Olivia didn't look away from Belenos' eyes. She understood what was unsaid between his words. He was probably the person who could relate more to her, as he was the son of the forest and lived in a very close relationship with the earth and Tartae. They were much the same, like the deer she saw in her dream, blended with nature and living as one.

"I do," she finally answered. "I'm not going to lie, this feels comfortable and full. I feel well like this, but I need to find a way to keep the connection more like how you do it. The way it is now is too dangerous."

"I agree," said Belenos, smiling kindly at Olivia. "Cordella and I talked, and maybe there's a way to help, but it will affect your connection at some level, I have no doubt about it." He paused as if waiting for Olivia to say something and continued. "Almost every day I visit some wild part of the Laliamo Forest and ground myself, strengthening my bond with all around me; it's a meditation very similar to the one other magical folk practice, but in my case, it's the source of everything I am. I experience the scents, the elements, the life around me in a deeper way, and I'm sure Cordella knows what I'm talking about. This sort of balance keeps our mind clear for spells."

Cordella nodded, and Olivia remembered their meditation in the woods so long ago.

"But you see, Olivia? There's a balance, a part of me that is always here in this level, and I believe most of you is in another realm," Belenos said.

Olivia widened her eyes, and images from her dream came to her mind clear and potent as a shooting star. "How—" she started, surprised.

"It's a blessed place, Olivia. Not many are fortunate enough to visit it and remember it. I believe you've spent too much time in there and some of you remained. We need to pull you out," said Belenos.

"And how do we do that?" Olivia asked.

"I brought you this potion." Belenos grabbed a small flask from his pants pocket, an amber-colored liquid inside. "You'll have to drink this. It's a potion I myself brewed, and it carries earthly magic, so you'll ground yourself and find your way back here completely."

"Does it hurt?" Olivia asked.

"No, I don't think so," Belenos answered.

"Will I be able to connect with nature again?" she inquired, already missing the sensation.

"We'll see," he said, smiling gently.

Olivia drank the potion in many sips, for it had a heavy and bitter taste and was hard to swallow. Every eye in the room was on her, waiting, expecting what would come next. She finished the whole thing, and her heart palpitated. Olivia held Belenos' hand, and the last thing she heard was, "It'll be okay."

***

Olivia woke up in her bed with a throbbing headache. She was alone and cold, even under her starred blanket. The sun shone strongly outside, and it made her head hurt more. She walked downstairs in her pink pajamas, which she didn't remember putting on, and found Trevor, Cordella, Belenos, and Alavro inside the library talking. They all went silent when she stepped in.

"How are you feeling, Olivia?" asked Cordella gravely.

"My head hurts," Olivia answered, bringing her hand to her forehead and massaging it. The light coming into the library from the window made her pain even worse.

Cordella ran her hand over Olivia's head, not touching it, but very close. A shock vibrated inside her skull, traveling down to her feet, extremely cold and electric.

"What about now?" Cordella said.

"Better. Thanks," Olivia answered. "What happened?"

"You're back," said Belenos.

Instantly, Olivia looked at her hands, and that greenish hue was gone. She scoffed, not really sure what to feel. Trevor stood and hugged her, relieved.

"You passed out after drinking the potion, and we took you to your bed, where you slept for a long time. I was worried, but Belenos said this was expected," said Trevor, his hands still over Olivia's arms.

"You were finding your way. Sometimes it takes a while," said Belenos.

"What about—?" Olivia started.

"You'll have to try it and see how it goes. But from now on, I say you don't let it take you over; you must control it. Try asking what you need clearly. Nature tends to hear us," said Belenos.

Olivia was afraid to try anything. She missed something in her and lacked the courage to verify what. If it were her magic, it would be too much to bear.

"Do we have news of Bran, Alegra, and Kirk?" she asked, changing the subject.

"Not yet, not yet …" complained Alavro, standing up from his chair and pacing. "Cordella, Olivia is well, Belenos is here … I can't take this anymore. I have to follow Bran and help him in this. I can't stand this wait."

Worry consumed Alavro, that much was clear. He wasn't himself in any way, and he even seemed smaller, as though what troubled him had outgrown his body, sucking out its life and covering him like a giant shadow. Everyone understood and encouraged him to go; he was aware of the perils of the road, but he was also a seasoned warrior and Guardian, so he knew what to do. He left without any fuss shortly after that, for his bag was ready and his heart already on the road.

Olivia and Trevor stayed inside the library; the fire was on and cozy, and Olivia stretched herself on the chaise, leaving one of her feet hanging. Cordella and Belenos walked Alavro outside and didn't come back, which somehow was more comfortable to Olivia. She'd just lie there mindlessly with Trevor for a while, something that she much needed.

"Oh, my mind needs rest," she complained, exaggerating her tone.

"At least you're not green anymore," Trevor scoffed. "Did you dream about something while you were out?"

"Nope … I was drinking the potion and then I blinked and woke up in my bed," she said lightly, staring at the ceiling.

"What was it like … I mean, what was *that* place like?" asked Trevor.

"It was awesome, Trev … Everything was part of the whole. It felt right," Olivia said, staring at Trevor and exchanging a profound look.

"Well, I'm glad you're back, anyways. … *This* is your place," Trevor said, sitting on the floor and resting his back against the small red couch facing the chaise.

"Tartae?" Olivia asked, a mocking expression on her face.

"You know what I mean …"

Olivia and Trevor stayed there for a long time, mainly discussing trivialities, like the plot of the book he was reading. It was the story of a man who got lost in the desert and found his purpose in life while trying to find his way back home. It seemed interesting and mundane enough to belong to Lucent Bookshop, especially if it didn't mention murmuring winds or elements that could be manipulated.

When boredom started to rise in Olivia and Trevor's bodies, they walked to the kitchen, still between laughs and carried away in light conversation. When they stepped into the room, Cordella and Belenos ceased talking abruptly. They both stood next to the kitchen window and were surprised by the arrival of Olivia and Trevor.

"What's happening?" asked Trevor, suspiciously.

"We must tell them, Cordella," said Belenos.

"Tell us what?" Olivia asked, emotion shaking her legs already.

Cordella and Belenos exchanged a look for a moment and didn't sound a word. That pause seemed to last hours, and the anticipation was about to give Olivia another headache.

"Don't you dare lie to us …," said Trevor. He took one step forward, and his expression was rebellious.

Cordella sighed, as though she were giving up. She closed her eyes and shook her head slowly.

"Lars has his people in Leve," said Belenos.

CHAPTER ELEVEN

NEWS OF LEVE

The ground underneath Olivia ceased to exist. She stuttered some words, which was very unlike her, and couldn't seem to find a train of thought to express all her confusion. She looked from Belenos to Cordella, expecting more information or at least something that wasn't so bad, but nothing came from their mouths.

Trevor remained silent too, frozen like a statue where he stood. He was so still that Olivia feared he would fall like a timber—at once and heavily.

"We don't know much," Belenos finally said. Breaking the silence with the exact words Olivia didn't want to hear. Cordella remained quiet, breathing heavily.

"What do you know?" Olivia asked, not really clear where to start.

"Why don't you sit down?" said Cordella, heading to the kitchen table and finding a place for herself in one of the wooden chairs. Everyone else followed her, except Belenos, who stayed by the kitchen window.

"Is anyone hurt?" Trevor asked, his voice trembling.

"We don't know much, Trevor," said Belenos, and Trevor shot him a menacing look.

"Cordella ..." pleaded Olivia, staring deeply into Cordella's eyes.

"When I went for Belenos' help, Mocer contacted me. The Council has been meeting without my knowledge, and in one of those meetings, they mentioned that Lars has sent some of his people to your world," said Cordella.

"We believe that their way in is through Leve, since he has managed Portals there before," added Belenos. "But that's not his goal; he aims for something higher, a way to infiltrate in politics, maybe. He wishes to spread fear so his name can be the only hope. We don't think his helpers are in Leve anymore; they probably arrived there and moved on to somewhere else."

Olivia and Trevor stared at Belenos and Cordella in dismay. It was a hard image to digest, Lars' people arriving in Leve through a Portal and then just trying to find their way into a place of influence.

"Is that all?" asked Olivia.

Cordella closed her eyes and took a deep breath. "I'm not going to lie or omit anymore. These secret meetings in the Council are a sign that Lars is in there as well. I wasn't the only one left out ... According to Mocer, there's no open talk about Lars being the savior, but it's all pointing that way: Only those who are uncertain are invited to the secret meetings. There's this unwillingness in the Council to pursue him, and they are saying now that the *future* arrived in your world. That's how Mocer discovered about what is happening in Leve ... That's why he started to ask questions."

"And what was he doing there? Can we trust him?" asked Olivia.

"He's playing along, gathering information," said Cordella.

"We are going to Leve," Trevor said, looking at Cordella and Belenos.

"Trev—" started Cordella.

"He's right, Cordella," interrupted Olivia firmly, leaving no room for negotiation. "And we need your help."

In moments like these, the slowness of Tartae got heavier. It seemed that time ran with no rush but in its fullness and importance as a piece of a puzzle.

The wind blew outside, and the leaves danced to it. Trevor fell deep in thought, bearing a blank expression that seemed a lot like shock. It was time for them to go back; it was right and needed.

Olivia had been through Portals many times, intentionally and unintentionally, but the idea of using them still brought shivers to her spine. It was like jumping into the unknown, unable to predict what was on the other side or if she would ever arrive there. At least now she'd have two of the most powerful wizards helping her, and she had learned plenty about the Portals. But on the other hand, they were erratic now, and the fact that Lars had been actively using and experimenting with them didn't help.

"You used to open Portals all the time, Cordella, you know how to do it," said Trevor. His voice with a mix of sadness and strength.

"I'm very uncertain about how the Portals are working after the destruction. I still don't quite understand how they were born again or even if they had never ceased to exist," Cordella said. "Belenos? Any ideas?"

He took a moment before answering; his face and his beautiful features twitched a little at every thought that crossed his mind. He approached the table where the rest of them were sitting, and somehow his posture changed, evoking action.

"Nature hears us. I firmly believe that we must make our intentions clear, and we shall be helped," said Belenos.

Cordella studied his face.

"Did you always use Keys to open them?" asked Olivia, and Cordella nodded. "In the Book, Ourivio describes the ritual for opening a Portal as a vote of trust; he then lists the actions needed: the spell, the Keys, and the willing witch. Is that what you did?" asked Olivia.

"Yes, I've always followed that," said Cordella. "We've adapted when we lost a Key, and it didn't take much to do it, only more of my energy."

"Your willingness," said Olivia.

"It's like what Belenos said; we need to ask for help and make our intentions clear," said Trevor.

"Is there something else about opening Portals hidden in the language of trees?" asked Cordella. She seemed hardened by her experience with the Portals, afraid of making any more mistakes, and Olivia could understand her, especially when Olivia and Trevor's safety were at risk, and not for the first time.

"No," answered Olivia. "But I think I have an idea." She stood up and got the Book of the Portals, bringing it to the kitchen and opening it over the table. The thing was so heavy with energy that the change in the kitchen was palpable but seemed a bit better after Olivia appeased it. "I like to calm it down," she said airily, while Trevor looked at her, puzzled.

Olivia opened the Book at a page where it read in huge flowery letters: *The Opening of Portals*. The writing seemed ancient and official. On the rest of the page was listed every ingredient needed for traveling between worlds, and the spell was explained in detail, much like a recipe. She pointed at the top of the page, right above the title, and translated something invisible to the others, written in the language of trees:

"Nature hears the witches' call,
Nature hears what witches plead.
Your way through all is easier when it's also what the moons need."

"Oh, this is an old saying in Tartae!" explained Cordella, examining the spot where Olivia pointed in amazement.

"It's like Belenos said," Olivia stated. "We do almost the same as you did, Cordella, which I believe was what Ourivio always did, but he also recognized the importance of nature in the equation. I just don't think he ever got to really understand it, like Belenos does. So, we do what you did, and we ask for permission. I think it will be safe."

"I agree," said Belenos. His deep voice sounded sure.

Cordella kept thinking with her hands together close to her chin, like in a prayer. She then faced forward.

"Very well, we shall do it," she said with courage in her voice. "Get ready to leave."

Olivia and Trevor didn't question anything, they just went for their weapons, and Olivia changed into something other than her pajamas, which didn't seem very proper for this adventure. When they went back downstairs, they found Belenos and Cordella in the yard. Cordella handed Olivia a piece of paper with the spell to open Portals written down.

"Keep it safe so you can open another one to come back," she said while holding Olivia's hand between hers.

They headed together to the woods behind Cordella's house and stopped at a place in the forest full of tall, thin trees. It was night, and the owls hooted loudly, while no other humans were around. They quickly found their positions in a circle, and Cordella said the spell by heart:

"The bridge, the door, our way in and out,
Allow us the passage to the City of Leve.
May we find our way to and back, safe and quick."

Belenos added solemnly:

"With the will of the Moons that blesses our skies,
To Nature we plea, give us a passage in this time of fear
We wish to help and only to heal."

Yellow dots appeared in front of them, translucent and multiplying until they clustered together and became a Portal: a round door into Leve, the same height as Belenos and wide enough for Olivia and Trevor. Its light shone brightly and resembled a replica of the sun rising in the middle of the Forest of Victro.

"Olivia do not forget your powers or your connection while you're in there," warned Belenos.

"Don't get distracted," added Cordella. "That's what Lars would want. Be brave, but careful. And be back fast."

Olivia and Trevor nodded and stepped in, enveloped by a warm yellow light and sucked into a rush of energy that made Olivia's stomach travel to her throat. It took them only moments to get to the other side, where they arrived abruptly in front of Lucent Bookshop, and the Portal dissipated behind them.

"I just hope we can open another one," said Olivia.

"I kind of hope we can't …" scoffed Trevor, looking at Olivia and shrugging. "What day do you think it is?"

"No idea …" Olivia whispered.

They stared at each other and went to their houses, following the same path they did on those much calmer days where they met after Olivia's shift and Trevor's classes. Leve looked the same; nothing strange seemed to be disturbing its calm streets and peaceful residents. There were people inside the houses going about their nights and cars passing from time to time. This weird sense of normalcy made Olivia uneasy.

They arrived at their street, and Trevor ran to his house, his legs so fast that they seemed about to detach from his tall body. He halted by the window, and Olivia was afraid to step closer to him until she saw his smile.

"He's okay," he said, smiling at Olivia. Mr. Meris was in his living room, staring mindlessly at the TV, with a book on his lap.

"Thank goodness. He doesn't seem very worried, Trev. That's a good sign."

"I guess …" he said, not convinced.

"Either way, he shouldn't see us. We're not staying. …" said Olivia.

Trevor was annoyed, but he complied. They walked together to Olivia's house so she could check on her grandma. The place seemed empty; only the porch light was on, and every window was shut. Olivia touched the door and used her powers to sense if there was life inside, much like she did when traveling through the forests of Tartae.

"Only bugs," she said, contorting her lips.

They walked inside the dark house, a harsh smell quickly filling their noses. "Come, let's find my computer. We'll check on Lara and the date and then we're out of here." She led the way to her bedroom, and Trevor followed.

"What is that smell?" asked Trevor as they got closer to Olivia's bedroom and the scent got stronger.

Olivia was already inside, connecting her laptop to power and turning the thing on. A month had passed since their Portal.

"But why did my father look so calm?" Trevor asked. He couldn't understand and kept asking Olivia to check if the date was right.

"Trev …" she said, fear rising in the back of her spine. "The slowness … It's here too."

"What?" said Trevor, grabbing the computer from her hands and visiting every news website he could think of. They all showed the same date.

"It's the only thing that makes sense. … Your dad would never—"

"He wouldn't …" Trevor interrupted Olivia, and his fingers finally stopped typing, resting over the keyboard.

After a moment digesting this information, Olivia read the news and recognized the man on the picture under the headline: "*New Minister of Affairs starting today.*" The man's hair was carefully groomed, and his gray expensive suit made him almost convincing as an upstanding citizen, but his smile was still foreign to his slender face.

"Baltazar!" Olivia exclaimed. A mix of relief and horror was inside her. He wasn't dead after all.

"They're in …" said Trevor, sadly.

The article didn't say much; it only described his career—all clearly forged—and had a couple of quotes from him and the president, both stating what a good choice he was and his amazing plans for the country.

"Maybe this is why he wasn't the one attacking me," said Olivia.

"If that is it, they have to have been here longer than we thought," concluded Trevor.

"I'm kind of relieved," said Olivia, and Trevor looked puzzled. "I thought I had killed him and, even though I was defending myself, it didn't feel right."

"What?" asked Trevor, widening his eyes.

"When the phookas took you, I was left behind and Bran was really Baltazar, remember? We fought and I struck him, and he fell …" narrated Olivia.

"Why didn't you tell me?" inquired Trevor.

"I was afraid that you'd judge me …," said Olivia.

"I'd never! You were a warrior, Olie! Chill. If anything, I'm impressed," Trevor concluded.

Olivia smiled, and a weight was lifted from her heart and her shoulders, but it didn't last long. She was quickly taken over by the realization that Baltazar was alive and had successfully infiltrated her world.

Olivia and Trevor researched more about any signs of Lars' influence, and the only thing they seemed to confirm was that people were also under some kind of Slowness Spell, for they didn't seem to notice anything out of the ordinary. They only had to discover if it was Lars' doing or only the Portals' erratic behavior spreading the same thing around their world. There was just the question if some people had managed to escape it.

After a couple of hours looking through many websites, they found some independent articles that mentioned a change in time and weird creatures growling under the shadows. It could be just the creations of an idle mind, but it sounded too close to what they knew to be true. "At least they are not attacking anybody," Trevor said.

"Maybe we should give Aeron a call; he might know something," said Olivia, looking for the gallery number online.

"Good idea. I'm going to call Lara too and see if she's alright," agreed Trevor, leaving the bedroom and heading downstairs.

Olivia closed her laptop. She looked around, and something seemed empty, like she didn't belong in her own bedroom anymore. Her things were the same way she had left them, showing that her grandmother hadn't touched any of it, which sparked something in her memory: Mrs. Halin was supposed to be home. Her last cruise had been about to dock when Olivia found the Portal and went to Tartae, which was a month ago.

A terrible feeling took over Olivia, and suddenly, the dark and quiet house seemed menacing, the putrid scent that lingered around finally having a source. "Phookas …" she said to herself, shaking her head, her fear rising.

Olivia ran out of her room and through the hallway, finding her grandma's bedroom door shut. She knocked twice and had no answer, and as soon as she cracked the door open, a strong smell of phookas found her nose. Olivia was ready to attack when she noticed there was no one inside, only her grandma lying as if frozen on her bed. Olivia turned on the light and got closer. Mrs. Halin was completely blue, and she seemed to sleep soundly with her frail hands resting over her stomach.

"May …" Olivia whispered, touching the elder's face, and as the cold skin encountered Olivia's warm hand, Mrs. Halin's body broke into pieces, like an ice sculpture.

Olivia stepped back in horror and screamed, bringing her hands to her face, clueless about what to do. Tears ran down her face as she witnessed the pieces evaporate like water under heat. She dug at the sheets desperately. Mrs. May Halin was gone.

Trevor came running and got only a glimpse of what had happened. He was paralyzed for a while under the portal door until he finally held

Olivia in an embrace that seemed to calm her down a bit. Olivia breathed hard, her eyes wide and fixated on the empty bed.

"Trevor … Trevor … did you see it? Did you see it?" she kept repeating. "Lars killed her," she finally said.

"I'm sorry," whispered Trevor.

"He froze her. There was no way of saving her … She had been frozen in here, alone!" sobbed Olivia. "I can't believe it."

"Olie, you know there was nothing you could do," said Trevor.

"He needs to be stopped," whispered Olivia.

"I know. … He does. Come on, Olie. They can come back. We have to get out of here," said Trevor, grabbing Olivia's hand and leading her out of the house.

Olivia's thoughts raced with images of Baltazar, the phookas dancing around her house, and her grandma there, forgotten, frozen in the dark. Olivia wished she could travel back in time so she could defend her somehow.

Olivia realized that they were now in Trevor's backyard, under the maple tree where his father had built him a treehouse many years ago. She followed him up the tree and inside it.

"Olie, I know it's hard now, but I need you to open the Portal. We have a lot of things to do in Tartae, so we can't get distracted, remember?" Trevor urged. He checked the windows of the small tree house and closed the plaid curtains. "I think we're safe here."

"Wait a minute, Trev. Your dad needs protection," Olivia said, opening the curtains in one of the small windows and facing Trevor's house. She raised her arms ceremoniously and closed her eyes, weaving a green smoke out of the grass and around Trevor's house. The thing created a shield and then disappeared. "Now we can go. He'll be safe," she said, smiling a strained smile at Trevor, who thanked her faintly.

Olivia reached for the piece of paper Cordella had given her before and recited the words. The Portal slowly formed before them, and they stepped inside while the sun rose in Leve.

CHAPTER TWELVE

CURSES OF NATURE

They were back in Tartae. As soon as Olivia walked out the Portal, she threw up, her feelings tearing her insides apart. They arrived in the Forest of Victro at the same place they'd left, but there was no sign of Cordella and Belenos; it was only Olivia and Trevor under the dark moonless sky, between the young trees of that forest. They walked slowly to Cordella's house, for there was no strength inside Olivia to run or hurry. Trevor examined the shadows around them like a hawk, but the only companions they seemed to have were the crickets and frogs that sang their wild melodies carelessly.

Olivia was still nauseated. The trip from one world to another, plus the sorrowful events mounted to an explosive reaction from her body, and her mind could barely think two thoughts together. It was all just a mess, and desperation took over slowly, like a poison spreading through her veins. Her face was all wet, covered in tears that she didn't even remember shedding.

Cordella's house finally appeared at the end of the trail made by dirt and small pebbles. As Olivia crossed the fence, it was like crossing a veil of energy: Cordella had put more protection around her home. Things might have worsened in Tartae too.

"It was bad," Trevor said to Cordella and Belenos as she opened the back door for him.

"Let's go inside. Hurry," Cordella advised. Her face was anxious and grave.

Cordella locked all the doors with a wave as soon as Olivia and Trevor stepped into her kitchen. She made Olivia sit down on her couch urgently, noticing her paleness and realizing instantly that something was wrong. She lit the fireplace with another spell that flew from her hands without any visible effort.

"My grandma is dead," Olivia blurted.

"Lars ..." Cordella sighed.

"Yes," said Trevor.

"He froze her ... When I touched her skin, she just—" Olivia couldn't finish it. She found Cordella's eyes and looked deeply into them, exchanging more than words. Right now, she wasn't crying anymore, but her face was still wet and puffy.

"Olivia, my dear ... It was already lost when you found her," said Cordella, getting closer to Olivia and giving her a hug.

"I'm sorry," lamented Belenos. His voice was sad and soothing as if it were enchanting Olivia in some way, farther from her misery. Her heart became lighter after his words.

"Cordella, Belenos ..." called Trevor. "You were right. Baltazar is now part of the government, and it seems that people are under the same Slowness Spell they are here in Tartae. My dad didn't even notice I'm gone, and it had been a month—my dad always worries. I've talked to Aeron and he said there are phookas there in hiding, waiting for their time."

"But that is not all, is it?" insisted Belenos, reading between Trevor's fearful words.

Trevor shook his head and continued, a somber quality over his face. "Aeron believes that the Portals are opening unexpectedly all the time ... Many people are disappearing. Some of them hadn't come back yet, but the ones who reappeared can't explain anything; it's like they had lost their minds. But even with all that, everyone seems too distracted to pay attention and things are just getting worse while nobody does a thing," said Trevor.

Olivia looked at him with desperation growing in her eyes. They hadn't had any time to discuss this before leaving Leve; it was all just a blur.

"What about Lara?" she asked.

"She's okay. I was able to talk to her on the phone. I was afraid that she'd be scared and desperate about what's happening after hearing about Tartae, phookas, and all, but she also seemed slower, out of touch or something. At least Aeron was normal. Normal and worried," acknowledged Trevor.

"It's like last time," Cordella whispered, her eyes blank as if she were looking elsewhere, far away from her living room.

"It's even worse, Cordella," added Belenos. "People are not even troubled this time."

"Is this spell part of Lars' plan?" asked Trevor.

"He might have added to it, Trevor. But I don't believe he's the sole cause," said Cordella. "This is because of the wounded Portals. What had Tartae's folk spellbound eventually befell your world too; after all, we're connected. Lars is taking advantage of it here and there, and I didn't expect any less of him. He was always smart and prepared. Maybe he's using other spells to make people even more clueless, and even though this isn't best, it isn't also that grave."

"Almost everybody in our world must be like that …" realized Olivia. She wondered how devastating Lars' doings would be and how quickly his power would lure people since they were all under that Slowness Spell that blurred everybody's minds and decisions. His influence had the potential of spreading like a fire in a forest.

"Some people in your world still believe and practice the old teachings. My hope is that they were protected, at least some of them," said Belenos. "I'll find a way to communicate with Aeron and other Tartae folks who live there. We must spread the word of what's happening and gather them as allies too."

"Good," replied Olivia as relief caressed her heart like warm honey.

They all ruminated on the newfound information for a while, deep in the silence, only interrupted by the sounds of the fire that cracked rhythmically, unaware of the sorrow and torment upon them. Cordella offered Olivia some tea, which she refused promptly, stating that she didn't have the stomach for anything right now. She wished to digest only her feelings, nothing else.

Two days had passed since Olivia and Trevor had left for Leve. Belenos and Cordella were quite anxious about how long that journey would take since, at this moment, it was even harder to predict how time would work in the two different worlds. Belenos explained it all after a long pause in the heavy conversation. He said that they had been waiting eagerly and were afraid that it could take *too* long.

During those days of waiting and hoping, he and Cordella were in touch with the others and learned that Alavro had found Bran. They were now off to see potential allies all around Tartae and spreading the word about all that Lars had done. Nothing was a secret now, and they'd decided to fight Lars' lies with the truth and were reaping the fruits of that decision. They had already found the support of the Willow Warriors, the centaurs, with whom Orion helped, as well as the Amazon Witches from the mountains, fauns, those who remain in Lirianthis, and people from Victro, Slintor, and Lotrien.

Unfortunately, they also had some terrible news. Lars' influence was getting stronger by the day; people were sympathizing more with his ideas and moved out of the shadows fast.

"He says he's the path to better days, to a better Tartae. With freedom and power to all … Even though he destroys those against him when he has the chance," said Cordella somberly. She paused as if to digest what she was about to say next. "That's what he did with his parents. Maleuca and Alcion were murdered."

Olivia and Trevor stared at her open-mouthed. It was as though the world around them was crumbling down fast, and there wasn't much they could do.

"He's targeting the Guardians again. Destroying us is a strong move for him, for it will minimize his threats as he dismantles a symbol. It will be easier for him to manipulate people without any hope or trace of what it used to be," lamented Cordella.

Olivia was afraid for her. Now, more than ever, Cordella was a target, but she didn't seem taken by it. Lars' threat on her life didn't hurt her or scared her as much as what he was doing with other people, with the Portals. It wasn't as bad as the lies he told all around Tartae.

"But Lars was betrayed by his own actions," continued Belenos, sharing a blink of hope. "He wasn't expecting the spread of the news that he was the one who killed the Arbres and Grondes, and with the death of his parents, everyone with sense ran the other way. This still wasn't enough to make the Council go after him or weaken him completely, but it was something in our favor."

"What should we do now?" asked Olivia.

"Now we must prepare to join Alavro and the others. But at this very moment, you go rest and sleep. No excuses … I'll bring you some allandrio tea in a minute. Go, go," said Cordella. The lady smiled with effort, observing Olivia and Trevor while they moved away. Olivia could almost see her smile fading as they stopped looking and all those worry wrinkles reappeared in the lady's face.

Olivia and Trevor dragged themselves to their bedroom. The tiredness was so heavy that it was even hard to sleep. Olivia lay in her bed under the dark blue quilt and stared at the ceiling for many minutes until Cordella walked in with the tea. She bid them a good night and closed the door behind her quickly. It wasn't long after that Trevor started snoring loudly on his bed, making Olivia more aware of how awake she was. The house went completely silent, and the night got old outside, windless and unstoppable.

Inside her—still—very active mind, Olivia kept piecing information together. Lars' steps and the bigger picture: the Portals and their unwillingness to close, to subdue to any who tried to control them. She figured that the Portals were much like a force of nature, impossible to cease and even hard to predict, like a storm or a hurricane. That thought led her to the next one, where she remembered how ancient people who worked in the fields and with the earth used to say that you should treat nature well, respect her cycles, perform seasonal rites in her honor, otherwise she would punish you; in that particular case, with bad crops, killing frosts and so on. Was this a response of nature for their offensive attempt to close the Portals? Were they being punished?

After losing all hope of falling sleep, Olivia decided to go downstairs to Cordella's library and read the Book of the Portals. Maybe there was something in there to point her in the right direction, some secret that even she hadn't found in there yet. She threw her quilt around her and walked carefully out of the room. The wooden steps creaked a bit under her weight, and the faint noise sounded strident, for the house was quiet; everyone was fast asleep, and the fire in the living room had died completely, making it all too dark.

Olivia reached the library after passing through the bedroom where Belenos was staying; she closed the library door slowly, avoiding any noises that could give away her late-night adventure. Once she was in, there was this feeling of safety that took over her, maybe because she was so used to be immersed in books and stories in another life. Olivia lit the fireplace and all the lamps in the room. The light revealed hundreds of books all over the wooden shelves. This place in Cordella's house was reserved only to knowledge and the written word, for all the walls were covered by shelves; there were no paintings or pictures around, only a desk by the window, a chaise and a small couch for reading. Olivia breathed the smell of books in, and it was like the world had stopped outside. She had the night to herself to mull over what bothered her heart and nagged her mind.

Before sitting down, she passed her fingers through many books' spines as if saying hello. *The Alchemist's Way, The Awe of the Times, The Awful Magician.* It seemed that Trevor had organized things here too, and Olivia chuckled. She found a book about ancient nature mythology named *The Gods of Green*, grabbed the Book of The Portals and perched herself over the chaise. The Book of The Portals was calm now, and it didn't require a lot of patting to release a lighter energy, which was great, because Olivia could just move on to her studies.

She shuffled through the pages multiple times, sometimes touching the parchment carefully to see if there was another message hidden between the threads. She read many passages over and over again, hoping to ease this feeling that there was something she needed to know. She then moved on to *The Gods of Green* and found a chapter on *Failed Celebrations and Their Consequences*, where Juno Southwood listed the effects of disappointing the deities of nature and many cases as examples.

Olivia fell asleep eventually while in the middle of chapter eleven, *Of Hexes and Curses.* She had dreams about the air and the fire, the Keys and what they really meant.

***

Light came through the library window filtered by the white curtains that adorned it. The sun rays woke Olivia from her sleep like motherly kisses, gently bringing her out of the realms she was visiting in her dreams. She sat down on the chaise, tired and groggy. "Maybe this wasn't such a good idea," she thought to herself. The fire still burned in the fireplace, and she turned off all the lamps before looking for some breakfast.

To her surprise, everyone was still asleep, and only birds sang outside, probably also tricked by the sun the same way she had been. It was supposed to be night still, she now figured. The sun wasn't yet a trusted sign of morning. She got ready for the day anyway, taking a shower and preparing a nice breakfast for the others, which she also thought would be a way to distract herself. Cooking wasn't her specialty, but she knew very well how to bake a banana cake and squeeze some oranges.

Olivia enjoyed this late night that gleamed like a fresh morning, for it was silent and everybody else seemed to be asleep not only in Cordella's house, but all around Victro, maybe all around the world. The moment itself was like a Portal, a hallway between two ends where she was lucky enough to get stuck for a while. There was this sense of calmness, joy, and time to spare.

While she waited for her cake to bake, she went to Cordella's garden and gathered some dandelion and rosemary; she realized everyone needed some happiness after the news of yesterday. Foraging for herbs made her connection with the elements arise again, and she allowed herself to sit and meditate between the flowers and leaves. She weaved some spells to make bulbs grow and help other plants find strength. Some of them were anxious and afraid, much like the humans.

Belenos greeted Olivia with a broad smile and headed to the yard; he needed nature as well, Olivia figured. He stayed there for a good while, facing the forest and grounded like a tree. Olivia had never seen him so simply dressed: He wore a white loose shirt and brown pants, and his hair was braided loosely.

The whole house awakened as well as the whole of Victro; noises found their way into Cordella's house, and people seemed completely unaware of the state of things, just strolling down the street with their carts, up and about.

Over breakfast, the group discussed some trivialities and how the sun kept tricking them into the weirdest mornings. Everyone seemed concerned about Olivia, but she said she was much better and dealing with her loss the best way she could. Unfortunately, there wasn't enough time to sit and mourn, and she was well aware of that.

They ate, talked, and rested until it was finally time to get ready and leave to meet Alavro and the others. As usual, Cordella had already packed not many bags, and they were all ready by the main door as soon as she called. Belenos had almost nothing with him, only a small black bag that he would carry across his chest. He was back again in his peacock blue cape and ready to leave. Olivia and Trevor were the last ones, for they didn't even know very well where they were off to. They were informed that they shouldn't bring much, only some clothes and their weapons and went upstairs running and started to fix their bags.

"Why were you up so early?" Trevor asked while picking up his backpack and filling it with a pair of jeans and some t-shirts.

"I had trouble sleeping last night," Olivia answered airily.

"Figures ..." Trevor said, shooting Olivia an understanding look. "You could have woke me."

"I wouldn't!" she said, smiling. "You needed your rest and not being dragged with me into my restless night ..."

Trevor smiled back and got more arrows from his trunk. Olivia sat on his bed with some bottles of potions in her hands, quite lost in thought and playing with the glass. She took a deep breath.

"This morning I helped some of the plants in Cordella's garden. I feel like I belong there, between them," Olivia said, deep in thought.

Trevor stared at her, sadness in his eyes and a glimpse of surprise.

"Things had changed now," Olivia said. "I don't have any family there anymore."

"You have me," Trevor said in a serious but kind tone.

Olivia chuckled and looked into Trevor's eyes; they were watering like hers.

"And you'll always have me," she said.

Trevor sat by her side and held her hand. "Think about it before doing anything, okay? For now, let's just get ready and hit the road!" They both laughed. Both knowing that things weren't so simple. They stayed for a moment there, holding hands tightly and unsure of what their future held, but then again, even though they were in an unusual situation for anyone who had ever lived in Leve, no one was ever sure about their future. It was always a surprise, a guessing game.

Time went by as quickly as it could after that, as if their quick heart-to-heart had given it permission to just unfold fast, bringing them to the next chapter of their journey. Before they realized it, they were out of Cordella's house, concealed under thick brown cloaks and meeting their horses again.

"Oh, it was about time, Lito!" exclaimed Trevor when he finally laid eyes on his huge brown horse. The beast was glad to see him and looked as majestic as ever, shining under the light of the sun.

Olivia approached her mare too; Myrrh was happy and healthy, and Olivia was relieved that the horse was well after all they had been through last time they were together: the demanding journey, parting ways without a goodbye. She was sure the mare felt the same, for her deep amber eyes gleamed at the sight of Olivia.

"Hello to you too. It's so good to finally see you, Myrrh," she said, caressing Myrrh's white mane.

Cordella explained that after the battle of the dark forest, they had galloped with all the horses to the Laliamo Forest, where they all spent some time recovering—human, horse, centaur, and eagle. They all needed a break to gather their strength and resume their lives. After time had passed, Myrrh and Lito didn't like much when others tried to ride them. They complained and sometimes rebelled, leading Firlo—who loved to care for horses and was responsible for looking after many of them—to believe that they wanted to be left alone to mourn the loss of their companions. Lito and Myrrh had lived a half-wild life after that. They would spend long periods in the forest by themselves and were back from time to time to the stables. It wasn't a surprise to Firlo when they appeared after the arrival of Olivia and Trevor in Tartae. They knew, and they were ready to be reunited.

Learning about that made Olivia's heart burst with joy; she kissed Myrrh's head and smiled. During that year she'd spent far away from Tartae and remembering everything, she missed Myrrh every day, and it pained her, the notion that she wouldn't ever see the animal again. She wished she had more time to ride her without worries through the forests of Tartae. Now, reunited, Olivia wished for that again and recognized that that powerful creature brought calm to her body. All her mourning from recent events and anxiety for what was about to come was softened by mere interaction with Myrrh.

Cordella and Belenos mounted their own horses—two tall and strong beasts, both black and incredibly shiny—and guided the group through the city of Victro at a fast pace, taking the right at Cordella's street and then another right, following a path with small houses of many colors on each side, where Olivia had never traveled before. The cobblestone streets of Victro became thinner and thinner, turning at some point into alleys, and those who crossed their way didn't seem bothered by them at all, maybe not recognizing them under their hoods, or not caring much because of the spell Tartae was under. The group entered a narrow street and kept going straight for a long time until they reached its end, where an unpaved street started.

Belenos and Cordella slowed their pace and looked back, a movement Olivia and Trevor repeated automatically, studying their surroundings. There was no one there. They resumed their journey, adjusting their speed again, and the scenery started to change more drastically as they galloped into a forest.

CHAPTER THIRTEEN

SLEEPY MOUNDS

The trees rose around them, getting higher and thicker, and, on the forest floor, stone, roots, bushes, and moss opened the way for the horses so unquestionably that it seemed the natural way of things. Pine and spruce trees spread all over, giving the group shade and shelter. Sometimes, Olivia got a glimpse of plants moving and shrinking slightly to the motion of their presence, and this simple realization made her heart glow. At least nature was waking again, maybe fully someday soon.

Olivia and Trevor galloped behind Cordella and Belenos into the woods they didn't know. They headed straight ahead for a long time until Trevor complained about his back and butt hurting so much that he was starting to see black spots. When they finally stopped to rest, they did it in a place surrounded by huge rocks, far away from any clearing or river, and where everything was covered in moss, from the ground to the trees. There were also mushrooms everywhere, popping out from every surface: small, big, of every color and shape.

"Where are we?" asked Olivia as she dismounted her horse. The forest was slowly introducing herself, presenting her scents, animals, and native plants.

"It's Fairwood. Victro is surrounded by forests, as you can see. When it was founded, it was a haven in nature, maybe in the likes of Lirianthis. But it grew too much and changed, as many things do," said Cordella, finding a rock the right height to sit on.

They all followed her lead and sat in a circle to eat some nuts and muffins they had brought with them, along with berries they found close by. They were again eating fresh and foraged things, back to living like birds in the wild as they did when they visited Tartae last time, a memory that sometimes seemed faded into the mixture of worlds and realities.

"And where are we going to meet Alavro?" asked Trevor, since that piece of information was never disclosed to Olivia and him.

"He's waiting for us at the mountains," answered Cordella, not paying too much attention.

"How long 'til we get there?" questioned Olivia.

"Two or three days. But there won't be many stops, so you might get yourselves used to it," warned Cordella.

"I wish we could meet the others at your house, Belenos," said Olivia.

"Too obvious of a choice," said Belenos.

"I wished to see your house again … and the Laliamo Forest," said Olivia dreamily, looking straight ahead as if her eyes could touch Laliamo, even from afar.

"I believe there will be plenty of opportunities." He smiled.

"Why didn't you tell us any of this earlier?" asked Trevor.

"We forgot, and you didn't ask," answered Cordella bluntly.

"Some things never change …" complained Trevor. And he was right. Once more, Olivia and Trevor were blindly following Cordella into some forest and deep into a dangerous journey.

They didn't stay for long at their resting spot and decided to move while it was still daylight. They resumed their quest at a slower pace at first, connecting once more with their surroundings and gathering enough strength to cast the same spell and manipulate the plants and roots out of their way. Before long, they were back again to riding as fast they could. Belenos got closer to Olivia and slowed down to a trot.

"Olivia, you should use your abilities to help us. Find a connection but control it. This is a great opportunity for you to practice."

She agreed, nodding, but inside her, excitement and fear rose together, both fighting for a chance to win her heart and take over. The conflict might have been transparent, for Belenos quickly added, in a kind, supportive tone, "I'll be right by your side."

Olivia pondered that this was possibly the safest way to try anything, since she was in the company of two of the most powerful people Tartae had ever seen. She closed her eyes and simply let the scent of leaves and flowers guide her. Her magic bloomed from inside of her; the elements came to life, and everything went numb for a millisecond until it burst into many sensations.

"Olivia!" Belenos' voice was far away, echoing between the trees. "Olivia! Control it!"

This time, the deep voice echoing around her got clearer, and she woke from a trance. A shiver ran through her body like a shock, and she found Belenos' face, staring at her from his mare.

"Maintain it. Find a balance, Olivia," he said, looking deeply into Olivia's eyes.

Olivia took a deep breath and centered herself, and for the first time, she understood what Belenos meant. The earth still pulsated with life around her, it still answered her call when she asked for clear passage, but they were not so intertwined. They were not one anymore and, in some way, Olivia was alone. Belenos shot her an approving smile and kept riding beside her, clearly still worried that her connection could take control.

They rode for hours, and the scenery around them didn't change much. The rocks got bigger and the sounds of wild animals louder. Sometimes, time seemed to run fast, and other times, they seemed to be in the woods for an eternity, riding on and on and never finding their way out.

When the night came, it fell at once over them, painting the forest in somber colors, and Olivia hoped to see the two moons of Tartae—a feeling she was so used to by now that she welcomed it like a dear friend. She dreamed about that vision even when she was in her world, that majestic confirmation that she was not in Leve, not living her ordinary life that seemed not to belong to her. But the moons never came, only those gray clouds, always heavy but rarely dripping a single drop of water.

The group stopped by some stones and bushes. Before getting ready to sleep, they ate some rosemary bread and mushrooms and drank fernolean sap (another one of Malva's teachings that Olivia thought would help them due to the energetic properties that plant had). They slept on the forest floor, very close to each other to avoid any surprises. Cordella drew some protection spells around them, and, before lying on the ground, Belenos warned Olivia not to let herself be lured into a deeper connection to the earth underneath her. She agreed and had many dreams of a forest spirit trying to woo her into the night, calling her to pass through the veil that covered the sky and into someplace where the two moons shone unapologetically.

They woke to some noises in the forest that turned out to be only foxes running around freely, but the scare was enough to shake away their sleepiness, and they resumed their travel in no time.

Before leaving, Belenos and Cordella asked Olivia about her night, and she explained that she'd slept well and had weird dreams, but nothing out of the ordinary. When they moved away from her, she confided to Trevor more details and her wonderings about what they meant, if anything.

"Don't you think it's just you wanting to see the moons?" he said, preparing Lito's saddle for the journey.

"I guess … That's why I didn't say anything before. Didn't want them to worry." Olivia shrugged.

"Worry more, you mean," added Trevor, laughing.

"At least *you* don't seem worried anymore." She laughed.

"Getting used to this weirdness, I gotta say!" Trevor said, mounting his horse and trotting away.

They rode deeper into the woods and, for a long part of the day, green and brown was all there was around them, but it wasn't tiring; it was beautiful and sometimes even hypnotic, like a mantra that repeats itself so many times, reaching the point it calms the spirit. The horses galloped loudly and no words were spoken for many hours, but even in the silence Olivia's mind didn't jump from thought to thought as it used to do. Somewhere along the way, between the worlds she had traveled and the many experiences she'd had, she learned how to dwell in silence.

The song of the forest was now known to Olivia. Little by little, she became acquainted with Fairwood, and even though she wasn't becoming the forest, she had a sense of what was around her, and that made her safe. She recognized the birds that lived around there, the noises from the tall trees.

When they slowed the pace to eat a little and drink some water, Cordella told them that she had traveled around Tartae many times during her long life, especially with her husband, Zervio, who was interested in finding and studying all the locations of the standing stones in Tartae. They also celebrated the Portals and the Seasons in pretty much every forest in Tartae, giving her much knowledge of those places.

Cordella's face glowed when she started, but a shadow made it change quickly—the realization that now, all she had were memories, possibly. That sudden shift in Cordella's face ached in Olivia's heart too, reminding her of her own losses and what was left for her in Leve. She had probably not only lost the last of her family but also any hope of resuming the life she knew in her world.

They took a right in the forest, changing sceneries and riding through a field of many nova trees that decorated the ground with their golden flowers until hundreds of hills appeared in front of them, spreading through the horizon and creating a spectacular landscape.

"Wow!" exclaimed Trevor. The image took his breath and words away; hundreds of green mounds stretched as far as the eye could see. The scenery seemed never-ending.

The sun painted the clouds with many colors, from purple to orange, in hues that seemed to change minute by minute. Olivia spotted a slice of one of the moons, faintly drawn on the day's sky, and a bit of hope rose inside her. The moons were still there, waiting for their time. The group chose a path through a valley with many trees, and some clouds hovered low over their heads, covering the top of the hills completely. It was as though the group was covered by a blanket, locked and protected inside a fort.

Cordella slowed the pace as they rode into the valley. "Let's not disturb the mounds," she said, leading the company into it.

Olivia and Trevor looked at each other.

"What do you mean?" Trevor asked. He studied the mounds, already afraid of waking up whatever that would be.

"The hills are sound asleep, have been like that for many ages. We don't want them to wake," said Belenos.

"Why?" asked Olivia. She held tightly to Myrrh, and deep down she wished to blend with nature again to understand that valley and those hills in a way no one could ever explain.

"No one knows how they will react," said Cordella.

"Good to know," joked Trevor.

"We just need to respect them," said Belenos. "We are safe here."

Belenos' expression was reassuring when he shot a smile at Olivia and Trevor. His face looked as refreshed as ever, as if he had just been vacationing and relaxing for days; his skin was glowing, and his wavy hair fell over his large shoulders.

The group galloped slowly, trying their best to move silently across the valley and leave all that surrounded them undisturbed. To their luck, many animals lived there and didn't bother the mounds, so all they had to do was to pretend they were not strangers to that land but just one more wild animal living their lives.

The valley stretched for miles and miles; they would have to spend a day in there—maybe even more. It depended on how fast they would have to go to keep the mounds calm and asleep. Waking them up would be a complete mess and a delay they didn't need in this pressing time.

The slowness of their travel made it much easier to actually see the wild woods around them, the many birds that chirped and played, dancing from tree to tree, the deer and foxes that ran around freely. The valley was beautiful, and they seemed to be locked somewhere with not as many worries, where the threats hanging over them had ceased to exist. The combination of that place, with that pace, in a Tartae that was almost dormant, gave an exacerbated sense of stillness in time and reminded Olivia of when she had just woken up from her sleep in the forest: how everything around her moved slowly and how connected she was to nature.

"How is everybody doing?" asked Cordella in a low tone. They hadn't said a word for a long time.

"Good," answered Trevor airily, nodding his head lightly.

"Very well, then. We'll keep moving," Cordella said.

"Is it safe to stop in this valley?" asked Olivia.

"Yes, we will just have to be respectful and careful," answered Cordella. "I don't think the mounds are that interested in waking up." She smiled.

Aside from the possibility of catastrophe, everything around them seemed normal, like in any other valley. Cordella explained in an extremely low tone—almost a whisper—how the mounds were a mystery to Tartae folk since they had been deeply asleep for ages; all knowledge about them had gotten lost and mixed. Some said they were giants who decided to sleep when the world became too small for them; others said they were dragons sleeping in cocoons made out of dirt and grass.

"How come no one does a scientific assessment to understand them and figure out what they are made of?" asked Trevor, intrigued and trying to keep his voice as low as Cordella's.

"They're afraid of waking them up, of course," she answered as if it were obvious.

"But—"

"Reports of what they are aren't clear," Belenos cut Trevor off. "But there's a consensus about the destruction they made. Whole cities were lost, many lives too. Our world is not prepared for something so big."

Trevor didn't say anything else. And Olivia wondered if they were actually so bad or if they just outgrew what was around them. Either way, she couldn't help the rising curiosity and temptation to see who they were. The amazement of meeting a new, strong, and wild creature of the valleys made her heart beat fast.

Cordella and Belenos exchanged some words about their plans, meeting Alavro, and the messages Cordella had received on her medallion, all saying everything was as well as it could be and that they had been successful reaching out many of Tartae folk. Things were starting to move, and Olivia wondered who she would encounter there when they found the others, who had decided to help them fight against Lars.

They finally stopped, and Cordella gave strict directions for them not to forage anything in there or drink the water from the creek. "Leave it to the animals. There'll be no harm for them," she said with a serious look that Olivia and Trevor knew very well.

As the night came, the mist that hovered over them fell at once, taking over the whole valley, thick and strange. It was also beautiful and raised in Olivia a desire to play with the elements like she hadn't done in a long while. She wanted to weave the mist, introduce herself, and understand why it behaved that way. She wanted to discover what exactly the mounds were underneath all that grass. It was hard to restrain herself and her impulses, but there wasn't any other way. She needed to mute the wilderness in her to avoid unleashing no-one-knew-what.

Olivia lay on the grassy ground and covered herself with a thin purple throw she had brought from Cordella's house. She kept staring up, breathing in the mist that was cold and smelled like nature, observing the treetops that disappeared into the heavy fog and imagining how it would feel to be like the mist: rising up with the night, spreading like a ghost and touching everything at once. She was carried into her sleep fast, not even noticing it.

"Olivia! Olivia! Stop! Stop it!" Belenos' voice sounded distant.

"Olie, wake up! Olie! Come on …" Trevor said.

And Olivia opened her eyes. All was blurry, but the ground trembled.

"What is happening?" she asked, coming to her senses and noticing the alarm in everybody's faces. Belenos and Trevor were over her, trying to wake her, and Cordella was standing with her arms stretched, waving them.

"The mounds … They're waking up," said Trevor, fear dripping from his big eyes.

"Olivia, you have to break it!" said Belenos.

"I'm not doing anything!" Olivia protested, not really understanding. She was just sleeping and dreaming with magic … Dreaming. "Oh no …" she sighed, and the forest trembled more. Olivia took a moment to think. "Maybe I can appease them … I think that's what Cordella is doing, right? I can do the same."

Olivia didn't wait for the answer; she got up at once and went to Cordella's side, not really sure of what to do. She observed Cordella for a while, but, on instinct, she kneeled to the forest floor and put both hands in it, as deep as she could. The earth covered her hands and fingers, its smell finding Olivia's nose and getting stronger. She closed her eyes and said silently:

"Sleep, under the warmth of the Sun,
Rest, under the light of the moons,
Be still underneath the grass and the dirt,
One day your time will come,
Until then, sleep, rest, be."

The tremors in the valley continued, but so did Olivia, still deep in her spell and into the earth, weaving it gently until the energy reached the mounds and worked its magic. From her spot, she could sense it touching all the sleeping creatures and spreading fast, connecting them to her. Slowly, everything calmed again, and the only things moving were the bats and the water that never stopped flowing in the creek.

Olivia removed her hands from the earth, breathing heavily. Cordella, Belenos, and Trevor got closer, and Trevor touched her shoulder in a fraternal movement. Inside Olivia, mixed feelings rose: her instincts were right, she knew what she had to do, but she also put the others in danger. Part of her was annoyed; controlling her connection to the earth only made it all the more uncontrollable. Why this need to tame everything?

"Can we just move on and resume our journey?" she finally said, standing and heading to her horse, which was lashed to a tree trunk nearby.

"Olivia, we must try to understand what happened in your sleep," said Cordella.

"There's nothing to understand. I was dreaming about my powers and I connected with them. The mounds must have heard. There's nothing to talk about," said Olivia, annoyed. She avoided looking into Cordella's or anyone's face. Anger rose inside her and made her want to scream.

"What were you dreaming about?" insisted Cordella.

"Please just leave me alone." Olivia sighed.

"We must know what happened. … Help us understand," said Cordella.

"I miss connecting with the elements in a deeper way, and I was dreaming with it. I was weaving the powers of nature, and I was happy." She looked straight into Cordella's eyes, making sure that she understood how frustrated she was. "Let's just go …"

Olivia mounted her horse and started galloping; the others soon caught her. It was still dark in those woods, but the heavy mist had lifted from the ground and was back again, hovering over them, filtering the first light of the dawn.

All of those feelings danced inside Olivia, clouding her judgment and her thoughts. Nothing was clear to her anymore, and annoyance only grew against everything, even Trevor, who rode next to her and watched over her with concern. It was time to leave that place, change the scenery, and maybe even discover more about herself and the right way to deal with her powers.

CHAPTER FOURTEEN

THE HOLLOW MOUNTAIN

After hours riding in complete silence, the mist over them became less thick, and the sun touched more patches of the valley.

"We're about to leave the valley. There are only a few miles left," whispered Belenos.

Olivia was instantly relieved. The thought of having to sleep in there one more night disturbed her, for she was insecure now, afraid of what she couldn't control. She hated this sensation and thinking that the connection she had with the earth was anything but special.

Mile by mile, their surroundings changed, and they arrived in an open field. The mounds behind them got smaller as the group galloped forward, and so did the threat they presented to their lives and Tartae as a whole. The mist still formed a thick blanket over the field they were in, and it stretched to the trees and hilltops behind them, reminding the group that at least inside that place they were protected. Lars and his lackeys, his phookas, would never venture in there to find them.

They galloped fast now, not afraid of waking up giants or dragons anymore, only focused on finding Alavro and the others as soon as they could. At a distance, mountains popped out of the field in front of them, completely covered in trees with some snow coloring their pointy tops in white.

The group reached the edge of one mountain when the sun weakened, venturing into the dense woods that climbed the thing. It was already late at night, according to Cordella, and the sun was just tricking them to think otherwise. They had been riding through the fields for long hours, never stopping, only slowing down their pace for water, a quick bite to eat, and some energy brew that Cordella had bought from Malva.

As they reached the insides of those woods, Cordella halted.

"Do you think we've been followed?" she whispered to Belenos.

"No," he whispered back.

"I don't think so either," Cordella continued. Her face was serious and didn't show any sign of relief.

Olivia and Trevor observed them and only exchanged a look of complicity.

Cordella led the group and never resumed her fast pace; she only trotted slowly over a faint trail on the ground and climbed the hill until they encountered many boulders piled up. Belenos dismounted his mare and closed his eyes, and after a second or two, they all witnessed an entrance opening into a dark cave.

"Come," Belenos said softly, walking in with his horse. They all dismounted and followed him.

The cave ceiling was high, and there was enough space for the group and the horses inside. After the dark hall they'd entered, it became some sort of labyrinth, with many hallways to each side, all completely dark. The cave seemed to occupy the insides of the whole mountain, and Olivia wondered if there would be an exit on the other side, somewhere far away from the field they were just in, like a massive tunnel.

Their way became brighter at some point as many torches appeared attached to the rough walls of the cave, showing that someone was in there already. Olivia feared for Myrrh; she had no idea if the horse would feel comfortable in that place, with less air and no field to run wild. When she was about to question Cordella about it, a voice broke the silence.

"Finally!" Alegra said. She ran to Trevor and hugged him, and then kept holding his hand while saying hello to the others. "Hey, everyone! They're here!" she yelled, leading them to their left, into a narrow hallway and then a huge room.

The place had some couches close to the walls, sleeping bags on the floor, and a huge wooden table right in the middle. It was all rough but kind of cozy, for it was very neat, and the smell of allandrio lingered.

There were no windows, and no light came from outside, only a fire they had made that Cordella quickly put out and replaced with some light blue spheres that hung over their heads and illuminated the place completely. "Much safer," she said, proud of herself.

Alegra, Bran, and Alavro greeted the group wholeheartedly and told them that they had been waiting for a while, planning and preparing. Bran offered to take the horses outside, where they kept them protected and away from any trouble.

The last days were so rushed that Olivia barely remembered her sadness or had any time for it. Thinking about that made the image of her grandmother, frozen and falling into pieces, pop into her mind, waking all those other feelings from their dormancy. Olivia found a place to sit on a flowery couch, running her hands over her face and sighing while listening to the others discuss the latest happenings. She wanted to be left out of it for once. Just in there with her thoughts and maybe fall into a nap.

"Hey, are you doing okay?" said Trevor, approaching her and finding a place on her side.

"Just tired …" answered Olivia, resting her back against the sofa and stretching her neck from side to side.

"Are you sure that's all, Olie?" he continued, his face full of doubts, staring at hers.

"Yeah, yeah …" Olivia sighed again. "I just think that holding off my connection is tiring sometimes, and I'm tired, and full of questions … And kind of pissed."

"What questions?" inquired Trevor, chuckling.

"Never mind … Many things happened these last days. My grandma and the fact that I didn't even have time—"

"To mourn." Trevor completed her sentence, twitching his mouth. "I see. I wish I could help."

"Thanks …" Olivia said, a faint smile on her face.

Bran came back with no horses and quickly joined the conversation Belenos, Cordella, Alavro, and Alegra were having. It seemed that Olivia and Trevor were in another world again, apart from the others and looking from outside while wondering about their place in all of it and how close they could be to the end. But then again, they could be mistaken. Destiny had misled them once before; there was no reason to believe that this time would be any different.

Cordella seemed to understand what was going through Olivia and Trevor's mind and decided that it was best for them all to rest, leaving the discussion to the next day. Olivia rejoiced and stretched herself over the couch, falling asleep quickly, like a tired child. She slept heavily and didn't even notice when the others followed her lead. She allowed herself to forget all her cares, at least for a night.

Olivia was awakened by Alegra, who just said, "it's time" and left her side, joining the others in their improvised kitchen. The scent of tea and boiled mushrooms took over the cave, and soon enough, they were all eating and drinking.

The talks about war took some time to start, but when they did, nothing could contain them anymore. Bran told the others that they had visited many folks of the forest, and they were all alarmed with everything they learned about Lars and his intentions, which made it easier for them to choose sides.

"Even in those tribes some people are bewitched, taken by slowness. But many chose to follow their warriors and chiefs, who are fully aware of what's happening," said Alegra.

"It was harder in the cities," Alavro said. "More people are under this weird spell and they paid no mind to what we had to say. You can punch them in the face and they won't wake up. It's sad and worrying. I tried to help but couldn't, and there wasn't enough time."

"Lars' influence is also stronger in the cities, and we had to be extremely careful not to approach those who believe in what he's preaching," continued Alegra.

Everybody listened with attention. In Olivia's head, she created that image, and it looked like a horror movie. People out of themselves, hypnotized, and unable to choose what was best for them, whatever that choice was.

"We also found this while in the city of Meadows," said Bran, shaking Olivia out of her wonderings with his words.

Bran put a flyer over the table. On it, a drawing of a happy family walking into a Portal with many riches on the other side, and around the image, the words: "In the name and honor of the old times, when power belonged to all. Hear Lars' words."

"That's horrible!" exclaimed Trevor, grabbing the piece of paper and looking disgusted. Alegra and Bran nodded.

"I'm afraid that something as simple as this can be very convincing to some people, and many must have chosen to follow him," said Alavro.

"Even with his empty promises," said Cordella.

"Even so …" added Alavro.

"So," continued Cordella as if trying to move on from the subject. "What's our next step?"

"Kirk is still at the Meadows gathering more allies," said Bran. "I say we move to the Moonsden plains and start to get ready. Set camp, prepare, and train while we can. We should let Kirk and all our allies know we are there and start to assemble. We must keep moving fast," he said firmly, sounding like a seasoned warrior.

"Can we move today?" asked Cordella.

"I don't see why not. It's early and we can reach Moonsden in a day if we go through the mountain," answered Bran.

"Bran, let's inform people from Lirianthis and witches and wizards of the cities. They should be the first ones to arrive at the camp, so they can help us with the protection and disguising spells," said Belenos.

"And what about Lars?" asked Olivia. "Has anyone heard of him? Do we know what he's up to?"

"No," answered Alavro.

"I don't think that's a good sign at all … Up to this day, he was always onto us. Why would that be any different now?" said Olivia. The memories of all of Lars' attacks were still too fresh in her mind. "We've been all around inviting people to a war against him. I know you tried to be careful, but there's no way we can guarantee that he doesn't know about it."

"I understand where you're coming from, Olivia. But we have no reason to believe—" started Cordella.

"We should find someone to go after him. A spy!" said Olivia, interrupting Cordella. Trevor agreed.

"What about Atlas?" asked Trevor. "She can fly and watch them from afar …"

"Or Mocer. He was trying to infiltrate in the secret meetings of the Council; he might be a good choice," said Olivia.

Everybody else went silent for a long time. Olivia only hoped they were pondering her idea, choosing to avoid more problems with Lars and failed plans. They had to agree that they had enough of those.

"We believe that Lars has infiltrated your world and is quite occupied with that. He's also learning what he can about the Portals, probably not caring much about our war, and he has been gathering his allies as well. As you see, many things on his plate," said Cordella. "But yes, I see no harm in recruiting Mocer as our spy and even trying to learn if Lars knows of our intentions of going to war with him before we want him to."

Olivia and Trevor smiled, satisfied with Cordella's conclusion. It would be nice not to be many steps behind Lars for a change, finally facing him at the same level. The man had been in silence, not even being chased by any of the Guardians—or what remained of them—he had time to plan and do whatever he pleased. They needed more information.

They left to Moonsden Plains later that day, sealing their hiding place with many spells cast by Cordella and Belenos before they parted. They exited the cave by the other side of the mountain, as Olivia suspected, cutting their travel time by many hours.

As they took the road again, Olivia kept retracing all she knew. Lars' attempts to make his power cross realms and take it all, and how scary this possibility was. The Portals opening without Keys, without control. The disturbing things she had read in The Book of The Portals, and how happy she was that Lars didn't know about it, and also the riddles Ourivio had in there. Something that kept creeping into Olivia's mind from time to time, like a puzzle she needed to solve.

The caravan moved through those woods at a steady pace, stopping briefly when the hunger and tiredness took too much of them. When it was already dark, and the sun had set like in a normal day in Tartae, they stopped close to a pristine and small lake, setting up a fire and preparing some carrot soup. Belenos manipulated a protection over them, and the smoke from the fire dissipated completely just above their heads, never leaving the dome they were in.

Olivia stayed for a while with Myrrh, caressing her mane and letting that strong presence of her horse draw calmness to her, appeasing her sadness and conflicted feelings. She also fed the mare carrots and apples.

"Brought this for you," Bran said, offering her a piece of honey cake that had seen better days and was already kind of dry.

"Thanks," she said airily, eating a piece of it and figuring it was still delicious.

"Don't you want to come with us and sit by the fire? We're just talking, nothing heavy, I promise!" said Bran, smiling.

"I've been thinking too much, Bran. Sometimes I feel like I just need to shut it all up," said Olivia, her heart shrinking and many thoughts flying through her head.

"My dad, Belenos, and Cordella already went to sleep, Olie. It's just us … You can just *be*," he said, an understanding look in his eyes while he stretched his hand to her.

She allowed herself to follow, and when they approached the fire, Trevor and Alegra were deep in a kiss.

"Oh my!" Olivia exclaimed, trying to contain her laugh but failing at it miserably.

Trevor and Alegra moved away from each other at once, widening their eyes in surprise. Their pale faces were illuminated by the fire in front of them.

"We didn't want to disturb … Sorry!" said Bran.

Olivia and Bran laughed hard, kind of embarrassed and surprised. But the simplicity of that made Olivia's heart shift and find peace, moving away heavier thoughts that were occupying every corner of her mind and leaving no place for anything else. Trevor and Alegra laughed too, and they all talked over the fire for a while, the two of them never speaking of what had just happened but never letting go of each other's hand.

The night was airy in the forest. The energy of it was easy and young, fresh as the scent of the pine trees around them. Olivia, Trevor, Bran, and Alegra fell asleep between giggles and woke up easily on the other day, for sleeping on the forest floor only seemed good to Olivia and Belenos. Trevor was back at complaining about it, and Olivia figured that he had had his share of nights in those conditions. The higher point for him now was that Alegra found joy massaging his stiff shoulders, which Olivia believed only motivated him to complain more, so he would get more of Alegra's desired attention.

Their journey inside that forest took three days. The place treated them like friends, and they hadn't met any challenges in there, not even wolves, which had many packs in that particular forest, according to Alavro. He was back to his bard storytelling style when he decided to tell the rest of the group the legend of the black wolves, who had lived there for many ages, always protecting the lakes and rivers.

"Strong and brave, those wolves are. Magical creatures that roam during the night in packs of thousands, like you will see nowhere else," Alavro said. "They howl to the moons as soon as they show up in the sky; they find those who walked in the forest uninvited, filled with ill intentions, and then they cast over them the spell of water, howling a magic song that transforms all those unfortunate souls into a mist, disappearing in the depths of the river."

"I just hope someone had asked for permission before entering here," mocked Trevor. And Alavro broke into laughter, making it impossible not to follow his lead.

As for Olivia, she could tell that those woods were young and happy still, even with all that was happening in Tartae, and even if she couldn't connect with them fully. But there was also something mysterious in there, and she had to hold herself not to try to discover what, and not to follow any clues in her sleep. She wished there would be a day when she would be able to roam like the wolves in every forest of Tartae, free and wild, part of the earth unapologetically.

Their journey ended on a high note, for everyone seemed happy and confident about their plans when they reached the borders of Moonsden. The main reason they chose those plains for camping and then for war was that they were far from cities, far enough from the forest—especially the Ancient Forest and Laliamo, both so important for Tartae—and a challenging place for Lars to get to, which would give them advantage. Moonsden also offered enough space for all their needs and troops.

The tents were set by Olivia, Cordella, and Belenos, who could do it by manipulating the air and were quite fast at it; in a matter of ten minutes, there were about seven tents around the place for them to have their meetings, meals, and sleep. It was all very organized and even pretty. The tents were dark green, matching the grass, and they were set close to a river so they could have plenty of water.

Everybody helped to organize the tents with the small tables they had brought, pots, pans, training equipment, and beds. Even though magic helped them carry it all in their small bags, the shrinking and feathery spell wasn't enough for everything they needed, and others would bring them the rest of it, including larger tables for meetings, wood stoves, and even bigger weapons.

Belenos cast enchantments for protection around the camp. He just sat down in the middle of it with his long legs crossed and closed his eyes. His expression was peaceful, and his mouth moved slightly, emitting no sound, but from him, yellow ghost-like streaks came out delicately, floating to the edge of the camp and forming a circle until it swirled and faded completely. Olivia observed, mesmerized, while a shiver ran through her body. Magic was all around them.

The weather was warm, and the sun was up in the sky, making it feel like old times in Tartae, but there was also a breeze that came often and traveled between them, not at all afraid of the protection spells around the camp. Those wind gusts were as cold as ice and chilled even the warmest thoughts they had, reminding them that Tartae was still not the same. It was their obligation to help, and for that reason, they had to keep going. Olivia wondered how things would be if Lars won this war. She figured that Tartae would burn down, succumbing to sadness due to all the fights and greediness around something that was always made to be so pure. They needed to end Lars' efforts, but also, they needed to discover a more respectful way to deal with the Portals, to handle the magic of Tartae.

Olivia was brought out of her divagations when Cordella called for help bringing water from the river, which Olivia insisted on doing the magicless way "to introduce herself first". Cordella concurred and left Olivia to it. She walked to the river with two empty buckets, studying the landscape around her: the green grass that covered the ground, the large river flowing nonstop, the rocks that decorated its edges, and the forests beginning again at a distance. She touched the water and said hello, asking for permission. Actions that came from her heart, without many explanations. She acted out of intuition, following the leads of her own nature and letting it run wild, at least with this small thing.

Both buckets were filled to the top; the water was clear and very cold, and something echoed inside Olivia: the voice of the river, greeting her back. She walked back to the camp refreshed.

This day moved slowly, allowing the group time to put everything together and arrange what they needed to start this new chapter that could mean the end of their troubles. When it started, the sun didn't take long to set; it seemed as tired as the group was and went to sleep as soon as it could. They did the same, just after eating some mushroom soup and talking very little, for even the words were tired.

Olivia fell asleep at once in the tent she shared with Trevor, Bran, and Alegra. They all had a small bed, much like the ones they used on their first journey around Tartae, and which Trevor seemed to love more than anything since it was his way out of sleeping on the bare forest floor. Everybody just dozed off automatically, not even stopping to choose beds or say good night; they just succumbed to their tiredness.

CHAPTER FIFTEEN

A NEW PATH TO LEVE

Training day. After everything they had been through—their journey to find the Book of the Portals, their fights with Lars and their attempt to destroy the Portals—they were back where it all started: training their war movements under the scorching sun. At least now Olivia and Trevor were not as inexperienced, but they were quite out of shape. They tried to explain to Bran and Alegra that in their world there was no constant training for fighting, no imminent risk of war at every corner, at least not like that, the way it was in Tartae. There was no fighting with swords, axes, bows, and arrows. In their world, the fighting was made more usually with words and guns, which Bran and Alegra had a very hard time believing.

"But there's not much honor in that," protested Bran, after learning how wars usually worked.

"I guess they really have forgotten the Old Ways …" added Alegra.

Olivia and Trevor were kind of embarrassed but said that many people were against those ways and much more invested in discussions and politics that could help more than just fighting, which led them to explain why Lars' move into their politics was so smart.

"Most of the time, that's the way to do things successfully in our world: with influence and deals," said Trevor, shrugging. "I think diplomacy can be the smart way out of many troubles," he added with a pompous tone in his voice, which made Bran scoff.

"Okay, okay … I don't think Lars is open to a lot of conversation with us. But I'll check!" joked Bran.

"Please, don't!" said Trevor, laughing.

They started their training, and Cordella, Belenos, and Alavro joined them. It was the first time they exercised their fighting skills together and, in order to refine their abilities on the field, no one used magic or any elements to help, only their strength.

Bran went back to basics when teaching Olivia and Trevor. He talked once more about how to keep balance, the importance of reflexes, and strategies for defense, and kept repeating that they should develop another sense almost, heightening their perception, and being able to predict what would come next. Olivia knew that her connection with the earth could be extra helpful in the battlefield, if only she could control it just a little bit and not turn into a plant completely, or not black out at the mere sight of phookas.

The session was hard and moved slowly, for they lacked the motivation to learn it all again. They just wanted to go back to the point where it was all easier and their bodies were so dexterous that they seemed lighter, like feathers moving to the wind.

"Can't you just manipulate the elements inside my body and mind so I can be better again?" said Trevor, out of breath.

"I can't, but we can call Freya to try something …" laughed Olivia.

"No, thank you … I guess I'm okay!" he answered, making a face, widening his eyes in shock and resuming his position, ready to avoid Bran and Belenos' strikes.

They stopped briefly at lunch for sandwiches and berries and drank bilboberry brew, which was supposed to give them energy for the rest of their session. Alavro left the pretend battle to rest and prepare some dinner, figuring they'd all be starving when this day was over. "I know I already am!" he added, going straight to the tent where they had an improvised and very ingenious bathroom where Cordella and Belenos had built a shower with the help and ideas provided by Olivia. After the time she'd spent with the river, she figured that they could make a shower using the trunk and leaves of a tree. The trunk would suck water from the soil and drip it out from its leaves, falling over one's body and creating a very refreshing solution for a recurrent problem in many camps. Of course, there was still the option of bathing in the river, but right now, it was a matter of choice, not the lack of it.

From time to time, Olivia noticed that Trevor would lose his eyes to the horizon with a blank expression upon his face, seeming quite detached from all that surrounded him. At those times, his arrow appeared to weigh a ton in his hand, and he'd let it fall to the ground carelessly. When the day was ending and Olivia had seen that same motion repeated many times, she approached him; they needed time alone, a moment to discuss everything that had been happening around them.

"Are you okay?" Olivia asked. She automatically thought that it was her turn to check on him for a change.

"Hey, Olie." Trevor sighed and forced a smile. "Tired yet?"

Olivia nodded. "Want to take a break? I don't think they will even miss us ..."

Bran and Alegra were deep into a fight with their wooden training swords, and Cordella and Belenos were talking about something fervently, but Olivia could not tell what from where she stood.

Trevor agreed, and they sat on the grass, the night taking over the sky, which was gray again and missing the two main components once more. Trevor was so tired that he lay down on the ground, letting out a deep exhale, resting his hands behind his head.

"I miss the moons," sighed Trevor, staring dreamily at the sky.

"Me too. It's always a reminder that something is out of place," said Olivia. "But seriously, Trev. How are you?" Olivia looked deep into Trevor's eyes, who now stared back at her.

"Not very well, Olie. I can't stop thinking about my dad and what happened to your grandma, and right now, there's not even talk about when we might be coming back to Leve ... We just seem to have so much to do around here ... It's not like last time, where our goal was to destroy the Portals and come back. Things are more complicated, I think. Not that they were ever easy."

"I see ... I sometimes feel like it's too much too, and what's happening in Leve doesn't seem to be their main concern with this oncoming war and all."

"Do you think we can find a way to check on my father without using a Portal or getting too much attention?" asked Trevor, sitting up again, and his eyes filling with hope.

"I mean, we can try," said Olivia. "We can talk to Cordella and Belenos and see if—"

"Can't you try it?" interrupted Trevor. "I didn't want them to know and to worry about me on top of everything else."

"I get it, but I don't have the faintest idea how, Trev ... And don't you think they'd like to know how Leve is doing, how our whole world is doing under Lars' influence?"

"I guess ..." Trevor sighed, disappointed.

"Come on, don't be like that! I'm gonna think of something and see if I have any ideas. Try to remember your readings too; we've spent so much time in Belenos' library, it ought to be worth something!" Olivia said.

"What about you? How have you been dealing with everything?" asked Trevor.

"I'm managing. Sometimes it just seems too much to handle. I didn't have the most perfect relationship with May, but she was the only family I had left. I feel bad, but it's getting better every day," said Olivia.

"I've told you before, she wasn't the only family you had. You still have a family, Olie, I'm right here," Trevor had a beautiful look on his face; his kind eyes gleamed with love, and Olivia smiled.

"There's also this uneasiness that had been growing inside me. I've been feeling ... I don't know how to put it ... confined, maybe. Like I need to be freed," added Olivia.

Trevor looked at her, pondering what to say next.

"Do you have any idea why?" he finally asked.

"Maybe ... Maybe it's because of this control over my connection to the earth. I feel bound."

"Don't you even start, Olie. Don't you dare become a plant again now that we're preparing for war and who knows what else. I can't even picture how many weird and evil creatures will be on Lars' side," Trevor protested, alarmed.

Olivia gazed at him, not saying anything. She knew that he was right, but she still wished to find a way between. Some kind of balance that could provide her with the right amount of connection to nature and control over it, shielded from the harsh influences of those with evil meanings. If only she still had access to Belenos' library. It was much more complete than Cordella's and bore many weird books about nature and its creatures; maybe she would find something she could relate to.

"Well," she finally said, moving away from that subject, which she clearly wasn't ready to confront. "At least now you have something to lighten up the mood." Olivia laughed.

"I knew you'd say something!" Trevor exclaimed, smiling back at Olivia, and his face glowing with joy, making him look younger, back to before this Portal madness started. "Alegra is the best. I missed her while we weren't here. I really wanted to see her again."

"And now that you did, you wasted no time!" joked Olivia, and they both laughed. "I'm happy for you, Trev." She smiled. It was clear that Alegra made things easier for him in Tartae. Made all the questions and insecurities he had bearable. Olivia was his best friend, but also a reminder of sad things that were happening in their world, and sometimes, even a source of more worries, especially when she decided to become a tree.

They talked a bit more before heading to dinner, including discussions about how good it was that Kirk wasn't responsible for their training anymore, for the man was borderline cruel with his tactics. They were also grateful that Orion wasn't there, since he had the crazy idea that one should train until blacking out, otherwise it wasn't a fruitful day. Orion and Kirk would make a great team of destruction, so it was better if they left their talents to the opposing troops.

Dinner was delicious; Alavro loved to cook and prepared a witch's brew, which consisted of vegetables with many healing herbs like rosemary, albion, falcon's eye and dewdrops. When Olivia and Trevor shared what such a name meant in their world, the others found it hard to believe. "How could they think witches would do such a thing?" Cordella kept repeating, and everyone else nodded in agreement.

Alavro went on to tell them how in Tartae they preferred to eat only life and that was why they had a diet based in plants with very little coming from animals, only milk, honey, and butter—but even those were always used with respect, he added. Olivia figured that Alavro was another man when his son was near him and well, which made a lot of sense and also made her heart shrink with pain thinking about Mr. Meris and Trevor. When Bran was around, Alavro was back to his bard oolf, telling many stories and finding pleasure in the smallest things, like gathering everybody around the fire for a nice pot of soup.

He shared with the others his ideas of writing a book about the folklore of Tartae and its many magical forests. Olivia was ecstatic about that. She wanted to learn everything about the inhabitants of those woods, mythical or not. And something told her that many stories would probably be far from folklore and very close to reality since the place bloomed with enchantment.

Before retiring for the night, Belenos and Cordella asked if Olivia wanted to train magic the next day, which she agreed to without having to think twice. According to both of them, and under the approving nods of everyone else in the group, adding a magical touch to battle was one more advantage to their side, and it was smart to use every single advantage they had.

Olivia stayed behind when all the others went to their tents; she headed to the meeting tent, grabbed a notebook and a lampion, resting it over the table close to her. She sat down and started doodling on one page, drawing, and writing many things, from pieces of what she had read in Ourivio's notes in The Book of the Portals to excerpts she remembered from every book she'd read about Tartae. She tried to organize her thoughts and maybe find a way to check on Mr. Meris without causing too much of a boast. She remembered this thing about words and their traveling power; could she use words to travel between realms? But how she would hear back from Mr. Meris? Not a very good option considering he wasn't magical at all. There was also this saying about rainbows being Portals, but that was proven to be just a myth. Everything that popped into her brain wasn't worth the try at all, and after a long time pondering many ideas, she decided to try something for herself. She figured every spell in Tartae was invented at some point, long back in time; maybe this was her chance to start working on her own enchantments.

Olivia listed things that she could manipulate into a Portal, a tiny one, only to spy without any fuss: a television, a mirror, a picture frame, a window, a dream … A dream! If she could visit Mr. Meris in some kind of dream, she would be able to check on him while still physically in the camp. The perfect solution.

"That's it!" she whispered to herself, and her voice was louder than she expected, interrupting the symphony made by the crickets and the frogs.

Olivia wrote down a spell that was very simple, just strong enough to safeguard her travel, and then she headed to their tent.

"Trevor," she whispered, shaking her friend out of his dreams. "Trev!" she repeated until he opened his eyes.

"Is everything okay?" Trevor said with a hoarse voice.

"Yes. I think I have found a way to see how your dad is doing, but I need your help," murmured Olivia.

Trevor quickly sat up on his bed and waited for her to continue.

"I'm gonna go there using my energy while I sleep. I prepared a safeguard spell, and you should watch over me, in case something seems wrong," Olivia said. "Let's go to the meeting room."

They walked silently through the camp, and Olivia found a bench inside the meeting tent to lie on. Trevor had this weird expression all over his face, something between excitement and fear, and Olivia figured that she probably looked much the same. She lay down and closed her eyes, taking some deep breaths to center herself, and then recited:

"Night, take me into your arms,
Bring me to Leve, so I can see Mr. Meris and how well he is.
Take me swiftly, awake in energy,
Bring me back safely, blessed by the night and the Moons that should always be in our sky."

As soon as she finished, it was as though she were washed over by a river. Her mind became unclear, moving fast through many places, memories, thoughts, and even feelings. After a while, everything turned orange and then back to the normal color of things. Olivia realized she was floating right outside Trevor's house. She didn't think much about what she needed to do, for she had no idea how long her spell would last or even the effects of a delayed stay in Leve. She thought about Trevor's living room and, automatically, she was there. The place was empty, all the lights off. She floated to the stairs and found Mr. Meris sitting in an armchair on the second floor, a thick book in his hands and a faint smile on his face. He was still unaware of the absence of his child, it appeared. He hadn't called the police or looked the least worried. Things were definitely out of place.

Aside from that, Olivia only paid attention to any sign that would show the state of things, but Leve seemed to be the same way they had left it. She had the urge to find out about Baltazar, and the things he would be doing as a minister, and as her thought jumped there, she realized she was already in front of him: His overly neat hair combed back, his strange features that seemed to mix a human face and something else far from it, and his empty eyes. The man wore a dark red robe thrown over his blue pajamas, and Olivia was floating inside what seemed to be his kitchen.

"Were you able to finish him?" a voice asked, coming from nowhere.

"Yes," Baltazar answered firmly, his voice scratching Olivia's ears.

"Good," answered the voice, and Olivia tried to figure out where it was coming from, since Baltazar was the only one in the kitchen.

"One less thing to bother me," Baltazar said with a laugh. "What about the other ones?"

"Leave that. Their stupidity is going to be their end," the voice hissed.

"Sir, what about the phookas? They're growing unhinged," Baltazar added, and his voice trembled a little. Uncertainty colored it.

"Let their fever grow," the voice said.

"But sir, we don't know how this world will affect them. They might not resist," Baltazar insisted.

"Don't argue with me. I made you and saved you. You owe what you are to me. Do as I say and never question," the voice barked, and finally Olivia recognized it.

"Yes, sir. I apologize." Baltazar's face twitched.

Baltazar was talking to Lars through realms. Lars' voice sounded distorted, but his ideas were clear. Olivia had the urge to flee, afraid that Lars' powers would sense her presence, but at the same time, this was too perfect an opportunity to dismiss. She could learn about their plans and what they knew; she could really give the remaining Guardians an advantage.

Both of them kept talking while Baltazar grabbed some fresh meat from his fridge. He seemed preoccupied and stopped, walking to the glass wall in front of him and staring through it.

"You should find a way to insert our advances in the presidential house. We need this for the new era," said Lars.

"Consider it done, sir," answered Baltazar. "What about the Council and the Guardians?"

"Their time is over. They will soon discover that as well. It's time for someone to show them the way out," said Lars.

Olivia's arm went numb, and soon after, it was her legs. She figured that she had been in there too long and was wishing to stay more, which certainly affected the spell. She moved to Baltazar's living room, a spacious place decorated fully with modern furniture and plenty of paintings covering the walls. She closed her eyes and asked for a way back, and everything blacked out again. When she opened her eyes, feeling her feet touching the mossy ground, she was in the middle of a dense forest, late at night.

Quickly she looked at the sky, searching for the two moons, but only stars gleamed there, and they were many. The forest was beautiful, and it sang a song that swirled around her. Many blue butterflies appeared and flew gently, as though the stars had fallen from the sky. As she looked down, she had a white dress on, much like a nightgown, something she didn't own and had never seen before.

"What a surprise to see you here," a warm voice said, echoing inside of her and making something bloom. Maybe the magic in her veins, she thought.

From behind a tree, Freya appeared, wearing a long, dark green dress that floated too much and unnaturally, for there was no breeze.

"You know what the forest needs, Olivia. Don't hesitate," she said softly.

Freya bore a smile and looked deep into Olivia's eyes, as she always did. Her hazel eyes sparkled, and slowly they became butterflies that flew right at Olivia, and everything blacked out at once until she woke under Trevor's vigilant gaze.

"What happened?" he asked, his eyes full of expectation.

"Was I out for long?" said Olivia, sitting up and trying to organize everything that went down in her dream, or whatever that was.

"Long enough. I was starting to get worried, but you woke up before I decided it was time to call Cordella," said Trevor. His face was still puzzled, waiting, expecting anything.

"Your dad is fine, but unfortunately—or fortunately—he seemed to have no clue that you're missing," Olivia said. "Leve seemed alright too, but I don't know for how long."

Trevor's face went from happiness to confusion in milliseconds.

"What did you see?" he finally asked.

"I ended up in Baltazar's home," Olivia said.

"Did he see you?" exclaimed Trevor, widening his eyes.

"No, I was just this energy. No one could see me, I'm sure. But things are bad, Trev. ... He was talking to Lars through realms ... like from a speaker phone. Lars was just this voice in the room, kind of distorted but there, and able to communicate very well. They know what they're doing, Trev," Olivia said, fear overflowing her voice and an alarmed look on her face.

Olivia told Trevor everything Baltazar and Lars had discussed, every detail she could remember. Trevor was amazed and scared. Knowing this piece of their plans made their imagination flow and created many other scary scenarios, which wasn't a good combination right before bed.

"We have to tell Cordella," warned Trevor. Olivia agreed.

Olivia didn't tell him about seeing Freya. Mainly because she didn't know what that was exactly; the whole thing could be just a dream she wandered into accidentally and carried no more meaning aside from that. But if it was something else, she wanted more time alone with it before putting it out into the world.

They decided they'd tell everything they had learned to the others as soon as everybody woke up, even if that meant getting an earful. Butterflies flew up and down Olivia's stomach; anxiety was like a beast inside her, looking to free itself. It was hard to keep it in, especially when fear and many questions were added like fuel into a fire. So many things she would have to shut down in order to sleep; it seemed an impossible quest. Olivia and Trevor crossed the camping grounds, walking carefully under the night sky. The air around them was freezing, making their breaths into smoke.

When the sun dawned outside, Olivia was sure that she had tried—unsuccessfully—to sleep for the whole night. Her head was spinning with new information, and ideas kept arriving, all piling up on each other and not making a lot of sense. She got up slowly, not sleepy but still groggy from the eventful night, and the trees outside called her. Something wild required her presence, and she didn't question much. She put on a large white sweater she had popping out of her bag and headed to the wild patch of nature in their camp, barefoot. The day was young and coral, and low, dense fog covered the ground.

The leaves and the grass were colored in a deep green, accentuated by the dew that dripped over everything. Between those trees, the world seemed to shift, vibrating into a different frequency so soundly that it echoed in Olivia's ears. She had this deep understanding of what was around her and, out of instinct, she blew slowly, weaving the air into a turquoise, pale tendril that danced around and into nature, traveling away between trees, protecting them all.

CHAPTER SIXTEEN

THE MISTY DOME

The camp woke soon after Olivia. The sun was still low in the west and the mist dissipated slowly, changing the feel of the morning into something more mundane. Everyone headed to the dining tent—as the group started to call it—and as breakfast was being eaten, Trevor let it out at once.

"We have news about our world," he said bluntly.

Cordella put down her mug and made no reply, only shot him a look. Anticipation filled all the space in the room.

"Oh, come on, boy! Spill it!" exclaimed Alavro.

"I went there," started Olivia.

"I beg your pardon?" Cordella was mad; her voice trembled and she had this outraged look on her face.

"No need to worry, people! As everyone can see, Olivia is fine!" said Trevor.

"Just listen to us, okay?" said Olivia, appeasing everyone's nerves as much as she could. "I don't think the details of how I got there are too important; no one saw me, and I was—and am—completely safe. The important thing is that Baltazar and Lars are able to communicate between worlds and they're planning something big," said Olivia.

"And also killing people there, as it appears," said Trevor.

Olivia narrated everything she'd learned and answered all the questions Cordella and Alavro asked.

"Did they mention you two?" asked Cordella.

"Never." Olivia shook her head.

"What did you say Baltazar was eating?" asked Bran.

"Raw meat, but he never actually ate it. It just seemed like he was about to," Olivia answered.

"And Lars said that he made him what he is?" Bran continued; Olivia nodded. Bran and Cordella exchanged a deep look.

"I guess Baltazar might be a phooka," continued Bran, hesitantly. "I think Lars transformed him into what he is today."

"That actually makes sense," said Olivia. "He shapeshifted into you, Bran, when we fought in the battle of the dark forest. Later on, when we were fighting, he changed more and more into something beastlike." Olivia remembered it all too clearly, Baltazar's nails piercing her arms, the fear growing inside her like a monster, Trevor's screams echoing in her head.

"There's danger in that," whispered Belenos. Every eye in the room turned to him and, as he continued, his voice seemed to tear the veil of fear around them. "It's not natural to perform something like that. You all saw how nature reacted to destroying the Portals, and we did it with the best of intentions. His magic shows no respect; it's disruptive."

"Should we do something about it?" asked Alegra.

"I don't think there's much else for us to do, my dear," said Alavro. "We must keep moving with our plans."

"Your world is in much need of protection, I know," said Cordella gravely. "I'll think of something that can help. Rest assured I'll find a way."

"And if it's not clear already, don't do that again," Alavro added, a serious frown on his small forehead, and Olivia was back again to being a child, reprimanded for trying something impetuous and adventurous. And potentially deadly, of course.

Soon they were back again in the field, training hard for the battles to come. The sun rose completely in the sky that day, the temperature as well. They didn't talk much during the trainings, but at every break they had, Alegra and Bran showered Olivia and Trevor with questions about their latest adventure.

"You should have called us," Alegra kept repeating.

Bran, on the other hand, seemed more bothered than interested, and stared at Olivia with curiosity, maybe making sure she was truly fine. The fact that she had come up with the spell by herself was a hit, and they all agreed with Alavro that she should not try that again. She wondered why … It made no sense that she shouldn't try something new, use more of her powers, understand and explore them more.

On their way to have lunch, the trees at the edge of the camp called Olivia again, a message that reached her heart softly, silently. She stayed behind and found her way inside that small piece of forest where the sunrays were filtered by the leaves.

"Do you hear its call?" asked Belenos, his voice mixing with the noises of nature.

Olivia nodded. "Can you hear it too?"

"Yes." He paused, looking around at the trees with a calm expression on his face. "How did you cast that protection?" he asked, looking ahead. There was nothing around, but Belenos could see all.

"It just came to me. I've woven a shield that traveled through these trees and reached the deep forests around us. I think the forest asked me to do so," said Olivia.

"Hum. Your powers are growing, Olivia. I'm here if you need to talk," said Belenos. He looked at her, staring deeply into her eyes.

Belenos looked straight ahead again, watching the birds play over the tree branches. His words echoed inside Olivia until they lost their meaning, and she wondered why he wouldn't just talk to her, share what he knew, for she didn't even know where to start.

They walked back to the camp, where everybody sat around the fire and food bowls were filled.

"Where were you two at?" asked Alavro. "Come, come. It's time to eat! I've made a pot of delicious onion soup with herbs I found right here. Do you know there is plenty of berberwood in these surroundings? Great herbs for seasoning, they are, and if you brew them … Oh, what a spectacular drink you have. Much superior to ale."

They ate and talked. Cordella had received many messages that day, and they were expecting company soon. People from Lirianthis would be the first to arrive, as Belenos suggested, so they could cover the place with even more spells and prepare with confidence for what was about to come.

There wasn't much talk about Olivia's energy travels. She figured that enough had been said about the matter, and maybe Cordella, Alavro, and even Belenos were still a bit annoyed with her, avoiding the subject before they could talk about it without emotion. It was usually like that with her parents: first the irritability, then some time to think, later on, the heart-to-heart talk, where they really made her understand her mistakes and the risks of what she had done.

Life with her parents was a faint memory, and every day they faded a bit more, it seemed. In one way, it was good, because it made it hurt less, but it was also painful, and she blamed herself for forgetting. Sometimes she wondered what they would think if they knew about Tartae and her quest. What they would say about this particular adventure.

Cordella went on and on about how the countdown to war had already started. A lot of allies would arrive soon, and they should be prepared to move on with their plans. She expected Lars to accept the call to war at once, since he had been preparing for violence for, maybe, his whole life. The new Guardians should be ready for that. Cordella missed Atlas and wished that the eagle would arrive sooner than later, for she was as smart as they came and very skilled in magic. An asset that they needed to have during battle.

Belenos alerted that the protections around them should be lessened, so the arriving troops could join them with no harm. He would do his part and asked Olivia for hers.

"What do you mean?" asked Cordella, looking from Belenos to Olivia.

Olivia sighed and squinted, preparing for a bad reception to her attempts with protective spells.

"I've woven some protection around the forest. I was asked to …" Olivia said at once.

"Oh, well. I'm afraid it's time for you to deepen your knowledge of witchcraft. Magic is calling you like crazy!" Cordella exclaimed.

Olivia was surprised. From all the things she'd imagined Cordella would say, that wasn't what she expected. She looked at Trevor, and he shrugged, smiling.

Cordella called Olivia to train her magic, and Belenos followed them. They headed to the river, so they could be near almost every element, which would make their training easier. They showed her strategies for battles, like channeling elemental energy for protection and attacking with gusts of air, all in a way that didn't hurt nature around them.

Unlike the last time she'd trained magic with Cordella in the middle of a forest, she didn't feel drained by it or at all tired. She was energized, ready for more and for running inside those woods, jumping into the river and meeting the spirits of the water, swimming with them to a place with even more magic.

***

Life went on in the camp, and they even found a rhythm and a routine for their activities there. They would train, eat, train, and sleep, so they could be ready to train some more the next day. Olivia spent a lot of time with Trevor, Bran, and Alegra, and even though Trevor and Alegra always escaped to have some time alone, they were always quite discreet and didn't bother the others with any displays of affection. Olivia talked a lot with Bran, and she got more used to his presence by her side. He never mentioned her memory again or had any expectations of her remembering anything from her past in Tartae. Now, they merely discussed sword training, phookas, and how Baltazar could have shapeshifted so successfully into a man. Deep down, Olivia feared their time had passed. Maybe he had even moved on to something else.

During those days at camp, Olivia kept on with her notes and drawings in her notebook. She would write down symbols, random words, sketches of anything that popped in her brain every day after her training was done, like some kind of homework. She hoped to find an answer and put an end to this idea that kept haunting her about something hidden in the Book of the Portals, and many times she wished she had brought it with her. There was something to discover right under her nose, but for some reason, she couldn't see it clearly. Until now, she had had no success, except discovering that she was a pretty fair designer.

On their third day of camping, the Lirianthis folk arrived in a caravan that was as splendid as the place they lived. Many white, brown, and black horses with the longest manes Olivia had ever seen paraded side by side, bearing no saddles and with their coats shining like satin.

There were about a thousand people, all walking slowly and dressed like magical warriors, in black, green, carmine, and brown. They had carriages made out of wood that kept their tents, food, and the weapons Lirianthis had many times designed to protect Tartae.

"A dangerous form of magic," Alavro said with a sigh as he headed to greet them.

Olivia quickly found Emma between all the people. The two of them hugged tightly and said no words, for so much had happened that it was hard to know where to start.

The camp filled with witches and wizards, and some of them joined Belenos in throwing around protection spells. As soon as they stepped into the camp, they were at it, leaving no time for chance. They made a huge circle around the camp, mouthing words quietly until a mist fell over them, but this time, it didn't dissipate.

"This will be our cocoon for a while," said Emma, staring seriously at the sky.

People were still settling when Cordella summoned many of them into their meeting tent, Olivia included. In there, they introduced Lidia Cernune e Lonel Carmac, who were responsible for the development of their weapons and for keeping the energy balance, and Melissa Luna and Iris Bulb, their fearless warriors.

Cordella discussed their plans from now on: they should expect many allies to arrive soon, be prepared to welcome them by weakening their magical defenses, and, as soon as they were all there, they should get ready for attack.

Up to this point, no one had heard anything about Lars and his plans, not even Mocer, who kept with his efforts as a spy. His only report was that things were getting worse, for Lars' influence was spreading fast, like a highly contagious disease, and more people were being lured into those ideas of regaining the power of the past, the old ways of the Portals—something that never existed. Cordella told the ones who'd recently arrived about Lars' presence in the other world and asked for their advice and ideas about what to do. They all discussed for many minutes, while Olivia only observed, and Emma, who sat next to her, bore a strange look on her face, showing that she wasn't expecting any of that.

When they started listing all the allies they had reached throughout Tartae, Olivia had the urge to speak.

"What about Freya?" Her voice broke through the murmurs of the room, and every face turned to her.

"What to say about Freya?" scoffed Lidia Cernune with disdain. Her voice was strong and low, and fitted her face perfectly, for the woman had strength in every inch of it. Her brown eyes were big, the color of the earth.

"You know how Freya is, Olivia," said Cordella. "She has chosen to preserve herself and her lineage once more. We won't be counting on her."

"Figures," sighed Trevor.

But something inside Olivia didn't settle. She remembered her dream and Freya's voice. Somehow, she knew there was something more.

"Can I try to talk with her?" Olivia asked.

"I'm not sure how this could help," started Melissa Bulb. She was tall and imposing, and she stood at once. "We have to get ready—"

Cordella waved her hand, interrupting Melissa. "Of course, you can try, Olivia. There's no harm in it." She smiled, looking deeply into Olivia's eyes.

Olivia smiled back, and Melissa seemed a bit annoyed, but she wasn't that bothered and quickly resumed her speech. In the end, when everybody disbanded around the camp and continued settling down, Cordella called Olivia and handed her a medallion messenger finely made, with the symbol for the Clan— a leafless pine tree with a flower floating on top—carved beautifully on it. Olivia stared at the thing for a while, passing her fingers over the drawing.

"I guess that doesn't stand for much these days ... Nowadays," lamented Cordella.

"Maybe there's something better on our way," said Olivia, dreamily.

"Use this to reach Freya; she will know it's coming from us and that she can trust it. Do whatever you think is right, Olivia. You're outgrowing my wits," added Cordella.

"Hardly ..." Olivia laughed. "I just ... I just feel there's something. Maybe I just can't believe she would be capable of doing so little."

Cordella scoffed and drew a deep breath from her lungs, finding a chair to sit.

"May I ask why you think there's hope?"

"I think she knows something we don't," said Olivia.

"About the war?" inquired Cordella.

"About everything. And I think she should be here. She is powerful, and Tartae needs her," replied Olivia, frustration dripping from every word she said.

"I hope you find out what you wish, but remember, you cannot force anyone into what you think is right." Cordella said it kindly and left the tent, patting Olivia gently on her back.

Olivia was left with her thoughts, and for a moment it was quite comfortable, even with her wonders being many and confused, all fighting for her attention at the same time. At least she was alone, which wasn't happening much these last days, and she was far from all the commotion outside—the noise coming from people, horses, carriages. It was all about to happen, and she wondered how close the end was.

A little before dusk, Olivia found her friends gathered by the fire, waiting for dinner that was now prepared by many from Lirianthis and Alavro. The food was seasoned with many magic herbs that made people stronger and more focused. Olivia had learned about all of them from Malva and Emma. Allandrio, which made people calmer and provided a nice night of sleep; berlion, to build strong muscles and stamina, which they would all need.

The energy was light, even though everyone knew what they were about to walk into, all the dangers they would encounter, and even the possibility that some of them might not survive. All those details seemed to be ignored in this fine night under the misty dome.

During their conversation over dinner, Emma told them about the terrible day when Diana left Lirianthis to accompany Lars and how Drusilla was heartbroken. She had now joined some other elders in Lirianthis, creating shields to protect the place and the Laliamo Forest. They didn't know much about Diana now, but they had heard that she was part of the closest allies of Lars due to all her powers.

"But that could be an exaggeration. I don't think anyone could know that. We know nothing about Lars," Emma said, an alarmed expression painting her face in somber colors.

Olivia told Emma everything she remembered after the battle they'd fought in the forest, how she blended with nature, being united with it as never before, her time with Malva—who Emma knew very well and loved learning from—and how she'd found a way to disconnect from nature. Olivia didn't share her findings in the Book of the Portals, for she understood that that information was too delicate, and if it were to be shared, it should be under different conditions and veiled in more secrecy than around a fire between thousands of people. She never touched the subject, but just remembering the Book made a shiver dance inside her, freezing her blood. There was something in there, a puzzle for her to solve. But the thought left her mind as quickly as it arrived, dusted away by more news about the state of Lirianthis, their travels, and the size of the fight they were waiting for.

When the night was as black as a beetle, the centaurs arrived. A space in the fog was opened for them, like a huge door, allowing them inside. They were many coming from the Laliamo Forest and Lotrium Mountains. Those centaurs lived deep in the woods and didn't have a lot of contact with humans, so they barely talked and deeply enjoyed caring for the horses.

Olivia invited Emma to share the tent with them, since there was plenty of space. They hoped to talk more, but before they noticed, they dozed off. When Olivia woke up the next day, the medallion messenger was the first thing she saw, and she figured it was time to talk with Freya.

It was hard to find an empty place in the camp now that everywhere was filled with Tartae folk. They didn't seem to pay much attention to Olivia, for they were all very much invested in their own activities, but Olivia wanted some privacy before reaching out to Freya, and, according to many, trying the impossible. She ended up finding a place close to the river, by some rocks where she chose to sit.

Olivia managed to send her a message, where she asked bluntly, "why don't you help?" After a while, Freya answered.

"It's not my time to get involved. I'm sure you will understand."

"What?" Olivia protested out loud, as though Freya were next to her and able to hear her complaints. How could she think Olivia would understand her unwillingness to help a land that was her own? This was outrageous. Olivia waited some more, thinking about what she would say next. Would she boldly call Freya out for her dismissive behavior, or would she try to convince her? But before Olivia decided, another message appeared on the medallion.

"You're right, Olivia. There's something else for you to discover."

Olivia stared at the medallion long after the message disappeared.

"How does she know?" Olivia whispered.

Many thoughts crossed Olivia's mind, most of them questioning Freya's behavior and if she had the ability to read Olivia's mind—which Olivia was pretty much convinced of by now.

"What do you know?" Olivia asked the medallion, her lips almost touching the thing.

"I know nothing else." The message gleamed and disappeared slowly. "This is yours, and for you to venture alone," it read again, long enough so Olivia could read it many times before it faded completely. After that, the object lost its force, and Olivia knew that she wouldn't read anymore from Freya. Not at that time.

The water in the river twinkled in the background, and the sounds coming from the camp got louder as Olivia dispersed her attention from the messages. She now looked around without actually seeing many things, only thinking, and thinking, creating space in her brain for what she had learned.

Did Freya really meet her in that dream, or was it nothing more than that. In it, she said something about what the forest needed ... Was it the protection that later that night became so clear to Olivia? She wished to see Freya in person and to be able to ask all the questions. But there was also no reason to be so dependent on Freya; she had always disappointed them, so Olivia just moved on.

"Any luck?" Trevor asked, as Olivia got closer to him, walking back to the camp.

Cordella was nearby, using her magic to help Trevor and the others train; she stopped and paid careful attention to Olivia's answer. Olivia only shook her head.

"What a surprise!" Trevor scoffed.

CHAPTER SEVENTEEN

THE CALL OF WAR

Olivia went back to her activities in the camp quickly. She helped two warriors, Juniper and Loane, load a carriage with many boulders—she used her magic to lift the rocks, making their work quite easier. Those boulders were to be thrown at the enemies during the battles and they would explode when touching the ground, releasing water seasoned with belgarium leaf, a special herb that had the power to temporarily paralyze everything it touched.

She intentionally kept herself busy to avoid thinking too much, but she was distracted during the whole day—and training—being the victim of multiple strikes from Bran, Alegra, and Trevor. They grew worried. Trevor was afraid that Olivia could be transforming into a tree again, which made his eyes very wide and attentive to any signs of greenery growing from her. Olivia assured them multiple times that it was just tiredness, probably a reminder that she needed to rest. There was no sign of flowers blooming from the flocks of her hair, no greenish tone in her arms.

More allies kept coming during the following days. Kirk was the first, and he was greeted with excitement by all. He looked somehow smaller and worn out. His time traveling around Tartae in search of allies was maybe too long and demanding, Olivia thought. Even that gleam he used to have for war had disappeared from his eyes, and he showed no interest in training with the others.

"I need to catch my breath!" he said, heading down to the meeting tent to see Cordella and Alavro and then leaving to his own tent.

The Willow Warriors and the Amazon Witches from the mountains came together through the mist long after Kirk. Their whole caravan passed calmly through the portal with the help of the three witches who guarded it. They also brought many carriages containing food and armory, and they dressed in tan tunics and pants, mimicking the earth under them. Alavro explained ceremoniously to Olivia and Trevor that they used this tincture to paint their clothes in order to praise the earth, for they considered it the most valuable thing around them. They were field people, and all their lives revolved around the crops and what nature gave them; it only made sense to worship it any way they could. For them, it was also a way to show respect for their ancestors and the animals, who blessed the earth before their time.

The beauty and profound meaning of those stories made Olivia wonder why the Old Ways were so lost in her world, to the point that it was even hard to imagine a day when this all fit there as naturally as it did in Tartae. Somewhere in the past, another kind of Slowness Spell might have fallen there, transforming all that was real into a forgotten myth, and that brought sadness to her heart.

After them, the Fern tribe, the fauns from the Summer Islands and sorcerers from Victro, Lotrium, and Slintor arrived in a group, and those were the last warriors Cordella expected. After they fully crossed their protections, Belenos manipulated more guarding spells, and the whole place trembled a little while he did it, settling down the energy after it flew around their heads in swirling clouds of blue and aqua.

All the chiefs of troops gathered inside the meeting tent, where Cordella laid out her plans for the attack so they could add their contributions and, later on, share everything with their troops. From now on, they all became one single troop, and Cordella was the head of it. Olivia and Trevor stood quietly at one corner of the meeting tent, not having a lot to add since they didn't bear a lot of knowledge about war and battles. It was agreed that they would use the plains as a ground for attack, and the forest nearby could come as shelter if they needed to flee. Their main goal was to capture Lars, for they firmly believed that his troops would be dismantled without him. Olivia wished they were right, and that his power would fade throughout the worlds. They were preparing for an attack with magic and brute force, and they would combine their strengths as much as they could.

Aside from Mocer, who was putting all he had into his double agent position, no other Guardians appeared offering aid. Cordella said that she didn't even try talking with many of them, for she knew they wouldn't be open to helping. They had left their position as clear as water during their latest meetings and now, more than ever before, it really seemed that the Guardians and all they stood for had been shattered to pieces. And they couldn't even blame the Slowness Spell for that lack of interest in the matters of defending Tartae and the Portals. The Guardians were so strongly connected to the earth and so aware of everything that they were all immune to that strangeness that had befallen Tartae; they just chose not to help.

Cordella also decided not to contact any members of the Council. The few of them who were awake had ambiguous positions on the matter of Lars and the menace he represented for all the worlds; they were also much into the politics of things and not very skilled warriors, so it wasn't that great of a loss.

Every group that had arrived shared that their troops were at least cut in half because of the Slowness Spell. Bran was glad that they were able to reach out to a great number of Tartae folk and that all of them agreed to help; otherwise, there wouldn't be any possibility of winning this battle. Lars had no respect and liked to prey on people's weaknesses, so he chose to take advantage of the cluelessness of those under the Slowness Spell to lure them into doing his deeds, which allowed him to recruit hundreds. He had no morals and only wanted power, nothing else.

The energy flowing around the camp weighed heavily, and the place was now like a pressure pot. Everybody was getting ready for war, and one could almost sense the blood boiling in the warriors' veins, hot and red, calling for their weapons. Anxiety and anticipation grew inside Olivia too. They were now only waiting for Cordella to send the call of war, and then they would be on their way in the biggest caravan Olivia had ever seen in her life, walking to meet Lars and his troops.

That night, one last ally crossed their protections: Atlas finally arrived, diving inside their nook and heading straight to the meeting tent. Cordella ran in there, and Olivia didn't wait for an invitation; she just grabbed Trevor's hand and followed.

Inside, Atlas was perched on the wooden table, her eyes shining with such a strong light that they seemed like the moons of Tartae. Unlike Cordella, Olivia couldn't speak the eagle's language, but by the gravity of her face, she knew that something bad had happened.

"Come on, you two. Maybe it's better—" started Alavro, as soon as he stepped into the tent and laid eyes on Olivia and Trevor.

"No, Alavro. Let them stay," interrupted Cordella, her voice falling to a whisper and her eyes never moving away from Atlas.

Alavro didn't say a word in response, only stopped by Olivia's side and waited for Cordella's translation.

"Good," she finally said. "Do you know how many people?"

Atlas looked at Cordella deeply, and sometimes she hooted a medley with long and short sounds.

"Thank you, my friend," said Cordella. She turned to the others with a calm expression. "Atlas managed to see Lars' army in his hiding spot around the Green Caves. There were many of them, thousands. But she doesn't believe his numbers are much bigger than ours. We are prepared now."

"The Green Caves?" asked Trevor. "Is that far?"

"Yes, it is. I believe we shouldn't delay this any longer. It's time for our call of war, and then we wait," answered Cordella.

"We must prepare for anything," whispered Olivia, her voice sounding unexpected even to herself. Her insides went as cold as a frozen lake, breaking in painful cracks.

"Yes, you're right," continued Cordella. "He's inside the elders of the Council, Atlas said. Many of them are already believing there is nothing bad in his intentions and they ignore crimes he had committed in the name of his own power. Our strength in there grows thin, because he killed many of those who disagreed with his ways."

"Who else was killed?" Alavro was alarmed.

"Cerceluna and two of the Council elders," said Cordella, her eyes filling with tears. "Atlas removed Mocer, and he is now in hiding. The man was about to reach his breaking point and burst into fear. It was only fair to let him rest, for he did his part. Hopefully, he won't have much to worry about soon enough."

"Oh no …" lamented Alavro, bringing his hand to his mouth. "Cerceluna … I can't believe it."

Olivia and Trevor looked at each other. Lars was advancing with his plans, destroying the Guardians one by one. Fear grew inside them, not only from all Cordella was sharing, but also from what their near future promised: one more battle, but at least they hoped this would be the last.

"How do you know Lars is going to come?" asked Olivia.

"Because power is what leads him, and destroying me would make him closer to all he desires. I've been always in his way. I've even brought people from other worlds to mess with his plans. Trust me, he will come," answered Cordella, curving her lips lightly in almost a smile.

"When is it going to be?" asked Alavro.

"Tonight, I send the call. There's no reason to wait," said Cordella firmly. "We must get ready and let the others know."

Alavro nodded and left the tent, and Olivia could tell even from afar the exact moment when he shared the news, for it all went silent for a minute until the voices rose again. Cordella didn't pay any mind to Olivia and Trevor and walked away deep into her almost silent conversation with Atlas, and only they remained under the inconstant light of many candles.

"I'm not even sure what to say now," said Trevor, his eyebrows raised in a very high arch.

"You're not the only one, my friend ..." Olivia said with a laugh.

"We've spent our days here training and talking about this, but I kind of hoped this moment would never come. I just wanted to read poets and novels and teach about them, you know? Being a warrior wasn't exactly in my plans," said Trevor airily.

"Not even when you were a small child?" asked Olivia.

"Nope. I wanted to fight only ignorance, and with words, not weapons," he answered.

"I guess we never know where life will take us ...," said Olivia.

"Oh no, we *definitely* never know that. Nope, not a clue!" Trevor laughed and shook his head.

Olivia laughed too, and they headed outside, where they met a very different picture than what they expected: People were gathered around the fire, pouring ale while they laughed heartily. A group of women approached the group with many instruments and started playing a beautiful and upbeat song that many followed out of tune.

Olivia and Trevor gazed at each other doubtfully and laughed, heading straight to where Bran, Alegra, and Emma waited for them.

"Here, drink some cider!" Emma handed Olivia a ceramic cup while she and Trevor found a place among them.

"What's happening here?" Trevor questioned, scooching beside Alegra and grabbing himself a cup of cider too.

"It's an old custom before battles for some of our people in Tartae," said Emma.

"We might see our last day soon, so we have to celebrate while we can," added Alegra.

"I'll drink to that!" said Trevor, and everyone followed his lead.

"Did you hear exactly when we'll leave?" asked Bran, speaking close to Olivia's ear so she could hear him among the loud songs and laughs.

"No, we still don't know when Lars will be arriving. He's at the Green Caves right now; I think it's far from here, isn't it?" Olivia answered. Being so close to Bran was sometimes distracting, and she had almost forgotten what color his eyes were. They sang the songs of the seas, and she was calmed by them—so blue and deep under the black of the night.

"Yes, it is," he continued. "My dad didn't say much about what was decided, only that the call was made."

"I understand. I don't see him around … It's not like him to miss a celebration," said Olivia, scanning the place and setting eyes on Belenos and Orion, but noticing that Cordella was still probably with Atlas and Alavro was nowhere to be found.

"He gave me a kiss goodnight and went to his tent," said Bran.

Olivia looked at Bran and smiled. She knew not everyone could ignore what was about to come to them and party without a care in the world. She herself felt divided in two, a half that needed to forget and another that feared their next moments and just wished to worry, nothing else.

The group moved into light conversation completely, enjoying the warm fire burning close to them and the amazing cider that the folk of the Fern tribe brewed. In joyful nights like this, the slowness of Tartae was a blessing, as it allowed them plenty of time to relax. Olivia finally let her mind rest fully, ignoring all that haunted her.

When they were already deep in the dark night, many women and men stood up and headed to the woods, crossing the thick mist that protected them.

"Come, Olie!" called Emma, standing up with a broad smile and grabbing Olivia's hands.

"Isn't it dangerous?" asked Trevor, quickly cutting short his conversation with Alegra and Bran.

"No, it isn't!" answered Emma casually.

Olivia followed, and between the trees of the forest, witches and wizards danced uncoordinatedly inside the veils of the night.

"You don't need to do anything special," whispered Emma. "Just let nature bless you and recharge you. Just dance around!"

Emma blended in the sea of other sorcerers, her body flowing between trees while she twirled around. Olivia took a moment, looking at them. Belenos, Cordella, and Atlas were there, mixed with the others and much into their own inner worlds, deep in that dancing meditation. After a while, Olivia let herself go, taking off her shoes and feeling the earth underneath her feet, the air all around her, and she just danced with the trees and the night.

CHAPTER EIGHTEEN

THE BATTLE OF THE PORTAL

Olivia woke with the others while light was still very faint outside. She sat for a moment in her bed while everyone else left the tent one by one and tried to recollect her dream, which was very vivid for a second and then started to slip away from her grasp. She fetched her notebook and drew the first thing that popped into her mind: a key with the face of a bearded man on the bow, waves in the ocean around it, and ships. She stared at it, waiting for the drawings to hypnotize her somehow, and she dove deeper and deeper into it, trying to find that ocean, the reason. But there was nothing more than that, only the certainty that she was being called to something. She closed her notebook and followed the others outside. Breakfast was served and she ate mushrooms with herbs, the kind of hearty and heavy meal she was now used to having this time of the day.

Everything moved smoothly that day. The weather was fresh and the training almost nonexistent since everybody was making the last arrangements before leaving for battle; Lars could answer their call at any time. Olivia, Emma, and Alegra found a space to train alone for some hours, for Alegra wanted the challenges of magic to strengthen her fighting abilities, and Olivia and Emma were happy to provide. They threw Alegra many small rocks and made her leave the ground, surfing a swirl of wind, but she always managed to find a way to save herself, whether striking every rock that came in her direction with her sword or jumping onto a tree branch and counterattacking. Olivia and Emma were able to manipulate the elements, but Alegra worked with them, taking their every lead and following that flow; her movements were precise, and she never fought the odds.

When Olivia wove the water from the river close by, planning to throw it at Alegra and playing with it like she used to do while she was at Malva's house—deep into the forest and into her connection to the earth—something moved inside her, cold and slithery, and the fear rising up her body made the water fall and splash all over them.

"Come on, Olie!" protested Emma.

"Quiet! Something is happening," Olivia warned. And they all fell silent expectantly. Not long after that, the dome they were in trembled.

They ran into the middle of the campsite, and Atlas was flying around in circles. Cordella shot them some fearful glance and yelled for all to hear: "GET READY! IT'S TIME!"

From that moment on, it was a mix of sounds and blurred images that Olivia could barely make sense of. She raced to Cordella, who was halfway to her tent, walking fast by Belenos' side.

"What was that?" Olivia asked, hurried.

"Did you feel it too?" Cordella questioned, not waiting for an answer and continuing quickly. "Lars is already here. What you felt was the Portal he opened for himself and his troops."

Olivia gasped.

"Go get ready, Olivia. The time has come," said Belenos.

At that moment, the camp didn't seem anything other than crowded. There were people coming from every direction, carts, carriages, many horses approaching from every side and assuming their positions. She had a hard time even finding her own tent, and even though all the sounds from outside were in there too, at least there weren't that many distractions to her sight, and she found a moment to concentrate, breathing in and out slowly.

She changed her sneakers to a pair of boots that would protect her feet more and never untie themselves during the battle, and she put on her sword belt. She had everything she needed.

"Olie!" said Trevor, as he entered the tent with a grave look upon his face.

"I'm here," said Olivia. "Are you ready?"

"As ready as I'll ever be!" answered Trevor, holding on to Olivia's hand and squeezing it. They were there for each other. "Olie, before we go, I need to know if there's anything you'd like to tell me."

"What do you mean?" Olivia asked, not quite understanding where Trevor was going.

"Anything that has been happening with you that I ... We all should know? Like flowers growing from you, voices you've been hearing, anything that could make us lose you in there ..." Trevor said, his eyes glowing with worry and love, and Olivia understood the depth of his concerns.

Olivia was torn. She never had to lie to Trevor before, but there wasn't anything clear to tell him yet; if she were to tell him about Ourivio's secret puzzle right now, it might just confuse him to no end.

"No," Olivia answered at once. "There's nothing to tell."

Trevor gave her a smile in return and sighed in relief, making guilt cut Olivia's insides like a pointy knife. She appeased herself, repeating internally that there wasn't actually much to tell, only pieces of a meaningless puzzle as of yet, and when the time came, Trevor would be the one to know, as he was her other half of this adventure.

The two friends walked outside and crossed the camp, passing by a huge number of people while they looked for Cordella, who was head of the company and who they would follow closely behind.

The protection around them fell slowly after Belenos raised his arms high and thanked the elements. It was the first moment of quiet after Cordella's call. Everybody stopped what they were doing to watch, mesmerized, while he untangled his many spells and they became a faint white smoke flowing high into the sky. Belenos' beauty was always quite impressive, but when he manipulated the elements, it became something otherworldly, even for Tartae's standards. Olivia imagined that this was how the gods from mythology should look: grand, gleaming, maybe far from human.

He found his spot right next to Cordella, Alavro, Orion, and all the other more skillful warriors who came from every corner of Tartae. Olivia, Trevor, Bran, Alegra, Kirk, and Emma were just behind them, and everyone started marching slowly, heading to the plain where they would meet Lars and his troops.

The walk to the battle seemed unreal. Every sound the caravan made resounded around them like a haunting echo, repeating itself until its message of doom became so clear that no one could deny it. They traveled slowly and, in some ways, being caught by surprise seemed better, faster. One would be deep into danger before even being aware of it, like removing a bandage at once. Olivia had so many feelings fizzing inside her that it was hard to know if she was scared. Everything was mixed into one ball of sentiments with no beginning and no end.

"Olivia, Trevor, beware. You're still Lars' target, don't make it an easy one," warned Belenos in a grave, deep tone while he slowed down a bit, pairing with them.

Olivia and Trevor nodded and looked at each other when Belenos moved back to his place in front of them.

"As if we could forget that," said Trevor.

The group moved on at that same speed for many minutes that felt like slow hours, and before they could see anything, a putrid smell took over their noses, announcing that they were now close. Everyone around Olivia set their posture straight, expecting what was undeniably there, waiting behind some magic trick.

Cordella stopped, and all the others followed her, halting at once and needing no orders. In front of them, an open field with only grass stretched until the trees rose in the distance. The dire smell lingered, betraying Lars and his company.

"LARS!" Cordella roared. Her voice sounded like magic itself, ancient like many of those woods they always walked through, like many of those trees with trunks as large as giants.

Cordella didn't say anything else. She just waited. Those moments stretched on, forever paralyzed in that place until, finally, something broke it. The roar of war made the spell Lars had cast disappear in front of them, revealing growling trolls, phookas, centaurs, many women and men on and off horses, witches and wizards who decided to turn, and Lars, seated powerfully over his huge horse, bearing a serious expression on his pale face.

There were no words after that, only Cordella's order for them to attack and soon; the fields were taken by dirt and the two opposing troops mixed into one intertwined mess. Alavro and Orion advanced strongly, wielding their weapons with no fear or mercy. Belenos and Cordella manipulated many spells to give their warriors time to gain ground. But Lars remained in the same place, observing it all from a distance. His disturbing face caught Olivia's attention, while it followed her around like a strange painting on a wall. He appeared to be annoyed and purposeful, a combination that made his face twitch in many movements making him even scarier: sometimes it was pure disgust, and other times, it was almost like a smile. Olivia wondered about the thoughts going through his mind now. Maybe he thought that she was dead and long gone inside that forest, or maybe it was just hatred against the ones he never seemed to get rid of rising inside of him like a forest fire, growing without control and ruining all it touched.

Fear rose in Olivia as she figured Lars was about to come for her and Trevor. Quickly, she looked for her friend on the battlefield and went to him in a sprint, opening her way with fireballs that she threw at every side.

"Trevor!" she yelled, squinting and defending herself from many arrows that were thrown at them. "He's coming for us!"

Trevor's gaze quickly scanned for Lars and found him advancing in their direction.

"OLIE, DO SOMETHING!" Trevor yelled. He was throwing many arrows around, striking phookas and Lars' soldiers.

Olivia didn't think much, she only stretched her arms and managed to dismount Lars from his horse with a strong gust of wind aimed at him. He fell onto the ground, standing with one quick movement, and his horse marched on in Olivia's and Trevor's direction. It was the first time Olivia had been able to attack Lars successfully, and she stared at her hands for a moment, finding what had just happened too hard to believe.

In a matter of a seconds, Trevor disappeared from her side and was already fighting some warriors dressed in scarlet colors with the help of Emma, Kirk, and Firlo. Olivia searched for Lars again and found him battling Belenos with many spells being cast from both sides; colors flew around them, making the show almost beautiful. As for herself, she wielded her sword and attacked the centaurs who had turned and now advanced over a group of wizards from Lirianthis. The centaurs were as fierce and graceful as the ones she knew, and there was this pain in their eyes, as though something corroded their souls. Olivia had to consciously avoid the connection with them, for she was about to dive into their profound eyes. She weaved a red flaming tendril that danced around her in circles, blazing fire and scintillating. It burned the centaurs, scaring them away far enough so the wizards from Lirianthis had space to defend themselves.

Once again, the battle was so heavy that only finding a place of tranquility inside her head made it possible, a trick Bran had taught her so many moons ago and was still the most relevant thing she had learned about war. She looked for him inside that sea of chaos and caught him striking a huge troll, moving quickly to his next target. Cordella was just behind him, braiding the elements so skillfully that everything around her seemed at her will.

Many phookas came into Olivia's direction, and one of them managed to bite her arm. The wound burned at once, weakening her strikes. She pushed the creature away with a ball of fire right into its face, and as it jumped out of her, others came, closing in on her, blood dripping from their fangs.

"Are you sure you wanna do this?" she said. They kept moving forward. "All right … But don't forget I gave you a choice!"

She weaved the roots hidden in the earth underneath her out of the ground. They sprouted through the surface, cracking and stretching upward before enveloping the phookas. The thin brown tentacles held the creatures tightly and close to the ground. At that moment, the belgarium boulders rained down, casting a shadow over the battlefield before meeting the troops. It paralyzed many of Lars' allies, which created the perfect opportunity for Olivia and the others to advance. Spells were thrown, along with arrows and many sword hits. Cordella's troops gained ground.

Sweat ran down Olivia's face, and her arms moved out of complete instinct, throwing hits with her sword, punches, and magic. Everything around her was tiring: the yells that she couldn't discern, the phookas' terrible smell, and the fear of losing her loved ones during that battle. She wished it all to end fast. When she focused her attention again, she noticed she had set a cloud of dust all over and around their enemies. This simple movement made Lars lose it. He rose from the smoke around him and, with a wave of his arm, freed all his allies. On his face, anger grew like a poison, and he burst into a guttural sound as deep as the night sky that made everyone stop. He then grew a blue translucent sphere between his hands, throwing it forward with no aim. The thing dissolved into multiple rays of electricity that found every single one of his opponents.

"WATCH OUT!" Cordella yelled, managing to block some streaks of lightning in a movement that protected herself and some of the others around to her.

Belenos and other magical folk did the same, but some of their allies fell once hit by the electricity. Belenos advanced in Lars' direction, but Olivia didn't follow what happened next, for many arrows found her on the battlefield. She avoided them all with her magic, but they cut very close. When she was able to take a breath and look for Belenos again, he was nowhere to be found, and it was now Cordella who battled Lars. Alavro and Bran were just next to them, fighting a gigantic troll that required the strength of two people to contain its menace. Olivia moved closer to them, and from the corner of her eye, she caught a glance of Emma casting one more spell that found many of Lars' allies and made them all collapse on the ground as if they had fallen asleep. Upon seeing that, Lars made one movement with his hand and shot something at Emma, making her fly back and fall.

"NO!" Olivia screamed. All around her trembled like an earthquake, and even Lars stopped and looked at her.

Cordella found Olivia's eyes, and they exchanged silent words; Olivia knew they had to finish this quickly while they still had a chance, and Olivia should use all she had. Lars followed their eyes and read their silence, and as he perceived his oncoming loss, he moved away from Cordella fast and began something that, at first, Olivia didn't recognize, but already feared. He closed his eyes and murmured something in an extremely low tone, and in the middle of the battlefield, a Portal started to open in the ground. At first small and contained, silver and sparkling, like fireworks. Olivia, Cordella, and Trevor stood back, witnessing the thing getting bigger and bigger.

"He's gonna send our troops through it! Run!" Trevor screamed, leading everyone he could in the direction of the woods.

Everyone started to run, even those on Lars' side. They ran and laughed loudly. The phookas skipped like children, playing as they had won.

Olivia didn't run. Something stirred inside her, and she moved forward, raising her arms high at first, and then lowering them as if to reach the Portal. She focused all her power into closing it, without using any spells or anything she had learned about them; what she was doing came from her heart and from the confidence that it would work. A sense of power she'd never experienced before. Everything around Olivia fell into oblivion, and after a while, her hands were connected to the Portal like white tendrils that extended from her fingers. She put all her strength into it while nature around her vibrated into one single energy thing, all connected. At first, the Portal grew even more, becoming wilder and green, and then it shrank fast into a spark that twinkled like a star in front of them. When it disappeared, Lars was just a couple feet across from Olivia, hate painting his face in threatening colors like never before.

Olivia didn't allow herself to fear him or to be slow; she had to take advantage of the connection she had just created. Light and power pulsated inside her and, at that moment, there were no limits for where she could go or what she could do. She gathered all that force that grew from her heart, incorporated the elements around her, and boiled them inside until she exploded in energy, making Lars fly many feet away from her.

Olivia smiled. Joy filled her heart when she realized that they had won; all they needed now was to capture Lars and move from that place. They were free to care for the Portals and be done. That sentiment lasted a flash. When Olivia finally looked around her, everyone had fallen just like Lars. There was no one standing, just bodies lying on the ground.

CHAPTER NINETEEN

MESSAGES IN THE RIVER

Slowly, some people sat up, and Olivia was able to exhale, relieved. She still stood at the same spot, unable to move, completely paralyzed by fear and the realization that she had caused it all.

Alavro was the first to stand up, and he quickly made others follow him, away from the battlefield. Some people needed help to walk, others to be carried, like Emma, who remained unconscious but still alive.

"Come, Olivia," said Kirk, resting his hand on Olivia's shoulder and guiding her out of there.

How Olivia got to the camp was a mystery to her. She was so taken by guilt and shame that everything that happened after they left the battlefield was a blur. She didn't see who they had left behind or what became of Lars; she only followed others' steps to their haven that was again under the misty protection.

Olivia went directly to the river to wash away those last hours from her body. She jumped in with the clothes she had on and, once inside the water, all calmed down. In the deep green of the river, submerged in the silence that only deep waters could provide, she wasn't so scared anymore. The voice in her head repeating "*what have I done?*" was muted, and she could just be flawed and strong like she was. The water around her understood, for they were much the same.

Olivia let her body sink down, observing the depths of the river while she traveled to the bottom. Something stirred in the water, making bubbles appear and dance around. Olivia followed it, swimming deeper. She stopped, and something moved again, so fast that she couldn't identify what it was. She kept following it, tracking bubbles until she reached the bottom of the river, where, from the sand, an image started to form: a man with a long beard walking into a dark and small cave, something that resembled the ocean and waves crashing on many rocks, and when one more image came to life, something pulled Olivia up.

"WHAT ARE YOU DOING!" screamed Trevor.

Olivia emerged and looked for Trevor's face.

"What the hell!" he continued. "This water is freezing; you could lose consciousness! What were you thinking?" he said heatedly and left.

Olivia stepped out of the river and followed him, unable to say a word and finding it all very strange, because, for her, the water was nice and cool enough only to refresh her thoughts.

"Come on," said Trevor, annoyed. "Cordella wants to talk to us."

They headed to the meeting tent, where Cordella, Alavro, and Bran waited for them. Olivia was afraid, unsure of what kind of reception she would find there, and deep down, she wished to flee, maybe to a place where nobody knew her and she could just forget what had gone down and the repercussions of it.

"What happened?" asked Bran as soon as he noticed Olivia and Trevor's clothes were dripping.

"Nothing. I jumped in the river, that's all," Olivia answered bluntly. "I'm sorry," she said, passing her gaze through everybody and finding that she was so sad that there weren't even tears to express it. It was just pain, crushing her heart into a million pieces.

"We're sorry too, Olivia," said Cordella with a sigh.

"What about Lars?" Olivia asked, hopeful. At least that could have been a success.

"He escaped once again," Cordella added.

"Did somebody d—"

"Not from your burst, no," Cordella interrupted. "But we lost some people to this battle, I'm afraid to say."

Olivia's heart dropped. Everyone's face passed through her thoughts.

"Emma was badly hurt, Belenos too," said Bran in a worried tone, running his hands against each other, much like his father used to do.

"Was there something good out of it?" Trevor said, his voice very low.

No one said anything in return. Silence covered them like a heavy mist for long minutes, and all inside Olivia went cold like the hours that precede the snow.

"We called you because we wanted to make sure you're all well, and because soon enough we'll need to get back on our feet. Are you two well?" inquired Cordella.

A million things popped into Olivia's mind: everything she needed to understand about her powers, everyone who was hurt, what was revealed to her in the river. But from her mouth, only one word came out. "Yes," she said, nodding. Trevor followed her cue.

"Good," Cordella stated. "I'll help the healers with the injured, but I don't want either of you to follow me. You need to rest and put your mind in order—"

"I know I need mine," said Alavro. His voice was fatherly as ever, but also strained, tired. "Go to your tent, sleep, and let the others be cared for. Soon enough we'll have much to discuss."

Cordella met Olivia's eyes and nodded slightly. Her face was dirty, full of tiny cuts all over her cheeks and around her eyes; her hair was messy, for her bun was almost deconstructed completely and patches of mud covered parts of it. It was as though some of the fight was still stamped over Cordella, telling the story of what they had been through.

The energy after the battle was burdensome, especially under these conditions. There were no winners, and their future became gloomier as this day came to an end. Olivia had no clue where this war would take them, and if this battle wasn't the one in the stars, what else waited for them?

Lars' wild fury was fueled, but he wasn't stopped. He was still a menace, walking around freely, recruiting more allies, spreading his beliefs, and messing with the Portals' energy. Disrespecting Tartae and nature at every minute of the day. He was at large, meaning that they still had the same problems as before, only now they had souls to mourn and an enemy preparing for even harder battles.

Trevor left the tent, saying that he needed to find Alegra. He still looked quite mad, but Olivia was happy to hear that Alegra was alive and paid attention to nothing else after that. It was a balm to learn that she was well, helping the wounded to walk to the healers. Kirk and Orion were also unharmed, bearing minor cuts that would heal in no time, Bran was glad to report. Firlo didn't share the same luck, and no one had seen him since the battlefield.

"Some have passed, but others are lost in the woods like Firlo. There'll be a search party leaving the camp soon," Bran said, hope gleaming in his eyes.

Olivia's heart shrank a bit more at the news.

Bran told Olivia about Belenos, who was injured by Lars but was already recovering in his own tent; he was strong and able to defend himself to the best of his abilities.

"I'm glad you're okay," Olivia said to Bran. Her eyes found his, and the joy of not having to worry about him took over her body.

"And how are you feeling?" asked Bran, gazing attentively at Olivia.

"I don't know," she replied. "What have I done, Bran?"

"You closed a Portal that would have hurt a lot of people and saved many by doing so. You used your powers the best way you could. You just have to learn more about them; don't blame yourself," he said.

"I hurt people." Olivia's voice disappeared into a whisper while she looked away from him. It was hard to face Bran and state that at the same time.

"We all did. It was a battle, Olie." He smiled kindly. "Come, you need to rest," he said, passing his warm arm around Olivia's shoulders, leaning into her and kissing the top of her head.

Olivia was now warmer inside; the freezing sensation of her fear and guilt had left her, at least for now. They walked together to the tent, and Olivia drew in a deep breath, a mix of relief, sadness, and fatigue.

"I'm going to get you some tea. I'll be right back." Bran shot her a smile and left, closing the tent's curtains behind him.

Olivia slowly changed into different clothes and combed her wet hair, which was all tangled. She crawled into her small bed, and before she knew it, she drowned in deep sleep.

At first, all around her was dark, as though she had her eyes closed and no thoughts in her head, deep in meditation, rooted firmly in the ground. For a moment, she hoped to be taken into that other level of Tartae again, where she could see the moons and the enchanted animals. But the darkness stretched on, soothing, taking her somewhere else. She eventually arrived at the river while the whole camp slept under the heavy protections Cordella manipulated. In her dream, Olivia could recognize Cordella's magic: It was deep, serious, and full of love, just like her. It smelled like jasmine blooming on a spring night. Olivia dove into the river. Its waters were now as cold as ice, and it didn't take long for the images from earlier appear in front of her once more. The sand rose into waves, a bearded man ran into a cave, many ships traveled side by side, and a whisper echoed in her ear.

"You *have* to go," it said.

Olivia looked at her side and behind her, searching for the source of the voice and finding no one. Her hair stood up at the sound of it, and she kept looking around, expecting something to appear.

The images now surrounded her in movements that exploded into sand, blurring her view. Olivia looked up, through the glasslike surface of the water, and the light of the two moons illuminated her from the sky. She swam upward, eager to catch them for the first time in a long while.

"You *have* to go," the whisper repeated. The voice *touching* all of her body.

***

Olivia sat up in her bed, gasping. Her eyes were so wide that they seemed about to burst. The night was old outside her tent, and her friends slept soundly in the beds next to her, unaware of the strange dreams she'd had. How long had it been since she passed out? She asked herself, scratching her head. The tent shook with the gust of wind that howled outside. Inside her, she knew that the elements had awakened completely.

She reached for her notebook, but before opening it, she realized there was no need to write anything down, and somehow doing it might ruin everything, spoiling what she had conquered and discovered in her last travel into dreamland. She cast her notebook to her side, and excerpts from the Book of the Portals came to her: *"The key is more than a key,"* she read once at the margin of one page, dismissively written down by Ourivio, maybe a mere note that he never thought someone else would read.

She wished to read the Book one more time so badly, and pieces of it kept coming to her.

"Portals are much like truffles.
One cannot grow them, they grow free."

That one made her laugh, and the note Ourivio hid using the language of trees made Olivia question his motives once more.

"*One cannot bind them. At least to this very day. I'll be the one,"* it read. And he managed to create spells to that end, keys that controlled the passages from world to world for many, many years.

"From rupture, peace is born."

That came from the Destruction Spell, and he couldn't be more wrong. There was no peace after the destruction of The Portals of Tartae. Tartae had never asked for a limit to its magic, and it protested when one was imposed on it. Maybe Ourivio didn't know better. His many pieces of research might have led him the wrong way; he wished to solve a problem by controlling everything, and that wasn't the path to take with the power of nature.

Olivia longed for days in the library, maybe Belenos' library, but deep down she knew that there wouldn't be much for her there. Maybe distractions, meaningful symbols, spells that inspired Ourivio back in his time, more about his history with the Portals, his history as a sorcerer. She wished to know how the Portals were handled before Ourivio's time; where did all the problems come from? No one had ever mentioned that. All the stories began at the rising issues coming from people's greedy intentions around the Portals of Tartae, how they were lost in the pursuit of power until Ourivio came and put an end to the mayhem. Olivia wondered who would know about what came before.

The cold breeze that howled outside finally found its way inside her tent, and shivers ran up and down her body. After so many thoughts, there was no way she could go back to sleep. Her bed was spitting her out to the world, and she obeyed, grabbing a green sweater from a chair.

The early morning wind smelled like winter, especially under the still-dark sky, giving the moment a mystery-like quality. Olivia walked to where the healers helped the wounded, and all was quiet at this time of night, but one healer was awake, dressed in black and manipulating small fires, like lamps, next to every bed. As the flames appeared, the place got warmer and more comfortable.

"Can I help with something?" Olivia asked. Her voice was low as the sigh of the wind outside.

"There's not much to do now. They're all resting and under heavy medication," said the tall man. His hair was curly and long. His beard framed his charming face.

"I'm Olivia Halin," she said, stretching her hand in his direction.

"I'm Night Adanesel. But you can call me Ade." He smiled gently, finding a place to sit. "But I know who you are, of course," he continued.

Olivia's stomach turned, visions from her burst coming into her mind.

"I'm sorry if I hurt you," she lamented, blushing.

"Oh, it's okay. I'm okay … But I hear you need to learn to control your powers," he said bluntly. He masked nothing between his words, saying it like a child.

"That would be good, for sure," Olivia scoffed. "Do you have any idea how to do it?"

"Ha!" he laughed. "I can teach you how to calm a wound or an illness; do you think it might help?"

"Oh, I'm open to trying!" Olivia answered. She had never attempted healing spells, and some witches had no powers with sicknesses or cures. She told Ade that she was able to help plants many times, bringing them back to health, and he replied that that was a good sign, for it was all life and connected to the same energy.

They both stood, and his fingers danced, one hand over the other, spinning the air like a fiber into many ice-blue sparks. They grew in quantity, concentrating between his delicate hands.

"See, now you send it to them. The relief is immediate," he said. He set the sparks free to flow all over the place, and they spun over half the beds. "Now it's your turn."

Olivia repeated his movements in detail, not looking away from her hands. The blue sparks were born from her energy; they came from her, from what she could not see.

"Now let them fly," Ade said, giving her arm a little nod when the cluster of sparks was concentrated enough.

Olivia's legs shook with excitement; venturing new magic was always like opening doors to the beauty of the unknown, and every time she did it, she was more complete. She shot him a smile, and he only replied: "Good job!" as if she were a kid completing a task.

They talked until the sun rose, which happened without any delay, but its light was filtered by the mist and by the great number of spells covering the camp.

"Don't they need the sun?" Olivia asked, observing the patients who slept soundly under the calming enchantments she and Ade had cast. Olivia had read and learned from Malva about the many healing properties of the sun, how all the humans and animals were much like plants and needed those rays to find life and nourishment.

"Yes, but I don't know how to do it. We also need all the protection we can get, and I don't see how we can have both." Ade's thick eyebrows made a stern arch; he was more serious now and stared at the patients with growing concern in his face.

"I hope we can find a way," Olivia murmured. She had the urge to try something, but fear made her step back, uncertain, afraid of what was dormant inside her.

Cordella stepped into the tent, bringing inside a scent of night-blooming jasmine that made Olivia recollect her dream and tremble at the memory of the magic. She seemed calmer and rested, wearing a light green gown, and a thick braid adorned her hair. She bid good morning to both Olivia and Ade, asking the latter about the patients. He explained that they were all recovering, as he would expect only a day after the battle, and that not even their hearts were far from the battlefield yet.

"I have called Olea and Malva. We'll have more help—and good help—soon," Cordella said.

She didn't say much after that and set on a round throughout the whole place, manipulating some enchantments over every bed. They fell over the patients, all green, and each one of them gained more color after it. Ade explained it was a kind of elemental magic that brought nourishment to sick people, drawing power from plants.

Olivia left when Cordella asked her to deliver some potions to Belenos and others who were hurt but well enough to remain in their own tents. She picked up the small bottles filled with a crystal-clear liquid and put them all inside a linen bag. As she traveled around the campground, entering many tents and walking into several conversations, she understood that the search parties had already left for the woods. They were expecting news at any time now, full of hope and praying to the moons and the sun.

Unlike Olivia expected, no one was afraid of her or mad. She was welcomed by everyone and they all seemed to be giving little to no thought to what had happened. She was relieved once more.

Belenos' tent was one of the last she visited. He was sitting on his bed when Olivia entered, wearing no shirt, his right arm in a sling and a brown throw around his shoulders like a shawl, protecting him from the cold that the night breeze brought to this day.

"Hello, Olivia," he said with a hoarse voice.

"Hi. I came bearing gifts." She smiled, handing him the tiny bottle.

"Thank you. Why don't you sit down for a bit and keep me company? I tried to read, but my head still spins," he said.

Olivia sat on a chair next to his bed, putting down the bag she was carrying. Having visited many tents, she noticed that Belenos' had more weed and wildflowers growing on the ground, like a natural carpet.

"How are you feeling?" Olivia asked, finally focusing her attention on him. Belenos' face had color all over it, and he looked almost the same to the untrained eye, but there was something less wild about him. Something was resting.

"I feel pain, and I'm tired," he answered honestly. "I would recover better in my home, but there's no way of doing that now."

Olivia had no response. She shot him a half awkward smile and wished deep down that she could help with more than some drops of "feel better" potion.

"What about you?" he continued.

"Have you heard?" Olivia asked, and he nodded. "I'm afraid, confused, guilty … mad. I feel that I'm stuck."

Belenos studied her carefully, paying attention to every word she said.

"You're afraid of yourself," he affirmed.

"Yes. Afraid of what I cannot control and, at the same time, feeling like it's disrespectful to control it."

"Unnatural …" Belenos added. "Can I tell you what I think?" he asked, seeming more normal than ever.

"Please," Olivia said, chuckling.

"I believe you're much like Tartae and the Portals: your powers shouldn't be tamed. You've witnessed all the mess we caused when we destroyed the Portals; Tartae rebelled, and she even brought them back because it's something larger than us, something that escapes our control. Your powers are being put to sleep inside you, and that's not what they desire … They are rebelling, and they will grow wilder, much like Tartae, I'm afraid," said Belenos. His voice was deep, and his eyes gleamed with light.

"Did that happen to you?" Olivia asked.

"No. I grew up deep in the forest, aware of my powers and the extent of them, and I don't think you should compare yourself to others. You're one of a kind, just like all of us," Belenos replied, not meaning anything special by it.

"Why did you help to tone down my connection to earth, then?" argued Olivia.

"For your safety. I don't believe that becoming a tree will help you either. You must find a balance. It's like I told you in the Laliamo Forest about Tartae and the Portals: There are gentler ways." Belenos smiled faintly, his face shining, for it was an idea dear and true to his heart.

Olivia took some time to think, and the sounds from outside became increasingly loud as she diverted her attention from the conversation. She looked through the tent wall, not actually aiming to see anything.

"I was thinking about Ourivio," she said. "Do you know of anything that happened before him? What were the Portals like, I mean?"

Belenos gazed deeply into her eyes, as if he were trying to read what lay inside them. "It's a misty history before Ourivio's time. We know very little." He shook his head with a blank expression, as though he were waiting to see where Olivia was going with that.

"I wonder how it was. You know, life before Keys and control," she said dreamily.

"I wonder about it too. But you must remember, Olivia, discipline must not be forgotten. Things should only be as wild as they should be."

Olivia had a hard time understanding that and frowned involuntarily, which made Belenos laugh, something that apparently hurt, making him bring his hand to his ribs and contort his face.

"I think it's time for me to leave. You should rest …" Olivia said. She got up and grabbed a blanket that was folded over a small wooden shelf. "It's getting colder outside," she said, leaving the blanket over Belenos' bed.

"Olivia," he called before she left the tent, making her turn. "Do what you find is right. Listen to your instinct and no one else now, for you seem to have learned more than you're letting on." He winked.

Olivia shot him a faint smile and left, halting just outside his tent and trying to figure out if she should go back inside and ask him exactly what she should do. Step by step, no space for improvisation. She decided to keep moving, delivering the potions to the remaining patients and consequently following Belenos' advice: She would trust her intuition and listen to no one else. She wondered if she had the guts for it.

That day moved swiftly. Trevor barely talked to Olivia and always had an excuse to flee when she was around; sometimes it was helping Alavro with the food, other times it was so ridiculous that Olivia concluded he wasn't even making an effort to hide his frustrations. At one point, he said that Lito needed a braid and left quickly, finding a seat just far enough from her.

That situation annoyed and haunted her pretty much all day long, making it hard to concentrate on anything else. Even her deep conversation with Belenos and her weird dreams moved to the back of her head. Trevor was the one she wanted to share everything with first, the most loving and trusted advisor, the one who held her hand throughout the worlds. Being shut out by him was hurtful. She knew she hadn't been sharing everything, but it was just a matter of time until she was ready to do so. She just needed a moment to figure things out, and she'd never expected this reaction from him, this harsh judgment for her uncontrolled powers.

She tried to keep herself busy around the camp, helping to care for the others, reorganizing, visiting Emma any time she was allowed to, and having light conversations every time she bumped into Bran or Kirk. Alavro and Cordella were very much into their own worlds, not discussing a lot with her about their plans. They only said that "time would come for them to regroup." So, they waited.

CHAPTER TWENTY

THE ACCIDENTAL PORTAL

The following days were calm, as if the whole campground were on some sort of bed rest, for they all needed to heal. Malva arrived almost a week after the battle, welcomed by Cordella, who opened a gate through the mist for her.

She arrived carrying many bags while Olivia observed from afar. A strong scent of mixed herbs and potions exhaled from them, reaching Olivia's nose at her tent's door. Malva went straight to the healer's tent, where nothing had changed, and there she stayed until that night. It was only then that Olivia could greet her.

"You sure look different, my darling," Malva said, holding Olivia's round face with both of her hands. They were warm and smelled like the earth.

Olivia smiled and they talked a little, being joined by Cordella and Ade. Malva told them about the world outside the dome they were living in, how the sun was back to its schedule, how the cold was falling over where she lived, how it was all moving again as it should. Because she lived isolated in the woods, she hadn't heard much about Lars and Greedy Factions gaining ground. She only told them that the forests were not all as happy as they should be with the awakening of the elements, so she knew there was fear and danger around.

She told Olivia the lake missed playing with her, and that it was so bad some days that Malva had to try it, spending many hours doing her best to make the lake laugh again. Olivia smiled, being taken by the amazing memories she had while she was there, missing the river and a time when she could be playful. Missing even the woods, for they hadn't been in any for a great number of days now. In some ways, it was like being back at Leve, far from wild nature.

Late at night, Alavro joined the conversation with some others from Lirianthis and the Amazon Witches, and they reminisced about the starry nights of Tartae, the great days of peace they had lived in their youth when they were blessed under the two moons.

Olivia merely observed, but she herself had fond memories of the moons and how wild it all was inside those ancient forests of Tartae. She dreamed about living that life again.

Olea arrived early the next day. The sun had not yet appeared in the sky when she was brought inside by Cordella, who had been waiting for her all night long. She brought with herself Agatha and Jasmi, and news about life in Lirianthis now. Olea had stayed there to help preserve the place and care for those taken by deep sadness, but things had gotten better, and the wounded after the battle with Lars needed her more.

Lirianthis was even more isolated now. Olea shared that they needed time to ground themselves and gather their strength; they had to stand with nature around them, with every tree and wolf. Every wizard and witch who lived in there were profoundly invested in protecting not only Lirianthis, but the surrounding woods, although most of the time, it wasn't clear if they were protecting the forests or if the forests were protecting them.

She didn't have much information about what was happening in the cities of Victro, Slintor, Lotrium or any other either. She knew even less than Malva, and the only truths she had were the ones she could tell about observing nature, like the fact that there was some balance again; the wind howled between the trees deep inside the forests, and the woodland lilies of the valley bloomed again. But just like Malva, she noticed things were restless once more. "There's this sadness hovering over Tartae, this thick cloud about to fall over our heads. This is beyond the dormancy. It's an omen of what waits for us."

Ade was the one who bore the news, and he told it to Olivia, Trevor, Bran, and Alegra in a hushed voice so none of his patients would awaken. He quoted Olea in such an ominous note that Olivia almost expected a resounding thunder after the heavy words.

"Uh, spooky!" Trevor joked.

Ade added that Olea went to see Belenos first of all, walking in his tent with Cordella, but he didn't follow. They were still in there, and Ade went back to his morning chores.

"Anyways … That's all I know," he said, holding a bunch of calendula flowers in his arms. "Any idea when Cordella will talk about plans?" he asked, his curious eyes traveling to all of them.

"She hasn't talked that much with me lately. I kinda think that means she's up to something big," said Olivia.

"I've heard nothing as well," said Alegra, shrugging.

Ade left the group to put some flowers close to the beds, the rest of them walked out of the healing tent and were quickly called by Alavro, who asked them to chop a mountain of wood for the fires in the camp. Now that the temperature had dropped, they would need a lot of it to keep everybody warm. "The warmth of spells is different than nature's. Not as comforting," he said dreamily, walking away.

The four of them kept a pretty good pace and system. Two of them would chop while the other two would organize the wood under an improvised tent—which consisted of a long white sheet over many tall sticks—and then, they would take turns at it. At first, Olivia and Alegra did the chopping while Trevor and Bran organized the lumber.

Hours went by, and the cold breeze that flew around eventually stopped affecting them as the warmth of the exercise took over. Olivia didn't use her magic for anything, only her whole body. There was a rustic, maybe traditional, flair to that activity, not to mention that it was also a great exercise. And sometimes, it just felt wrong to cut corners with magic, especially now that she feared her powers.

They talked and even sang a little during their chore; Alegra and Bran shared some songs that were common in Tartae, some pieces they used to hear while growing up, like "What To Do Now That The Moons Are Gone?" and "You're The Wolf Of My Heart." Trevor didn't want to sing anything from their world, and Olivia lost the will for it as she noticed how her friend was still acting around her. Alegra and Bran resumed their singing to distract from the tension between Trevor and Olivia. Hearing them singing those never-before-heard songs was nice and made the time chopping wood quite enjoyable.

When it was probably afternoon, for the sun was high and warmer in the sky, the group that went out on a search-and-rescue mission arrived. They were led by Aster Gran, a centaurid who was widely recognized for her wits and abilities to search for those who were lost. She was tall and strong, and her black hair hung wildly down her shoulders in curls. They crossed the mist slowly, pulling a carriage with many people inside and halting at once. Kirk ran through the camp fast, approaching and helping the group. Olivia walked there with the others.

There were around thirty people squeezed together in the carriage; they were all wounded, and some couldn't even open their eyes. Firlo was in there, conscious, but his leg was broken, and he had a bad injury in his stomach.

Cordella and Alavro joined the others, and everyone helped to move the wounded warriors to the healing tent that eventually had to be expanded to accommodate all who needed a place.

Malva, Olea, Cordella, and Ade got to work quickly, and when things were pressing like this, they always asked to be left alone. Even Olivia, who had recently discovered some healing powers, wasn't allowed to stay. They needed only the most skilled healers, as these moments were critical and there was no time to waste.

The hours that followed fell into silence and anxiety. There wasn't a soul in the camp who wasn't worried, and they were all reminded of the misfortunes the last battle had brought to them. Bran reminded the group there was still much to do, and they headed back to their chopping chores, but it wasn't as gleeful as before. There wasn't a song or many words, and Trevor's quiet behavior toward Olivia could even become imperceptible if she didn't know him so well.

Malva walked out the healing tent later that day; Olivia was eating by a fire with Bran and Alavro. She looked tired but hopeful and told them that it was a blessing that those people were found when there was still time for healing, for they were all spread out in the woods, hidden and afraid, and that combination could be more poisonous than the venom of any snake.

Malva rested with them for a while, joining some light conversations and eating a bowl of warm soup that Bran had brought her. Before leaving, she asked Olivia to forage for some herbs she needed: greenflower for fear, eye of the night for open wounds, and turmalina for fast recuperation.

As soon as they were finished with their meal, Olivia went to the edge of the river, the wildest part of their camp, to try to find the herbs Malva asked for. It was a small patch of the forest, and even after looking carefully through it many times, she was still missing the greenflower, an herb that grew between barks in tree trunks. The scent of the forest called her outside, and she figured that this was the perfect opportunity for some freedom. She walked toward the mist, which was dense and cold, like a thick white wall, and it opened for her without fighting. Olivia found herself deep in the woods, where birds sang loudly, and the colors were darkened due to the setting sun. There was a deep pink and purple hue painting the grass, and tiny bunnies feasted unafraid out of their holes. She quickly spotted greenflowers blooming out of an oak tree trunk and collected them carefully until she had enough for the potions Malva would brew.

Olivia took a while to realize that there weren't such deep woods at the edge of their camp. When they arrived, they had been traveling through a field with just a few trees. She studied her surroundings and looked back to where she came from, and there was mist flowing around, dissipating slowly in the air.

"Oh no," she whispered.

It dawned on her that she went to one of the surrounding forests, but she wasn't sure how. The misty protection was miles away from her, and it would take a long time to walk there by foot, maybe an hour or two if she was lucky enough. Olivia ran back to where she last saw the mist, but nothing remained. Even so, she tried stepping across an imaginary wall and into the camp, but she was still there, very much in the forest. She tried everything that came to her mind, meditating, asking nature, and only avoided calling her connection to the elements because she was afraid of what it could bring. And when nothing else worked, she decided to run.

She grabbed her basket of herbs and flowers tightly in her hand, as it could save her life, and allowed herself to try one little spell so she wouldn't take the wrong path back. She called the elements and asked for guidance.

"Please, take me to the camp," she murmured. A gust of wind shook the trees around her; leaves swirled on the forest floor, up, down, and finally forward, and she followed.

The leaves flew high at the height of her nose and then guided her way. The night came completely when she entered the field, which wasn't so green anymore, since its grass had dried up, gaining a beige color for something that started to resemble fall.

As Olivia crossed the field, fear grew inside her, for she had no cover. She broke into an even faster run, following the leaves that flew in front of her and trusting that she was on the right path.

The ground under Olivia trembled due to the heaviness of something moving. She halted and scanned for anything around her that could offer some cover, finding only a couple of trees that were too far away. The sound of galloping horses got louder and closer, and Olivia ran faster, hoping to reach the camp before anything else could reach her. The tall grass wiped her knees, and the night breeze embraced her face, cold. In her ears, the sound of gallops and the wind were mixed together, reminding her that she needed to go faster.

"Stop that madness!" a familiar voice said, coming from the shadows right behind Olivia.

She hesitated but kept running. What if it was a trick or just wishful thinking? She couldn't risk it. Olivia marched on, focused, not even looking back, and the dried grass tangled around her legs, making Olivia drop like a statue on the ground at once.

"For Ourivio's beard!" Cordella said, dismounting her horse and nearing Olivia. "Come on, give me your hand."

"Did you need to do that?" Olivia protested as she stood and cleaned the dirt from her pants and hands.

"I'm sorry, but you didn't stop! What are you doing here?" Cordella asked with a puzzled look.

"Er … I went to find some herbs for Malva, and I ended up deep in the forest," said Olivia with a weak voice.

"How?!" Cordella shrieked in a very high-pitched tone.

"Would you believe if I said I've no idea?" Olivia said with a half-smile.

"Why doesn't that surprise me?" Cordella rolled her eyes. "How did you pass through the protection spells?"

Olivia shook her head.

"Alas … I'm afraid you have no answer for me. Come on, let's go back," sighed Cordella.

Cordella mounted her horse, and Olivia did the same, quickly heading back to the camp at speed and crossing the protective gates cast by Cordella a while later.

There was a big reception for them when they arrived, but with no happy faces. Alavro, Bran, and Kirk approached Cordella's horse and showered them with questions, which Cordella answered loudly, aiming her reply for everyone else who was waiting.

"She is fine! We're all fine! You can all go back to your things now!" she declared, and most dispersed, not giving it too much thought.

"What happened, Cordella?" inquired Alavro.

"She crossed the protection and … I don't know … made a Portal?" Cordella answered, puzzled.

Olivia gazed at everyone with unsure eyes and a broken smile that meant to say she was sorry. Trevor stood far back, next to Alegra, and after scoffing and shaking his head profusely, he left. Alegra met Olivia's eyes and shrugged, and Olivia didn't even hear what Cordella and Alavro were saying anymore. She left Malva's basket on the ground—which had almost nothing inside after Olivia's adventures—and followed Trevor.

"Hey, wait!" she yelled, walking fast to reach him. "What the hell are you doing?"

Trevor stopped, annoyance covering his face, and he shook his head again, about to resume his walk.

"Why are you avoiding me? You don't talk to me anymore. Everyone else is treating me fine but you. Why can't you even look at me? Are you so disgusted by what I am that you can't stand my face anymore?" Olivia barked.

"YOU ALMOST DIED, OLIVIA! YOU KEEP ALMOST DYING! I'VE BEEN WITNESSING YOU ALMOST DIE FOR FAR TOO LONG!" Trevor exploded.

Olivia got smaller and stepped back.

"I've never done it on purpose, Trev," bargained Olivia.

"I know," sighed Trevor, still avoiding Olivia's eyes.

"It's my powers— I can't control—"

"I know! And you should!" Trevor roared again, his voice louder and his eyes wide.

"I don't know what to say …" Olivia said, unsure.

"If you don't know," he started. "Just give me some time, will ya?" Trevor said before Olivia could say anything else. He stared deep into her eyes for a long time, and there Olivia found doubt and terror.

He went into their tent, and Olivia did what he asked, walking away to the meeting tent where she thought she could wait for a better time to go to bed. She had never given too much thought about any of this from Trevor's perspective. How it must have felt to see her flirting with the unknown so many times, fighting Lars, becoming a plant, opening Portals, getting lost.

It was hard to give him time; all she wanted was to talk to him about this, about it all. The events of this night made her aware of all the information she kept from Trevor, of how deep she was into many strange facets of her powers, and how fear was not protecting her but actually leaving her more exposed, without his support and without his words of guidance that she much needed.

By the time she decided to go inside the tent, Trevor was already sleeping, snoring slightly, emitting a very low sound. She crawled into bed, tired from the day of many adventures that seemed to have lasted ages, and Bran and Alegra entered just a while later, walking swiftly.

The night outside had owls hooting and the howling of wolves in the distance, faint, like a song playing in the background. Olivia had this weight pressing her heart that made it very thin and small. Falling asleep that day was a challenge, and she could tell when everyone else in the room did: first, it was Bran, then Alegra, and then there was only the hooting owl and that pack of wolves far away. This sadness in her chest was aggravated by all that she knew was coming, what she couldn't avoid.

CHAPTER TWENTY-ONE

A NEW QUEST

Six days they spent in the camp after Olivia stepped out of their protection. Days that were still slow, stretched, but mostly back to what they used to be before time went off track. Emma had regained consciousness but wasn't yet herself. She was out of the healing tent and ecstatic about that, but there was still recovery time ahead: her wounds were healing slowly, and her magic was erratic, needing rest.

Cordella and the other healers concluded that the injures caused by Lars and his allies were deeper and more persistent than normal. They appeared to have a life of their own, refusing to leave the wounded, persisting and rotting like a poison, and it wasn't like that the first time he'd attacked. His powers were growing and were so vicious that they evolved into something corroding. Thankfully, they could count on dexterous healers.

Belenos recuperated fast; about seven days after the battle he left his tent and went straight to the edge of the river, where he spent many hours under the sun dipping his toes in the water. After that, his face shone again and even his broken bone was almost mended, leaving him with no pain at all, only a sling out of precaution until he was fully recovered.

Firlo and the others who were found in the woods were gaining strength, and every day brought them some hope. Olivia visited the healing tent any time she could and helped with potions and spells whenever she was asked. But she never again went to forage for ingredients.

Life in the camp found its rhythm once more, and after a while, the pressure of the wait of what would come next left them, leaving space for training and full mental recuperation. They didn't have any news about Lars. Atlas looked for him, but there was only silence now. He retreated, and they knew that they should prepare for the worst: There was a haunting note in that silence that guarded a fierce plan of attack, especially now that he learned he could be defeated.

The camp was overly protected now, and they also had guards at some points. After Olivia left so effortlessly, many feared that the place could be invaded, a notion Cordella appeased by mounting enchantments over them daily. She figured there was no harm in that, and it would be harder to explain that what happened to Olivia was something else and, probably, none of those spells would ever be capable of holding her.

During those days, many more people became acquainted with Olivia; she met the fauns from the summer islands, the Fjorts from Lotrium, a group of sorcerers from Victro. But none of them filled the void she had from her broken relationship with Trevor, who was still very closed and weird around her.

As soon as night fell and all the fires were lighted around the camp, Cordella asked the leaders of the troops to follow her. Olivia exchanged a look with Bran and Kirk and stood at once, heading to the meeting tent where Cordella led them all. Olivia, Bran, Kirk, Trevor, Alegra, and Alavro found a place in a corner under the dim light in the tent.

"We must prepare for attack again," Cordella announced, her voice firm and clear. "This is the war we wished to avoid, and we must *make* the next move, not wait for it."

All the women and men in the tent paused; some murmured indecipherably, others remained in silence. Olivia's heart beat fast.

"What is your plan?" asked Lidia Cernune.

"Do we know where to attack Lars?" added the leader of the amazon warriors.

"What should we do about those who can't go to war?" questioned Orion.

The room broke into noise, and the voices were inflamed. All had something to add, something to question, something to fear.

"We need to start from the beginning, taking one step at a time," Cordella said, still calm, indifferent to the commotion taking over the room. "I say we send our scouts out for him while we get ready. We're also here to decide on a plan together. We were all there in the same fight, we saw what he was capable of, but also what our people are capable of. No one better than ourselves to come up with a strategy," continued Cordella.

"I suggest we form small groups of skillful warriors to search and mitigate clusters of Greedy Factions. That might dismantle some of his power," contributed Alavro, walking closer to Cordella and gesticulating.

"I've heard that he keeps many of his allies around him, like faithful protectors. If that is true, I'm not certain that it would be wise to divide our warriors," said Orion.

Some agreed, others complained, and they decided to vote. Alavro's idea was accepted, and they moved on. They discussed gathering more allies and asking them to be ready for war at any moment.

"Lars opened a Portal right in front of our eyes last time. How do we prepare for something like that again?" said Lidia, clenching her fists.

"I've heard that Driona and the Wood sisters went after iron to make new Keys for the Portals. Shouldn't we wait for them and do something about that?" proposed Kirk.

Olivia's stomach turned at the sound of that; she looked down, staring at the floor, and then she found Belenos' face, gazing back at her.

"We don't know how long that would take, Kirk," said Cordella. "And there are no guarantees …"

"What about Olivia?" said Aster Gran. "She was able to close the Portal. She can do it again!"

Every eye in the room turned to her.

"Yes, but at what cost?" argued Milo Trelion, the head of the Willow Warriors. "That blast of energy hurt many people. We must find another way! A way that is safe."

"We don't have many options to choose from, Milo. Someone could train her, and we use her like an asset," added Aster.

"I'm not going to war," Olivia whispered, shaking her head.

"What was that?" asked Milo, standing.

"I'm not going," Olivia said firmly. Everyone stared at her in silence. Cordella and Alavro frowned, puzzled. Belenos kept looking at her.

"WHAT NOW?" Trevor fumed.

"Calm down, Trev. You're coming with me," Olivia said it with a low tone, touching Trevor's arm. She then turned to the others again and continued. "There's something else I need to do, something for us to find, and we can't join you. Now, if you'll excuse me …" She left the room after Trevor, who had fled already.

Bran, Kirk, Alegra, and Alavro followed them to one quiet corner in the camp, next to Alavro's tent.

"Please, everyone, just listen to me," began Olivia. "There's a *key* to the Portals, something else completely, something that will help us fix this mess and bring balance to the Portals. And when I say balance, I mean something we've never seen in our lives."

"A key? Like the one we're planning to forge?" asked Alegra.

"It's not an actual key …" answered Olivia.

"What is it, then?" said Trevor.

"I don't know exactly, but I know I must find it. It probably holds many answers to my powers too … And we all know that I am out of balance, and kind of out of control. I fear every impulse I have, all magical thought I think," Olivia confessed.

Trevor was paying profound attention to her words, looking into Olivia's eyes deeply. His face bore no doubts or anger anymore, and just by witnessing these changes, Olivia already found refuge there; before he said anything, she knew she could count on him.

"Olivia, you cannot part ways with us and go out on a mission like that. Where did you learn all of this?" warned Alavro, shaking his head lightly.

"I've received many messages. I'm sure this is the right thing to do," stated Olivia.

"Olivia, you can't—" Alavro started.

"I'm going with her," interrupted Trevor, his eyes locked with Olivia's.

Olivia shot him a smile in return.

"Alavro, I understand your concern and I truly appreciate it. But I'm certain that this is the right thing to do. I must trust my instincts on this," explained Olivia.

"Ok, Olie. What do you need from us?" Bran offered.

Alavro sighed, defeated, and lowered his head.

"Are there pirates in Tartae, by any chance?" asked Olivia, uncertain. Kirk, Bran, Alegra, and Alavro exchanged a puzzled look, and Olivia changed tactics. "I mean, groups that live mainly on the sea trading; they would have fleets of big ships, that kind of stuff."

"Yes! The sea folk! They spend their time on land at the wild beaches of the north, the wild sea," said Bran.

"I need to go to them. How do I get there?" said Olivia.

"I can take you there," Bran said, excitement growing in his voice. "Hear me out! That's the same way to the Astar tribe. I can take advantage of that to talk to them, ask for help during this war."

They all ceased talking and looked at Alavro, who ran his hands through his hair and exhaled loudly.

"What was all of that?" Cordella inquired, approaching fast, Belenos right after her.

Olivia told Cordella all she needed to do and how she had come to that decision. Cordella listened to her in silence, weighing every word. When Olivia was done, Cordella passed her gaze through everybody, lingering on Olivia.

"I agree you must trust your intuition. Your mind is made up, and I won't hold you back. I trust you; I always have." Cordella smiled kindly. In her eyes, Olivia could read many other things: love, worry, pride. "Come on, Alavro. It's time to let them fly a bit." She passed her arm around him and they walked away with Belenos.

Bran, Kirk, and Alegra explained all they knew about the sea folk and the path to where they moored. It seemed that they were travelers, and a mystery to all.

"I feel you'll like them, Olie, they're adventurers," Bran said, smiling.

The complicity of that phrase and the moment they were building together made Olivia's heart dance inside the confines of her chest. For the first time in a long while, she was unrestrained.

The path that was going to lead them north through the forests was heavily used for travelers looking for the ocean when times were lighter in Tartae. For that reason, they would be able to find well-drawn roads that would make their travels easier, at least for a part of their journey. They wanted to leave no later than tomorrow.

They decided that Bran was the only one who would accompany Olivia and Trevor on that quest. Alegra and Kirk would stay behind, helping the troops and preparing for the next steps of the war against Lars.

When it was late at night already and the wolves howled again, Kirk left for his tent, excited for the war ahead and resembling the old Kirk Olivia knew, with energy boiling in his veins and eyes looking attentively for action. Bran wanted to talk to his dad before retiring for the night, and Alegra left with him, for she had questions about their next steps. They headed straight to the healing tent, where Alavro and Cordella had walked to earlier. Olivia and Trevor went into their tent, where Emma was deep asleep.

Olivia had this relief in her body that made it so light, she was about to fly. The certainty that they had chosen the right path, a feeling that was so intense and warm that it guided her forward with a different kind of energy, something close to plentitude. She was about to go even deeper, touching truths no one even knew existed, but which were calling her incessantly.

"I'm glad you're coming with me." Olivia smiled, finding Trevor's eyes.

"There could be no other way," he answered.

Olivia told him everything that had been happening with her, from the first dream she had with Freya to her wonderings about how the Portals behaved before all the control imposed by Ourivio. Trevor listened to all of it. He didn't question Olivia's conclusions, not even the fact that she had waited until that time to tell him; he just sat across from her and listened, and Olivia was assured that he comprehended how confusing all of that should be, the fact that she needed time and sometimes that was the only thing that could make things clear.

Olivia wanted to sleep fast, but the anticipation for the next day kept her awake for longer, like a child who was about to go on an exciting field trip.

***

Preparations started as early as the sun. Olivia didn't know how long their travels would take or where she would go after they met the sea folk, which made it quite hard to pick what to bring with her. She decided on the basics, even less than she had brought with her to the camp, and she couldn't forget her sword. The weapon had its own power by now, even there, and even when quiet, inside that tent during a peaceful morning; it carried the memory of all they had been through, even what Olivia couldn't remember. She looked at it for a while, and it was like an extension of her arm, a sharper, physical version of her magic. Just behind Olivia, Trevor got ready as well, and when he grabbed his bow and arrow, they exchanged a look and a smile. In a way, it was like they were back at the start.

They shared everything with Emma as soon as she woke up. Olivia could tell she had many questions, maybe hesitations about their journey, but she understood that that was something that needed to be done. Emma was still weak and didn't say much. She bid them the best of luck and said that they would love to see the wild waters, for it was beautiful like a dream. Alegra gave them advice about traveling alone in Tartae, like *"always trust those who travel in the sea, but never listen to a mermaid. A merman is even worse."* She rolled her eyes while saying this, and Emma agreed. Olivia and Trevor found it a weird piece of advice, but they knew nothing about either of those creatures, so they made a mental note while nodding along.

Trevor and Alegra went to find somewhere more private to say goodbye to each other, leaving the tent holding hands discreetly. Emma complained about feeling cold, and Olivia covered her with some more blankets, also weaving some fire by her bed that flew just above the floor, contained in a small flame. Emma fell asleep again instantly, and Olivia kissed her forehead gently, wishing to see her again soon.

Outside, Olivia found much of the same routine, though some people were looking at her askance, and that part was quite new. She walked straight to the healing tent, looking for Ade and Malva, and said goodbye between hugs. Malva gave her concentrated versions of potions to be diluted in water and drunk for rest and strength. The healing tent was getting less crowded by the day, and that was something that on its own already made everybody lighter and more receptive to farewells.

After that, Olivia was called by Cordella into her chambers. The place smelled like magic, a mixture of jasmine and sandalwood, and it dawned on her that she had never been in there before. The inside of the tent already carried the same energy as Cordella's house, inviting, interesting, already charged with something not physical, but palpable enough to be undeniable. Her bed was neatly done, covered by a deep brown blanket, made of something like velvet; some papers were on the bench by her bed, and an old trunk rested by one corner. Cordella opened it, grabbed something, and closed the thing with a wave, sitting on it.

"Sit," Cordella said, smiling and pointing to her bed.

Olivia followed her command, resting her hands over her lap. And still looking around the place, as though there was more in there to discover.

"I would like for you to have these. First, this medallion messenger that I had made for us." Cordella handed Olivia a beautiful bronze medallion, quite small and carved with an olive branch on one side and a flower on the other. A very delicate silk rose ribbon held it; it looked like the wind itself, so flowy and thin.

"It's beautiful, Cordella!" Olivia exclaimed.

"And useful," said Cordella, in a very practical tone. "And I would like for you to have this as well. It will protect you from harm and from the cold." Cordella handed Olivia a sage green cape with embroidered flowers, leaves, and twigs crowning the shoulders.

"This is just perfect! I've always wanted a cape!" Olivia laughed, standing up and throwing it over her shoulders. As she dressed, a warmth touched her body, and it was like a shield surrounded her.

"There's magic in every stitch of the embroidery. It will protect you like I've always tried to do. It's an honor to see you and Trevor growing into your powers right before my eyes. I don't know what you're looking for, but I know there's something out there for you to find, and I know you'll do it; I've never doubted you," Cordella said kindly, finding Olivia's eyes.

"Thank you for everything. I'll send as many messages as I can, and I hope to be back soon, with an answer for us. Just promise me no one will try to forge a key. There's a better answer out there, and I'm going to find it," pleaded Olivia.

Cordella agreed and guaranteed her that nothing of that sort would be done; they were still a team, even if now working on separate paths, and their goal was still the same. Olivia explained to Cordella every piece of the plan they had put together, and Cordella suggested that they should bring some allandrio tea, which was hard to find when living so close to the sea, and the sea folk loved gifts. It would be a good way to guarantee a welcome during these uncertain times. Olivia also shared her growing concerns about what had led Ourivio to control the Portals, the extent of the truth in what they knew, and how she wished to find a clue about how life was before he created keys and disturbed the Portals in such an intense way.

"Well, I guess we've never questioned that. We've been so profoundly deep into this notion of Ourivio bringing order and that being the way of things that our visions were clouded; we've never wondered how it was before the mess. I hope that there was peace and we can find it again," Cordella said.

"What was decided about the war and the next attack?" Olivia asked.

"We will prepare for another attack, and some groups are going to search and capture Greedy Factions. But what I aim for is to find Lars where he's hiding and attack him where he's weak," answered Cordella.

"What if he attacks using Portals?" continued Olivia, frowning.

"I'll have to deal with the risk. I won't play with the Portals like he does; that's disrespectful, and nature doesn't dwell in that, and right now, I lack the power to open or close a Portal. I was taught to do that using Keys, spells, with a purpose," answered Cordella.

Olivia listened and hadn't much to say in return, and before the silence became too much or too heavy for both of them, Cordella stood.

"Let's go. You have a journey ahead of you and many people to say goodbye!" she said, walking Olivia outside.

They headed to where Alavro, Bran, Kirk, Orion, Alegra, and Trevor—who had a very similar cape on, only his was the same sage green but with embroidered light green clovers and silver leaves—were. Trevor and Bran were also ready to go and seemed quite calm, not very bothered by the quest ahead.

"I got the horses ready. We can go anytime you choose," said Bran, looking at Olivia.

"Thanks." Her gaze traveled over everybody in their group, and then the camp, and her heart flipped. "I didn't see Belenos today. Did anybody?"

"He headed to Laliamo. Belenos needed the forest to heal completely. Here, he asked me to give you this." Orion handed Olivia an envelope.

"Thank you," she said and put the envelope in her pocket without opening it. "I guess it's time," Olivia sighed.

"For a change, I don't have many words in me," said Alavro. "What I'll say is that I believe in your quest and wish you don't take long on it. Take care and be brave!" His voice trembled, and his eyes were sincere, shimmering under the sun like two sapphires.

He took a long time saying farewell to Bran; he said many things that Olivia couldn't hear from where she stood and squeezed Bran's face between his chubby hands many times. Bran laughed and kissed his father lovingly, saying that he would be back with more help in a jiffy.

The goodbyes went on and on until there was nothing left to say and no one else to hug. Something inside Olivia shifted at that moment, moving her out of her calmness and to a place of a warm void; the part of her that wished to stay and already missed all those she loved. Something called her, pulling her to a path she knew was hers, but a piece of her stayed behind with each one of those people, leaving her with an incomplete version of herself that longed, and only that.

She took a deep breath, from where she gathered the strength to say the last farewell and mounted Myrrh, crossing the mist with Trevor and Bran, never looking behind and letting the coldness of that thick fog embrace and then release them into the world.

As they stepped outside, still galloping slowly, Olivia opened Belenos' letter and read in his flowery handwriting:

"You know your instinct, and you know it's time to follow it.
Trust yourself and what unfolds for you; it's your path.
I'll be seeing you again soon,

Belenos."

CHAPTER TWENTY-TWO

THE GOLDEN FOREST

The group picked up speed as they passed through the plains, quickly diving into the woods and traveling at a high pace amidst the mossy knolls and the trees that had started losing leaves. The cold air touched Olivia's face intensely, reminding her that the warm days were being left behind. Bran and Trevor galloped beside her, focused on the path ahead that was still spacious and easy to follow. Eventually, they would have to choose more challenging ways to cross the forests in complete secrecy.

The way to the sea folk took five days at a demanding velocity; they were to cross the Hollowtree forest, the fields of Lorne, and up to the Astar cliffs, where Bran would stay behind to discuss an alliance for the upcoming war. Olivia wished that she could open a Portal and save them that precious time, jumping straight to the beaches where they hoped to find the sea folk moored.

Around them, the forest was calm and almost soundless, making the noise of their horses quite loud, echoing around the place, trembling the ground and disturbing the animals who slept or rested inside the bushes. In there, far away from anyone else, where the birds sang cheerfully and the flowers bloomed again, Tartae seemed back to its wholeness; the days were still slow but passed accordingly, and only the nights brought a big reminder that things still needed fixing. And the first night of their journey wasn't any different.

They still rode many hours in the dark until finally choosing a spot to rest. The first day was a complete success, for they had covered many miles from the Hollowtree wood and would soon be at its border, according to Bran, who had already laid down to sleep nestled between tree roots that popped from the ground. Olivia and Trevor ate before following Bran's steps. They found some nut bars in their bags and washed them down with apple cider brewed in the camp. Neither of them talked much, for they were tired and still processing their day and having to leave everyone behind. Olivia wondered how Trevor might be feeling about Alegra but didn't want to pick at that wound yet, which was still so young and open, so delicate.

They fell asleep under the moonless sky and woke when the sun was still young, wishing for a smooth day of travel like the one before. Their breakfast consisted of drinking the whole contents of a bottle of strength brew that Malva had prepared for them, and after feeding the horses, off they went again across that same road, passing by different trees and creatures of the forest.

Their surroundings had gotten wilder, and Bran warned Olivia and Trevor about wolves who dwelled in that area and advised them to stay close the whole time—getting lost in those woods was the last thing they needed.

"Tell me about it," joked Trevor, finding Olivia's eyes and widening his.

Olivia scoffed and moved Myrrh a little bit closer to the other two; she now rode on the left of the group, and Trevor was in the middle.

The weather was agreeable, quite chilly sometimes, with the wind blowing mercilessly, but the cape Cordella had given Olivia helped. The falling leaves started to paint the forest floor with yellow, burgundy, and brown colors, but many trees still had their branches covered by them. Autumn was just starting, much like their journey.

At mid-afternoon, Olivia slowed her pace and called for a break. Her stomach howled loudly, for she hadn't eaten since that morning and was lightheaded. She jumped off her horse, caressing Myrrh's white mane and exchanging some energy with the horse, which always seemed so balanced and calm that it emanated that energy around.

"Here, my friend." Olivia put down some water and an elixir for Myrrh and kissed her forehead, heading to a rock next to them and sitting down.

"How are we doing, Bran?" asked Trevor, finding a place near Olivia.

"Great. Better than I expected, actually. We've covered a lot of ground," answered Bran.

"Do you know what you'll say to the Astars when you get there?" questioned Olivia.

"The truth …" answered Bran. "Lars is a huge menace to them and the land where they live, of course. We thought that we might not need to bother them for help, but here we are."

"Very convincing …" chuckled Trevor. "Add to that some somber song and you have the prelude of doom," he joked.

Bran laughed. "I don't think there's anything else I could say to make this more colorful … But I don't think they have a lot of options either. What can they say? That they would just wait and see?"

"I don't know, Bran. Take Freya as an example. She's not helping at all, and she is one of the most skilled witches in Tartae," said Trevor.

"I think there's more to Freya than what we know," said Olivia. "Not that I am defending her … No. I don't agree with what she's doing, but sometimes I feel like she's in my head."

Trevor and Bran looked at Olivia with puzzled eyes.

"And why is that?" asked Bran.

"I don't even know how to explain. But she knows she has that power over me, because when we met her as soon we came to Tartae again, I could tell that she was entering my head," said Olivia.

"That's creepy!" exclaimed Trevor. "I don't know if that's good, Olie. Have you mentioned that to Cordella?"

"It's hard to mention something when you don't even know what it means or how to explain it. But every time I've heard her in my head, she was trying to help me. So I guess there's no harm," continued Olivia.

"Do you think she knows where we are going?" asked Bran.

Olivia shook her head. "I've no idea."

"My dad finds Freya very weird. After last time, they barely talked with her or about her," said Bran.

"My dad would find her EXTREMELY weird!" said Trevor.

They all laughed, and Olivia continued.

"I don't see how she can be so indifferent. I guess she wouldn't resist if Tartae doesn't recover completely."

"Do you think she'll die?" asked Bran.

"Yes," Olivia answered bluntly. "Do you remember what happened to me last time we were in a forest? I almost died myself by the mere presence of phookas and their evil intentions. Her connection with nature is not so deep; I've never seen plants growing from her, but I think it's the same principle. I believe that the magical beings will perish first, and those who work intrinsically with the earth, the first of all."

"Like Freya and Belenos," said Bran.

"Like you," concluded Trevor.

Olivia nodded.

"But that's just what I think. I might be wrong, for all that we know," said Olivia, trying to make the mood a bit lighter but failing miserably at it.

"So, why say it at all?" inquired Trevor.

"Because I might be right, Trev. And if I am, there's no point in pretending it's not true," Olivia added. "Come on, it's time for us to go!" She got up and smiled, offering her hand to Trevor and Bran, helping them get up.

The horses appeared to be fully recharged again after minutes under the shade, eating and drinking. The humans, on the other hand, left their break spot drained after Olivia's last words—which wasn't her goal at all. But every day that passed, Olivia was more certain of this: Just like the trees in the most magical and ancient spots in Tartae were the first to perish, the witches and wizards would be too. She just didn't know what effect this would have on Lars himself, for he was deeply connected to all elements, but he was also the cause of much of what afflicted Tartae at that moment.

They resumed their journey and soon left the path, turning right by the biggest oak tree Olivia had ever seen and finding their way inside a dense forest. No one dared to ask Olivia for her help opening the way for them, and she herself was hesitant to try it.

The trees around them were close together, and the noises of the forest got louder and more present. Olivia was suddenly aware that this was not her home; she had just stepped inside someone else's territory, surrounded by trees and animals that had never heard of her. Naturally, their speed slowed, allowing each of them to look around and breathe in that place with all its life and many noises.

"Have you ever been here?" Trevor asked Bran.

"No, I've never been to these parts," answered Bran, his head turned up, staring at the sky through the many leaves and branches of the tall trees closing over them.

"Is it safe?" said Trevor.

"Yes. For the looks of it, there are only forest beings around. Let's move," Bran said and guided them forward.

They reached a part of the forest that was completely colored in the golden tones of the fall. The ground was a carpet of yellow leaves, and the treetops were covered by the same tone, transforming the hue of the forest around them.

"I guess it took a while, but now fall is coming with all its force," stated Bran, while he studied the place.

Olivia remembered her time with Malva when she suspected it was autumn by the quantity of pumpkin and squash in her harvest. She wondered if fall had taken all this time to stick and roll, or if it was paused, like many other things in this world. Her mind quickly moved to the Tartae of before, with balance and so much respect for all that lived.

They were still in the golden woods when night ordered them to stop with its freezing winds. Every single one of them had learned to not defy the powers of nature in Tartae, so they all agreed to stop and chose a small cave under many huge boulders, all covered in moss and coral bells.

There, Olivia went back to her silent dreams again, which she reported to Trevor as soon as they woke. Those were the dreams of a tree, she had learned, and whatever connection she had with the earth right now, it was starting to call her, luring her into that world again. Olivia could tell that Trevor was afraid, but he didn't make any warnings this time; he only said: "You do what you have to do. Just be very careful."

And that was what she did. With yet two days ahead of them, she figured they needed speed, and she accepted the invitation of the trees—at least, as willingly as she could. She channeled that connection, weaving the earth elements and asking for a clear way as well as a safe road, and the path changed for them, opening clearly before their eyes. Bran and Trevor looked at her, but Olivia didn't look back. She concentrated on that spell with all she had, not letting it take over her, not letting it *become* her. She could still will the obstacles out of their way, she could ask for the wolves to take another path, but she wasn't the earth underneath their horses this time, she wasn't all spread around the forest, pieces scattered before and after them. Olivia was now controlling and weaving, too concentrated on not diving too deep in that connection to think of anything else.

Olivia's spell allowed them to go even faster, and she remained in a constant state of meditation the whole time. They moved for the next two days rapidly, like a pack of wolves themselves while Olivia led the group, galloping fast. She enjoyed running free with Myrrh in that forest, and its images and colors passed by her all mixed and blurred into one thing. Nature around her vibrated with life and pleads for help, warnings of a somber future and memories of a past of mishaps.

CHAPTER TWENTY-THREE

THROUGH THE WATERFALL

They arrived at a great waterfall; the veil of misty powerful waters came from the top of a rocky tall mountain. Along its surface, patches of maroon, green, and brown painted the huge rock. The water came down violently, leaving no doubt of its strength and the size of what was in front of them. Olivia, Trevor, and Bran halted next to the river where it fell, drops of water splashing over them. It was the night of the fifth day and the coldest of all they had spent during their travel.

"Are we close?" Olivia asked Bran.

"Yes, the way up is through the curtain of water," he answered.

"Can we do it?" said Trevor, his eyebrows raised. "I'm afraid we'll freeze to death."

"I can help," stated Olivia.

She neared the waterfall, thinking. As she got closer, the energy of the water enveloped her at once, wild and boundless; she trembled and joined it in its strength, allowing it to run through her body in waves. Olivia stretched her arms while she sat tall on Myrrh, and an invisible arch held the water; it opened a portal to the path under it.

"Come, it's safe for the horses," she said, leading the way.

The others followed her slowly through a path of earth she created to the portal; it was as though the horses were walking over the waters that were very deep and held unknown things. They reached the rocky path under the hill, all wet and mossy, following it in the dark until it made a slight turn to the right and then went up, out of the cave. They continued to go up for many minutes at a slow pace, for the path was winding and hard. When they finally reached the top, the ground was flat again, and down the tall cliff, laid out on a calm, dark blue carpet, was the sea of Tartae.

Olivia was completely bewildered. It was as vast as her dreams, and its waters told the stories of ancient times. There were slight waves that came and went rhythmically, breathing in and out the life of Tartae. She stared at it as if hypnotized, and the clouds that spread out so heavily in the sky above them moved, some of them lowering, showing pieces of the dark night sky.

"What's happening?" whispered Bran, staring at it, mouth half open.

The clouds continued to move, dissolving into the sea or into the wind, opening up more pieces of the sky, showing more stars shining for all to see until they appeared: the two moons of Tartae in full, shining brightly, casting their glow over the waters and the sky.

Instantly, the waves got stronger, crashing violently against the shore and the rocks, making a shiver run down Olivia's spine as it awakened something inside her.

All three of them remained silent, observing the scene that unfolded before them, witnessing every star reappearing in the sky until it was completely cleared.

They finally looked at each other, laughing loudly, and that took them many minutes, as though they needed to shed through laughs the apprehension of those last days and the bothering feeling of not seeing the moons for such a long time. In that laughing state, they didn't notice anything else until there were many horses around them and arrows pointed right at their faces.

"We mean no harm," warned Bran. His voice was soft and broke the silence of the beautiful night around them. He raised his arms, showing no weapons, and Olivia and Trevor did the same.

The arrows remained pointed at their faces and hearts.

"I'm Bran Talbote, son of Alavro Talbote, and this is Olivia Halin and Trevor Meris. We are passing through and mean no harm. We are on our way to the Astar folk; we seek their help," he said, and nothing changed for many minutes.

"You are the son of Alavro Talbote, one of the Guardians of the Portals?" said a voice Olivia couldn't place, blended with so many faces in the darkness.

"Yes. And may I ask who you are?" said Bran.

"I'm Lilith Drat." A short woman walked forward. Her hair flowed in the wind and her features were hidden under the cloak of night. "I am the head of the Astar. How can we be of service?"

"We need your help to save Tartae," Bran said bluntly.

All the weapons were lowered after Lilith waived a sign to her troop. She didn't ask any questions after that, as if knowing that little was enough; Olivia, Trevor, and Bran dismounted their horses to introduce themselves properly, shaking Lilith's hand and apologizing for entering their territory unannounced.

"If you mean no harm, there's none done," she said. "You've arrived with the moons, and that must mean something good."

Lilith led them to her village, which at first Olivia thought it was a trap, for there were no houses anywhere to be found, no fires lit. But little by little, the secrets of the Astar folk revealed themselves, showing many tiny cabins hidden under mud, grass, and hundreds of other plants, nestled among the trees, completely covered by nature and sheltered.

"Our huts … for us, it's just home, but people think they're magical just because they are hard to spot," said Lilith, noticing their amused faces.

"Sounds much like people from my world," joked Trevor.

Lilith laughed along, but Olivia wasn't sure if she quite understood. From what Bran and Alavro had told her, they didn't have that much contact with the rest of Tartae; Bran didn't even know if they were aware of the last battle and the current state of things.

Aside from Lilith and her troop, there was no one around. Olivia, who wasn't sure what time of night it was, wondered if everybody was already sleeping or just afraid of them. Lilith walked them into the biggest hut of all—which was still quite small—and only three of her people walked inside with them. The place was quite dark, humid, with some small wooden benches arranged in a circle and no windows. Mushrooms popped out everywhere.

"Please, sit," Lilith said. She never introduced the other women and man who walked in with her. Now in the faint light, her hair was as white as the moon, and she was very young, with many freckles on her face. The others had fair hair as well, and they all dressed like warriors.

"I've come to ask for the help of your people, Lilith. I don't know if you're aware of what has been happening—" Bran started.

"We've also suffered under the Slowness Spell, Bran, and we know it all," she answered, gravity weighing her every word.

"Why didn't you come to help?" Trevor asked bluntly, and Bran shot him a look.

"You've seen my people out there, the ones who welcomed you? Do you think those would be enough for a war?" Lilith asked.

Trevor didn't answer, only passed his gaze to the other three warriors.

"That's the part of the village that is awake. We're all there is now. We have to protect the others from everything because they're well enough to keep up with chores and routine activities for our village, but they don't see danger anymore. And besides, no one asked for our help. We hoped we wouldn't be needed," Lilith shared.

"We need everyone who can join us now. Lars is getting stronger," Bran said.

"His promises are getting louder," Olivia added. "Which I think is even worse. He plays with the elements and the Portals with no respect, and we're the only ones in his way. We must join forces."

"I see." Lilith sighed. "And you're the two travelers from another realm?"

"Yes," answered Olivia.

"I heard you're powerful. Did you bring back the moons?" Lilith asked.

"I'm afraid not. I just watched them coming back with amazement just like you," said Olivia.

Lilith remained with her eyes locked on Olivia, deciding whether she should believe her or not. Her gaze lingered on Olivia long enough for her to be uncomfortable and twitch in her seat, smiling flatly.

"I'm happy that we will be walking into war with the travelers," Lilith finally said.

"Actually, we're not going with you," said Olivia. "We need to find the sea folk. We hear that they moor near here, is that right?"

"That is correct. But why aren't you joining in a moment like this?" Lilith inquired.

"We have another piece of the puzzle to solve ..." answered Olivia.

"I understand. You're in luck; the sea folk are by the shores at this moment. But it's late at night, you should rest, and tomorrow I can point out the way. We have a hut for visitors. It's at the end of the village, and you'll find the door open for you. Your horses are resting right next to it, you won't miss it," Lilith said, leading them to the door and pointing out the way they should follow.

The hut was extremely tiny, with a fireplace and tree beds made with only rugs on the ground.

"At least it's warmer than the forest," Trevor joked.

Olivia managed to do that same old trick for fluffier beds, because at least now she had the rugs to work with. Trevor chose his bed and dove into sleep, while Olivia and Bran were still calming down from the eventful night.

"Do you trust Lilith and the others?" Olivia whispered to Bran as she lay on her bed and stared at him by her side.

"Yes. I don't think there's a reason not to," he answered, his eyes clear under the firelight.

"Good. Be safe here, and be safe leaving here too," she said.

"I will, but you're not going to the sea folk alone. I'm going there with you," Bran said.

"You don't need to! You've enough on your plate," Olivia added.

"Yeah, but I have to see the sea folk from up close! I just have to!" He laughed, and his whole face brightened.

Olivia laughed too, and her eyes quickly weighed down, relaxing into sleep. She reached for Bran's hand, and they intertwined their fingers, falling asleep like that.

CHAPTER TWENTY-FOUR

THE SEA FOLK

There was a knock on the hut door, and they were up with a halt, forgetting that they were safe in that place and not sleeping in the wild. It was still dark outside, and the sea breeze was cold and salty, kissing their faces as they walked out of the cabin.

"The sea folk will leave today. You better hurry," warned Lilith, who wore a blue tunic and carried a torch that lit her face, as though she were a mythical messenger who appeared from the depths of the night.

Olivia and Trevor went back inside and gathered their things, throwing the cape Cordella had given them over their shoulders as a sign that they were ready. Olivia said goodbye to Myrrh once again, and to Lito as well, for they would be going down the hill by foot and the horses needed to be left behind. Bran promised to take Myrrh back and protect her, assuring that she would be well taken care of during their travel back to the camp.

It was still the middle of the night when they left; there was not even a sign of the sun in the sky, and that energy of mystery that only the night can provide still hovered all around them. Olivia thanked Lilith before leaving, Trevor did the same, and the three of them headed out of the village by themselves, carrying torches, looking for a path that would open to the right, winding down until it reached the beach.

The sound of the breaking waves got louder with each step they took, pairing with their breaths in synchronicity. The way down was full of tall grass and steep, and at one point it was covered in very thin sand, like salt under the full moons of Tartae. As they reached the beach, the scent of the shore caressed their noses, and the water was wild, breaking into tall waves that reached their feet reduced to foam. They walked along the water until splashes and voices broke the night; soon enough, as if appearing out of nowhere, a fleet of many black ships revealed itself and, little by little, as they got closer to the ships, a veil lifted from their eyes and their ears, completely showing them the sea folk of Tartae.

"Wow!" exclaimed Trevor in a very low tone, studying the size and strangeness of those ships and the people on the sand, who danced around a huge fire dressed in flowing clothes as though they were made of water and air.

The ships were as black as night, and they bore no flags, only black sails, as flowing as the clothes the sea folk wore. The three of them were suddenly aware of their small size and the fact that they had never been invited to this feast. Olivia hoped that they would be welcomed and that the sea folk would understand why she had to go with them.

Olivia, Trevor, and Bran approached quietly, Olivia walking in the front. No one had even looked at them yet.

"Hi!" Olivia said loudly, interrupting the low song they were playing. Everybody stopped and looked at them. "Any chance I can get a ride?" She smiled.

As soon as they turned their eyes to her, she realized she was in front of something mythical. There were about thirty of them, women and men all dressed the same, and, even though they were humans, there was something quite different about them; their eyes were bigger, watery, and their faces glowed bluish under the stars and the moons.

The one who was playing an instrument that resembled a guitar neared Olivia bearing a smile—which made Olivia instantly more relaxed.

"Hello," he said, studying the group and taking his time. No one dared to say a word. "I'm Linthony Seawaken, and you are?"

"I'm Olivia Halin and these are my friends, Trevor and Bran," Olivia answered, pointing at the two of them. "We're not here for fighting or anything of that sort; we only seek your help."

"I know, I know," he said. "That much I know. I see you're much like us, huh?"

Olivia frowned, puzzled by his statement, and mumbled an incomprehensible answer, to which he laughed. He then handed his instrument to one of the women, and the music resumed.

"You can put down those torches. The moons are—finally—light enough," he said, and they obeyed, putting the fire down in the sand. They walked by the dancing folks and closer to the sea. "We're celebrating our travel to come, blessing the ships and the elements. That's what we do before going into the unpredictable ocean."

"It looks lovely," Olivia said.

"Tell me, Olivia Halin, why do you need our help?" he questioned.

"I need to find something. I'm not sure exactly what, but I've been called here, to you," Olivia answered, confident, but as she mouthed the words, she realized how weird this might sound.

"You look for a key, isn't it? But not one that was forged in metal, but a key to solving a puzzle," he said dreamily.

"Yes!" Olivia exclaimed. "How do you know?"

"I've been called too, my dear. That's why we are here," he answered in his deep silvery voice. "You're welcome into our ship. We leave at dawn," he said and left, rejoining the others in the dances and jumps around the fire.

Olivia, Trevor, and Bran were left speechless, staring open-mouthed at the sea folk and their ethereal dance under the moonlight. So many things ran through Olivia's head, but mainly the fact that she was actually closer to figuring this out, to discover what had been waiting for her somewhere in the sea of Tartae.

"I guess we came to the right place," said Trevor with a sarcastic tone. "I'd say that that was luck, but—"

"But it wasn't," completed Bran, looking at Olivia. "It was you."

"And how about that opening? *'Any chance I can get a ride?'*" Trevor laughed. "Couldn't you think of something better to say to those mythical creatures dancing around a fire in the middle of the night?"

"Nope, that was the best I could come up with. What was I supposed to say?" Olivia answered, laughing too. "I haven't been on a ship since I was a child, with my parents."

"I've done some cruises with my dad," Trevor said.

"At least that is an improvement, something that you two already know." Bran laughed.

Linthony called them to the fire, offering all three a drink that was strong and scratched their throats. Olivia learned that the ocean people were born under the star of the sea, and they were deeply connected to it, needing saltwater to thrive. They didn't fish or look for treasures, unlike the pirates of her world; their purpose was to discover new things, new places, draw maps for travelers so no one would get lost in the sea, and always nurture their connection with nature.

Bran was excited to learn about them; he was about to jump in the ship and join Olivia and Trevor in their quest, but the sun pointed at the horizon, reminding him of his own path. The sea people ran to the water, blissfully diving deep—unafraid of the huge waves—and then rising high above the surface, doing perfect backflips and diving again. They danced with the water under the open sky while the colors of the night and day mixed together in a painting made by nature in all its glory.

"What are they doing?" Bran asked.

"They're reconnecting," answered Olivia. Amazement and familiarity filled her soul.

"I guess it's time to go," said Trevor as Linthony headed to one of the ships. He hugged Bran tightly and they didn't exchange a word other than 'bye', for there was so much to say that there wouldn't be enough time in any world. Trevor walked to one of the boats heading to the ships.

Inside Olivia, something stirred crazily, and all her feelings came crashing down. She realized what she was about to step into and how lonely it would feel without Cordella, Alavro, Belenos, Emma, and having to say goodbye to Bran; it crushed her heart. The ocean in front of her was endless, much like a symbol of the unknown she was going headfirst into.

She looked at Bran, his eyes expecting hers and trying to hide his own uncertainty and anticipation.

"Be careful," she said.

"You too," Bran said, smiling. He leaned over, kissing Olivia's lips gently.

Olivia let herself go into that kiss like it was the sea and she was floating around in its waters. She was all happiness; there was no fear of what waited for her in her mission, only the promise of the future that depended much on what she was off to do.

"Come back to me," Bran said as their lips parted.

Olivia only smiled in return. She walked to the boat fast, catching the last one of them, and as it floated away, Bran got smaller until he was a tiny dot on the shore, waving farewell.

In front of her, the sun rose, flaming orange in the sky; the ships appeared to be even bigger up close, even blacker and more powerful. The smell of the ocean was intoxicating and there was no end to any of it, all was grand and seemed to be there to show how small Olivia was compared to nature, how little she knew.

She looked ahead to what was about to unfold in front of her, unable to foresee any of it, as if it were all hiding under the profound sea; she looked ahead to what the future held beyond those cliffs and beyond the life she knew in Tartae. She was stepping into the unknown, unexplored waters. But she had to answer the call. The Portals needed her.

THE ADVENTURE CONTINUES IN BOOK THREE OF
THE PORTALS OF TARTAE SAGA

Coming soon.

ABOUT THE AUTHOR

Marcia Soligo grew up avidly reading fairy tales and watching The NeverEnding Story movies. Creating worlds and stories was an important part of her childhood that led to an interest in fantasy literature and myth, which she has continued studying until today. Marcia was born in Brazil and majored in communications and journalism. She currently lives in California with her family.

For more stories, free content, and giveaways, subscribe to the newsletter at marciasoligo.com.

If you loved The Portals of Tartae: The Language of Trees and want to spread the magic, leave a review on Amazon.com. Great reviews help authors keep writing stories and readers to find their next read.

Thank you!

Made in the USA
Las Vegas, NV
03 November 2025

33575288R00136